Elizabeth Krall

Too
Close

THE GREATEST TABOO

Chapter 1

"THE NEW GUY is hot."

Nicola frowned at her computer screen. That analogy she had drawn between the crescent moon in the sky over Istanbul and the crescent moons on the city's mosques had seemed almost poetic in a jet-lagged daze over the Atlantic Ocean at 35,000 feet, but now it seemed contrived. She tapped at the delete key. "Hmmm?" she replied, only half-listening to the woman who had spoken to her. "What new guy?"

Kylie put her hands on her hips, sheathed in a skirt one size too small. "Really, Nicky!" she huffed. "That new guy in finance. Don't you read any of your emails?"

Nicola admitted defeat: she was never going to fix this article as long as Kylie was bent on Monday morning gossip. She had never been able to understand why Kylie thought that she wanted to hear all the gossip in the first place, but she could never be rude enough to tell her to go away.

She turned from the screen. "There were, I don't know, 150 emails in my inbox this morning, Kylie. You'll have to forgive me for not reading them all closely. But I think there was one regarding a new deputy financial officer. George?"

"Greg," corrected Kylie. She perched on the edge of Nicola's desk, revealing a long leg that ended in a shoe with a heel far higher than Nicola would ever consider wearing. In this crowded corner of the third floor of the office building housing the *San Francisco Age* newspaper, home to the writers for travel, fashion, gardening and lifestyle, more than one set of male eyes were drawn to that leg.

When the younger woman had joined the newspaper's fashion team three years ago, Nicola had, for a time, felt like a drab sparrow beside Kylie's flamboyant canary. Her own carefully chosen pantsuits, even her occasional skirts, had overnight seemed dull and sensible. And from the way Kylie's eyes were narrowing, it looked as if another fashion lecture was coming.

"Nicky." Kylie's voice held disappointment, and she plucked at Nicola's sleeve. "How many times have I told you that caramel is not your color?"

"Ten?"

"At least! We got some cute tops in last week, try one," suggested Kylie.

Nicola knew that if she ever dressed in something Kylie described as "cute," such as today's leopard-print mini-skirt and low-cut orange blouse, she would feel ridiculous.

Kylie gave in with a smile. "I guess you travel types just have no sense of fashion. Anyway, back to much more interesting things! Greg came to Friday drinks at Casey's. He's 33, and moved here from Seattle a year ago. Built like a...well, I'm not sure what, but it's all muscle. Even though he was wearing a suit, I could tell. He has blue eyes and hair so dark it's almost black." She cocked her head, a look of faint surprise on her face. "Like you, actually. Though he's better looking. In a guy way, I mean!"

The fashion editor, who sat in the cubicle opposite Nicola, called out, "You girls talking about Greg? I met him in the elevator this morning. He can audit my books any night!"

Kylie cast one swift, dismissive glance towards the partition that blocked her from her boss's view, and muttered, "As if." Then, in her normal voice, "We're going out tomorrow night."

Nicola laughed, and thought, Another victim for The Man Eater! "Does he have any idea what he's in for?"

Kylie shrugged. "If he doesn't, he sure will by the end of tomorrow night!"

Trying to stifle a yawn, Nicola smiled with sympathy for the unsuspecting man.

"When did you get back from Istanbul, Nicky?" asked Kylie. "You look tired."

"After midnight."

Kylie shook her head in disapproval. "Why didn't you work from home today? Your body's got to be messed up after a five-day trip from here to Turkey and back."

Nicola felt more awake just thinking about her stay in Istanbul, and she grinned. "A day or two of jet lag is fair exchange for a free stay at that resort on the Bosporus. Five stars do not begin to do it justice."

"One of the perks of being the editor, rather than a lowly

writer like me," grumbled Kylie. "The editors get all the good assignments. Guess who goes to the fashion shows in Paris, and who goes to them in LA?"

"Poor Kylie," Nicola replied. "Don't you have a trip to Madrid in a few days?"

"Thursday." She looked underwhelmed at the prospect of Spanish fashions.

"That still gives you time to ravish poor George before you go," Nicola pointed out with a sly smile. "Cheer up."

"Greg!"

Nicola shrugged. "Sorry. Your men all blur together, I guess."

"You can refuse to get involved with a colleague again, but that doesn't mean I'm going to take the same stance," said Kylie. She lowered her voice. "Of all the co-workers you could have fallen in love with, you chose Andrew! Nicky, the one good thing that jerk ever did for you was to run off with your boss. She got your man, but you got her job."

Nicola could not help but laugh at Kylie's attempt to look on the bright side. "So true. And I've got a lot of work to do, so if I want to keep that job, I'd better get back to it." She jabbed one finger at her computer. "I suspect you've got work of your own to do," she hinted.

Kylie slid from the desk and tugged the skirt back into place. "Yeah. Research into the latest styles of flamenco dresses, or whatever they wear in Spain." She minced to her own desk at the other end of the row of cubicles.

Nicola turned back to her screen, but her mind was no longer on Istanbul. She wished Kylie hadn't brought up Andrew. Yes, he had been a jerk, and she was over him now, but she didn't like to be reminded of him. After he and Brenda had disappeared, it seemed everyone at the newspaper had treated her with the utmost delicacy; she could almost hear them calling her "poor Nicky." It didn't seem to bother Kylie in the slightest that everyone called her something far less flattering, but she was made of sterner stuff than Nicola.

* *

On Wednesday morning, Kylie again perched on Nicola's desk, but this time her face beneath its permanent tan was white with fury.

"George turned you down?" repeated Nicola in surprise. This was worth losing a few minutes' work to hear. She pushed her chair back to see Kylie better.

"Greg!" The blonde hair was tossed back. "Said he wasn't 'that kind of a guy,' can you believe it? I'll bet he's gay."

"Why on earth would he have gone out with you if he was gay?"

Kylie examined her red-painted fingernails. "To make people think he wasn't, obviously."

Nicola laughed. "In 2011? In San Francisco? I don't think he needs to hide in the closet!" She felt a small surge of admiration for Greg, whoever he was. In the three years she had known Kylie, no man had ever turned her down. "Maybe it was a misunderstanding?"

Kylie stared at her. "A misunderstanding? When I put my hand on his thigh in the restaurant, he actually moved away. But when I suggested a nightcap at that little jazz bar near my apartment he agreed, and in the taxi on the way there he sure didn't move away when I kissed him. But then when I put my hand on his—" she stopped abruptly, looked around and leaned closer. "His, you know, he plucked it off like it was a dirty rag. Then he gave me the 'not that kind of a guy' line, had the taxi driver pull over and got out! And he's a lousy kisser!"

The laughter that had been building in Nicola throughout this story spilled out. "Oh, poor Kylie!"

"Easy for you to laugh, it wasn't you sitting in a taxi with a smirking driver," muttered Kylie.

"Maybe you'll find someone who is that kind of a guy in Madrid," suggested Nicola, although the laugh still lurked in her voice. "How's your Spanish?"

Kylie rolled her eyes. "If it takes words, I'm definitely doing something wrong."

* *

"You coming, Nicky?"

She looked up from the drift of papers and receipts on her desk. It was 6.00 on Friday evening, and people were heading off to Casey's for the ritual drink. "In a minute, Max," she replied to the man who had paused in the doorway to call back to her. "I want to sort out this Istanbul stuff. Accounts is on my back about it."

With most people gone now, a peaceful stillness settled over the office. She could hear someone's rapid tapping on a keyboard a few cubicles away, and over the hum of the air conditioning came the faint noise of traffic. Evening sunlight fell in golden stripes through the half-drawn blinds. Nicola liked the office at this time of day, in part because fewer people meant fewer interruptions. More than once she had considered changing her work hours, to start later and finish later, but as much as she liked the quieter office, she liked the evening at home more.

Casey's was a block from the *Age*'s building, and on this gentle May evening the walk seemed too short. Nicola lingered, looking up at the pale blue sky and savoring the warm breeze. Even in downtown San Francisco, the change of seasons could not be held back. She opened the door to the sports bar, and spring disappeared like a light going out. Casey's was heaving, as usual, smelling of beer and fried food, full of the workers who had spilled from their offices and were intent on loosening their ties and letting down their hair at the end of the working week. Nicola pushed through the noisy crowd to the back, where the *Age* group always gathered, but kept one eye on the big screens to see how the Giants were doing. Still in a slump, apparently.

Her colleagues and friends made room for her, and someone handed her a glass of white wine. On the other side of the group she spotted Max, talking to a man she didn't recognize. The stranger's back was to her, and her first impression was of big, straight shoulders, his torso tapering in a V down to narrow hips.

She wondered if this was Greg, the only man ever known to say "no" to The Man Eater. She tried to remember how Kylie had described him. Muscles...yes, the bulk of his torso, the strong forearms below the rolled-up white shirtsleeves, hinted at a life beyond balancing the books. He was a couple of inches shorter than Max's lanky six feet. When he turned, Nicola saw the straight nose and the strong, sculpted features – and saw, too, the relaxed, expectant expression, saw the smile hovering on his lips break into a grin as Max delivered the punch line to the story he had been telling.

He was easy on the eye, she admitted. Very easy.

Max waved her over. "Nicky, have you met Greg yet? He started in finance a week or so ago." The woman beside him tugged on his sleeve, and Max turned away.

"So you're Greg," Nicola commented, holding out a hand to shake.

One dark eyebrow rose as he took her hand. "I admit it. Has my reputation preceded me?"

Too late, Nicola realized she probably should have settled for saying hello. "Uh, no. Someone I work with mentioned you, that's all." His hand felt rough, the fingers callused; not what she would have expected from an accountant.

He regarded her with curiosity.

His eyes are the color of the sky just before the evening light fades, thought Nicola. And then she looked hastily away, wondering what had brought on such a fanciful idea.

"Someone you work with?"

She sipped her wine, praying for inspiration. It didn't come. "Kylie. She said she met you here last Friday."

One side of his mouth quirked up. "Is that all she said?"

"What else would she say?" Nicola asked with a smile, responding to the humor in his face.

"Nothing very flattering, I imagine," he said dryly.

Nicola laughed, liking the way he wasn't trying to play down what had happened with Kylie. "No, not very," she admitted.

"Is Kylie your friend?" His eyes, over the rim of his glass, looked doubtful.

Nicola did not want to gossip about Kylie behind her back, but she also did not want Greg to have the wrong idea. "She latched on to me when she started at the *Age* a few years ago. I was never sure why! I wouldn't describe her as my friend, though.

More of a colleague. You're stuck with them, whether you like them or not!"

His eyes lit with laughter. "That's true! So you know what happened?"

"By now, I suspect the whole company knows what happened! Kylie is not big on secrets."

"Is she always like that? Or was she blown away by my irresistible charms?" His lips turned up and his eyes looked down, and his expression was of such absurd modesty that it was clear he was mocking both himself and his charms. Not waiting for an answer, he asked, "Were you not here last week, or did I not see you?"

She shook her head. "Not here. I do drop by most Fridays, but not all. And I don't stay long."

"I suppose you have a family to get home to?"

"No, I'm just not into the noisy bar scene. I take it you aren't, either?" She gestured to his glass of Coke. "Don't you drink?"

He smiled. "Oh I do, and I would love a beer right now! But I'm driving home, and I have an early start tomorrow."

"Is it a long drive?"

He shook his head. "Not bad, 30 to 40 minutes depending on traffic. Across the bay, in Richmond. How about you?"

"Polk Gulch."

"I love that name!" Greg exclaimed. "When I moved here from Seattle, I thought it sounded like a Wild West town. You can walk home from here."

She pulled a face. "Yeah, uphill the whole way. I think I'll settle for the trolley. The last stop is a couple of blocks from my apartment. Whereabouts in Richmond are you?"

"Bayside Yacht Harbor," he replied.

Nicola frowned. "Is that one of those new condo developments on the bay?"

He laughed. "No, it's a marina. I live on my boat."

"You live on a yacht?" Her voice rose in disbelief.

The laugh grew louder. "You're thinking of a shiny white monstrosity with a helicopter pad, and a crew in matching uniforms, aren't you? My boat is a 30-foot sailboat. No helicopter, and I'm the only crew."

A waitress was worming through the crowd, tray of drinks held high, and Nicola moved aside to let her pass. She caught the tail end of an old joke someone was telling, and laughed. She was torn between staying with this group and returning to Greg; he was new, and it wouldn't be fair to abandon him in a crowd of strangers. He was interesting, too, she admitted. A glance at Greg showed him standing by himself, looking around with that air of someone wondering what to do next. Then he met her eyes, and smiled, and the next thing Nicola knew she was back beside him.

"I've never met anyone who lived on a sailboat," she said, picking up the conversation. That would explain the tan on his face and arms.

"It wasn't my plan to start with," Greg admitted. "I'd already spent a year on the boat before I ended up here, and I did intend to find an apartment. But I never seem to get around to it! And it is convenient: when I get home from work and want a quick sail on the bay, all I have to do is swap the suit for shorts, un-moor her, and I'm off."

She could not imagine being on a 30-foot sailboat for a day, let alone a year, let alone two years. "Can I ask why you had already spent a year on it, or am I being too nosy?"

Greg shook his head. "Not too nosy. I took a year off. Dropped out of the rat race and sailed south along the coast from Seattle, down into Mexico and the Gulf of California. It was wonderful," he confided with a grin. "No work, no commute, no suits. Just me and the sea. But all good things must end, huh?"

"So how did you end up in San Francisco?" she asked, then with a laugh, "Did you take a wrong turn on the way back to Seattle?" What she really wanted to ask was "Why did you take a year off? What happened?" but those questions seemed too personal for such a brief acquaintance.

"I made the turn on purpose, but I didn't intend to stay so long! I have some good friends in San Francisco so I stopped off for a while to see them. They suggested I should get a job here but I didn't take it seriously, until one rainy day I had nothing better to do than check out job openings on an accountants' website. I found what I thought was a great one, with one of the mid-tier firms. So I bought a suit and went in for an interview."

Something in his voice told Nicola there was more to the story than this. "And?" she prompted.

"And it turned out to be not so great. After a while I realized things weren't as rosy as I had been told, and a few months ago the word 'downsizing' started doing the rounds," he said.

"Uh oh."

"Yup." He nodded, smiling ruefully. "Last in, first out. So here I am in the newspaper business! It's very different to what I'm used to. Interesting, though."

Nicola's mind was still struggling with the idea of spending so much time on such a small boat, and alone. "Did you sail all that way on your own?"

"Mostly, but sometimes friends would join me, and my parents came down once," he replied. "Do you sail?"

Nicola was taken aback at the very idea. "I've never been on anything smaller than a ferry in my life!" she said.

"I'll take you out one day, if you like," he offered. "Everyone should try it."

"I'd be totally useless!" she protested. "And seasick, no doubt."

Greg smiled at her. "Don't worry, she's rigged so I can manage her on my own. You can lounge around on deck. And take seasickness pills." He tilted his empty glass. "I think I'll get another Coke. You want anything?"

She shook her head and held up the glass of wine, still half full. "No, thanks. Nice talking to you."

"You too."

Nicola heard someone say, "The Giants are out of it!" and she turned quickly.

"I still say they can take the Series this season!" she declared, jumping into the conversation.

* *

At the bar, Max sidled up beside Greg as he waited for his Coke. "You're wasting your time there, buddy," he advised.

Greg looked at him in silent query.

"Nicky. She won't have anything to do with anyone from the *Age*. If you want to get any closer than Casey's on a Friday, you'd better find a new job. She has a strict 'no colleagues' rule. Turned me down flat. Twice," he added. "And I'm not the only one."

"What's with the rule?"

Max drained his beer and waved at the bartender for another. "Three years ago she started going out with a guy named Andrew, one of the news journalists. After a year, they moved in together. And a year after that, she comes home one day to find all his shit gone. Not even a note. And what do you think? He'd been screwing Nicky's boss the whole time and the two of them took off together. She was married, by the way."

"That bastard," growled Greg.

"Oh yeah, man, you won't get any disagreement from anyone at the *Age* about that. Nicky swore off dating colleagues after that. She said if her love life was going to end in humiliation, she didn't need the whole company knowing about it," Max said. "And some good came of it. She got her boss's job. Now Nicky's the travel editor."

"I'll bet that keeps her warm in bed on a winter night," retorted Greg.

Max raised both hands in a peaceful gesture. "Hey, I'm only bringing you up to speed on the Nicky thing. You wouldn't be the first guy at the *Age* to fall for her pretty face and big blue eyes, but I'm warning you, it ain't going to go anywhere." He took his beer from the bartender and moved off.

Greg turned back to the crowd. More people had arrived, jostling and talking loudly, and he couldn't see her. Had she left? No, there she was, laughing at something a woman he didn't know was saying. Her dark hair gleamed and her sapphire eyes were alight with humor. He couldn't imagine how any man could be such an ass as to cheat on her, and go off with someone else.

Nicola looked at him then, as if the weight of his stare pulled her eyes to his, the straight fall of her hair like shining curtains framing her heart-shaped face. She held his gaze for a moment or two, and then smiled.

His heart skipped a beat.

* *

Nicola left the bar when her glass of wine was empty, after refusing offers of a refill. Outside, it was almost dark and a north wind stole under the hem of her short jacket. The balmy spring evening had given way to a cold night.

She was lucky: the trolley was approaching the stop as she hurried around the corner, and she managed to find a seat inside. It was touristy, yes, and some days she had to resort to a bus, but she had loved the trolleys since she was a child – and this one stopped, as she had told Greg, only two blocks from home.

He's nice, she thought. She could see why Kylie had been so attracted. Although Kylie probably had been more interested in his muscles and his good lucks than in his personality and his conversation! She smiled as she imagined that scene in the taxi.

But what, Nicola wondered, was the truth behind that glib "dropping out of the rat race for a year" story?

Chapter 2

GREG GLANCED at his watch. The meeting at the auditors' office, with the newspaper's chief financial officer and chairman, had gone on longer than expected. Once he'd got over the strangeness of being in an accounting firm's office as a client, rather than as an employee, he had struggled to focus his attention. The meeting hadn't been necessary, in his view, and very little had been accomplished.

The taxi stopped near the *Age*'s building, and Greg was first out. If he was quick, he could still get to the marina in time for a sail. He began to walk around the taxi, and his eye was caught by a flash of color in the mass of people streaming along the sidewalk. He'd seen that yellow jacket before, when Nicola put it on to leave Casey's last Friday.

"Please excuse me, gentlemen, I must speak to someone," Greg said over his shoulder, and he plunged into the crowd, following that jacket, without stopping to question why.

She was half a block ahead and everyone between them seemed intent on getting in his way, but he closed the gap. Ten feet behind her, he was forced almost onto the road by a group of gawking tourists. His knee bumped hard against the corner of something solid, and he glared down. A planter full of marigolds looked back at him.

He finally caught up to her at a red light. "Hi."

"Oh! Hello, Greg," Nicola replied. She smiled at him, which he thought was a good sign. Or maybe she was just naturally polite. "Do you go this way too?"

His mind was blank. Great. *I walk away from my boss and my boss's boss, chase this woman for two blocks, steal a flower, and now I can't think of a damned thing to say.*

"Sometimes," he said weakly. Then he laughed, and said, "No, never. I wanted to give you this. It matches your jacket." He held out the yellow marigold.

Surprise, wariness, pleasure – they were all plain on her face. She looked at the flower, and then her eyes, as blue as the sea far from land, flashed up at him.

The light changed and the waiting crowd surged forward, jostling them.

Then she laughed, too, and took the marigold. "Thank you."

Greg watched her walk across the street, and all the witty, amusing, sweep-her-off-her-feet things he should have said crowded into his head. Too late. But she had accepted his flower, which was something.

* *

Midway through Tuesday morning, Nicola became aware of someone standing behind her chair. She looked over her shoulder, and there was Greg. The pinstriped suit fit perfectly and the white shirt emphasized his tan. She told her stomach to stop its absurd fluttering. Yes, his eyes were darker blue than she remembered, and his shoulders broader, but he was just another colleague. There was no need for this silly happiness at the unexpected sight of him, just as there had been no need to think of him as often as she had since he'd given her that flower yesterday.

"Hello," she said. "Are you lost?"

"I was looking for you, and I've found you, so I don't think so," he replied.

"Why were you looking for me?"

His face took on a serious expression. "There's a discrepancy in your Istanbul expenses."

"Hey everyone, Nicky's been fiddling the expenses!" called out Max from the next desk. People all around looked up with interest.

"What kind of discrepancy?" asked Nicola, who was secure in the scrupulousness of her expense recording. Fairly secure.

Greg withdrew a sheet of paper from one pocket and studied it. "You claimed that you paid $14.25 for lunch at JFK airport, but according to the receipt it was $14.20." From the same pocket he pulled out a coin, and handed it to her. "The company owes you five cents."

Laughter from the surrounding desks, and someone advised, "Keep it, Nicky, it's the only bonus this company is ever likely to hand out!"

She turned the nickel over in her fingers, looking down at it so he wouldn't see her smile. "You didn't have to come down here and give me this, you know. And is checking expenses the sort of work a deputy financial officer does?"

He leaned against the low divider between Max's desk and her own. "On a slow day, maybe. But it really was a transparent ploy to see you again," he admitted, speaking quietly.

Dismay fought with pleasure at this admission, and to Nicola's chagrin the pleasure won. "Greg, that's very flattering, but I don't get involved with men I work with. It's a rule I have." A rule that was a lot easier to stick to when the men who asked her out didn't interest her in the slightest.

He smiled. "So I was warned. But fools rush in, you know. Why don't you have lunch with me today?"

She cast around for an excuse to say no, and saw it sitting on her desk. "I brought my lunch. Look, there it is."

"Bring it outside. We can sit in the park," he coaxed.

"Greg," she began, but he held up a hand.

"Do you object on principle to eating lunch outside?"

She shook her head.

"Do you think every person in this building who is having lunch with a colleague today considers it a date, or a declaration of some type?"

She shook her head again, struggling to stop a smile creeping over her lips.

"Do you have a prior engagement? A meeting to attend? Urgent calls to make?"

Again, she shook her head, the smile bigger now.

"In that case, Nicola, I believe you must agree to join me for lunch."

She laughed, and gave in. "I believe I must."

The small park was wedged between buildings, crowded by their glassy soaring height, but its trees and benches offered a respite from the recycled air of offices. Tubs held clumps of flowers, bright splashes of color among the greens and browns of the trees. A woman sitting in the middle of a bench moved over to make room for them.

"Did you have a good weekend?" Greg asked, before taking a bite from his sandwich.

She smiled, thinking that she had heard more original opening gambits. "Nothing special. I went for a run Saturday morning with a friend, did laundry and groceries and cleaning in the afternoon. On Sunday, I went over to my parents' house in Sausalito for the day."

"So your family is here?"

Nicola nodded. "Yes, none of us kids strayed far from the nest. Want to see us?" Before he could answer, she put her lunch to one side and dug in her purse for her smartphone. "Here," she said, when she'd found the photo she wanted. "This was last Christmas, a picture without the spouses and kids."

Greg leaned closer to see the screen, which brought his thigh into contact with hers. Nicola fidgeted discreetly. Moving away would seem rude, or give the touch a significance he couldn't have intended; and, really, what harm could it do?

He made a small grunt of surprise. "You don't look much like them," he commented. "They've all got red hair, apart from this blonde lady whom I assume is your mother."

"Her name's Gwen. My dad is Arthur. And my brother Bill, he's 39, and my sister Alison, who's the same age as me. Well, she's five weeks older, actually. It was her birthday on Sunday, so for the next five weeks she's 36 and I'm only 35. When we were kids, she kept insisting that she was the oldest by a whole year, so she was in charge!" Nicola was full of laughter at the memory.

"Nicola?"

"Hmmmm?" She took a bite from a cold chicken drumstick.

"How can your sister be five weeks older than you?" Greg asked, frowning. "I find it hard to believe that you hung around inside your mother's womb for that long after she was born."

She laughed at his look of confusion. "Oh I'm sorry, Greg, I always assume that everyone knows I'm adopted!" She patted his hand in sympathy. "I was nine months old when they adopted me. I've always admired Mom for that, when she already had a baby girl not even one year old."

The confused look had given way to interest. "Really? That's something we have in common. No, that's not strictly true; my mother is my real mother, but my father is my stepfather. They married a few weeks before I was born. She's always refused to talk about her life then, or my natural father, and, frankly, I don't care. Dad – Edward – is my father. He taught me to sail, helped me with my math homework, and gave me a good talking-to when I needed one. Or rather, when he thought I needed one!"

Nicola nodded enthusiastically. "Yes! That's it. I know absolutely nothing about my natural parents, and don't want to. This is my family." She stabbed at the cell phone. "They are the people who have loved me my whole life, and whom I love. What's DNA got to do with it?"

She grinned at him and he grinned back. The awkwardness she had felt when they sat down was now gone in this discovery of shared family life.

Around a mouthful of roast beef, Greg said, "Have you ever considered living in another city?"

She shook her head. "Never. I can't ever imagine leaving San Francisco. I love this city! It's my home. Although I do like to travel to other places!" she enthused.

"Hence the job as travel editor," he remarked. He tossed a crumb to the pigeon pecking at the ground near his feet.

"I started out as a writer, of course. I became the editor a year ago."

Greg paused, then said with deliberation, "Yes, I know."

She turned to face him. "I'll bet you know the circumstances, too."

He nodded.

"So now you understand why I don't get involved with colleagues any more," she said firmly.

He sounded as firm when he said, "No, I don't. You can't put us all into the same basket. I've never cheated on any woman I was seeing, and I can't imagine starting with you."

She rested her fork on her salad, and tried to explain. "It wasn't only the cheating, although that was bad enough! It was the way everyone treated me with kid gloves for weeks after, so careful not to say the wrong thing or upset me. I knew they were all talking about me."

"They care," he said lightly. "You should be pleased to have so many friends. Tell me, if I worked somewhere else, would you go out with me?"

Nicola was so surprised at the directness of the question that she answered, "Probably," then looked away, embarrassed. She expected Greg to pounce on this inadvertent admission that she wasn't indifferent to him, but he chewed in silence, his eyes on the fountain where water splashed over a sculpture of jumping frogs.

"I owe you an explanation about Kylie," he said abruptly.

"No, you don't. I know what she's like," she assured him.

"You know what she's like, but you don't know what I'm like. You'd be justified in thinking 'Oh, that Greg, last week he went out with one woman and now he's after me.' I'm not. Well," he corrected with a laugh, "I am, obviously, but not like that. I said yes when she asked me out because I'm as weak as the next guy when a woman comes on to me, and yes I kissed her, but when I realized all she wanted was casual sex, I left. That's not me, Nicola."

His eyes held hers so steadily, so evenly, that it did not occur to Nicola to doubt him. Nor to wonder why she was so pleased to hear him say that.

"By the way, should I call you Nicola, or Nicky?" he asked. "Everyone at work calls you Nicky, maybe you prefer that?"

"I don't mind which," she said. "My family and some friends call me Nicola, but almost everyone else uses Nicky."

"Then as someone who aspires to be at least your friend, I'll stick with Nicola," he said. The lazy grin spreading over his face gave him the look of a mischievous boy planning an escapade.

He is ridiculously good looking, thought Nicola. He even has a dimple when he smiles. There was a fleck of mustard on his upper lip, and she had the impulse to wipe it off with her finger. Where on earth had that crazy thought come from? "So, uh, was your weekend more interesting than mine?"

"No groceries and no laundry. No family because my parents are in Seattle and my sister in Chicago. No running because I was sailing, and also because I'm not a great runner. I'm more of a weights man than a marathon man. A lot of cleaning once I got back, however. What do you think, does it sound more interesting?" he teased.

She placed the half-eaten drumstick on her salad while she considered. "Yes, I think it does. Not so...so ordinary. Maybe too much sailing, and from the sounds of it too much cleaning, but no dull chores."

He laughed. "I'm afraid the dull chores were only postponed! No escaping them. Perhaps I shouldn't admit this, but I'm a fairly ordinary guy."

Nicola slanted a glance at him, laughing too, but something told her that Greg was possibly the least ordinary man she had ever met.

* *

Greg leaned against the bar in Casey's. He was talking to Max, but he was watching Nicola. Since that lunch on Tuesday, he had wracked his brain to come up with the least threatening, least date-like way to spend time with Nicola alone. She would, he knew, dismiss dinner or drinks or theatre out of hand. He thought he had the answer, but he had no intention of suggesting it in here, shouting over the noise of people, televisions and music.

She had that look of someone on the verge of leaving, playing with the clasp of her purse and listening with partial attention to Kylie. He frowned in Kylie's general direction; he couldn't believe he had ever gone out with that woman. Well, yes, he could believe it: she was pretty, in a flashy way, and he hadn't known anything about her. And he'd always been a sucker for a woman who made the first move. Greg wished Nicola had come to Casey's on his first Friday, for he would never have looked at the blonde if she had been here and he wouldn't now be wondering if it was a strike against him.

There! Nicola had stood, and was saying goodbyes to the people at her table. She glanced over and waved at him and Max, then began to thread her way through the crowd. Greg let her get to the door before he followed.

"You're wasting your time," came Max's voice from behind, in a "didn't I tell you already?" sort of tone.

It's my time, thought Greg, and I can do with it what I want.

Outside, he called, "Nicola!" and she looked back. Her expression held not the slightest trace of surprise, and she smiled at him.

"What a coincidence – that you should leave so soon after me, I mean," she observed.

He grinned. "It is, isn't it?"

"Where are you headed?"

"Wherever you're going," he replied. "What else would I want to do on a spring evening other than walk with a pretty girl?"

She shook her head at his foolishness. "You could go sailing?"

"I've got a whole day of that tomorrow." He had a sudden image of this beautiful woman sitting on the deck of his sailboat, wearing no more than a swimsuit, her dark hair blowing in the breeze, and smiling up at him. Greg cleared his throat. "Do you like penguins?"

In a tone of amused surprise, she said, "I suppose."

"Three eggs hatched at the zoo a few weeks ago. The chicks are completely adorable. You should see them," he added, sounding casual.

"Maybe I will."

"Thing is," he continued, "they're in a special area, not open to the public."

She glanced at him in puzzlement. "Then I guess I won't."

"If you went with me, you could see them."

"Oh? Are we going to scale the walls at night, and break in?" Nicola teased.

"We could, if that's what you want, but it might be easier to swipe my security card at the door. I volunteer at the zoo, 10 hours a month," he explained.

She turned to look at him, eyebrows raised. "Really?"

"Really. So showing the penguin chicks to you would be no different than showing them to other zoo visitors." Like hell it wouldn't. "Not a date at all. Nothing more than two animal lovers looking at animals."

She was considering it, he could see. What woman could resist animals, particularly cute baby animals?

"Did I mention how adorable they are?"

The look she gave him said that she knew exactly what he was up to. But she was smiling, too.

* *

As Nicola walked from the parking lot to the gray wooden building housing the zoo's ticket office, she reminded herself that this was not a date. She wasn't certain what it was, but it was not a date.

She bought her ticket and went in and there was Greg, sitting on a bench by a cluster of trees. He was wearing faded jeans, and a powder-blue polo shirt with the zoo's logo on his chest. Above the logo was pinned a badge with his name and the word "volunteer." He rose smoothly to his feet and pushed his sunglasses back onto his head, and smiled at her, and her heart gave one mighty thump.

Who was she fooling? This was a date. She hadn't taken so long to decide what to wear simply to go look at animals. It was worth it, though, to see how his gaze ran over her sweater and down to the jeans that hugged her hips.

"Hi," he said. "You look different."

She laughed. "Not as different as you!" She pointed to the badge, not quite touching his chest with her finger. "What do you do here?"

"I'm a docent," he said, and taking her arm he steered her towards a path.

"A what?"

"A docent. I lead educational tours about the animals. For school groups, and general visitors," he explained.

Nicola stared at him. "What, you're a zoologist in addition to being a certified public accountant?"

He shook his head with a smile. "No, the zoo provides a training course. Anything you want to know about lions or meerkats, I'm your man."

"I like elephants better," she said.

"Wrong zoo. We don't have any."

They skirted a family clustered around their foldout map, arguing directions.

"Shouldn't you offer to help them?" she asked in an undertone.

"I'm off duty. You are the only one I'm helping this afternoon. Not about elephants, though," he added.

He led her on a winding path around the zoo, showing her Chinese Fire-Bellied Newts and Double-wattled Cassowaries and Black Lemurs, telling her things about the animals she would never have imagined. Who knew, for example, that gorillas liked cottage cheese?

When they stopped at a café, Nicola secured a table outside while Greg ordered. Looking around to make sure he wasn't watching, she plucked at the V-neck of her sweater, fanning herself discreetly. Why hadn't she worn a shirt under this sweater so she could take it off? Vanity, that was why, as she very well knew: she hadn't wanted to ruin its smooth lines.

The loud laughter of two young women at the next table drew her attention, so she happened to be watching them as Greg walked towards her and she saw how one of the women, a skinny redhead, ran her eyes over him in appreciation and nudged her friend.

"Here we go, two iced coffees," said Greg, as he put the drinks down and slid onto the chair opposite.

"Thanks."

His right hand rested on the wooden table, and she noticed the angry red mark curving up from his palm and running across the back of his hand. "Ow," she sympathized. "What happened? Did an animal scratch you?"

He laughed, and flexed the hand. "No, *Drifter* did! *Drifter's* my boat," he added. "It's a rope burn from yesterday. I was in a race, and did something stupid trying to win."

"Do you sail every day?" She couldn't see why anyone would want to do that.

"I don't have the time. And when it's cold and wet, sometimes even I would rather stay at the marina, reading a book or something. And what with three hours here after church this morning, and now the afternoon with you, I won't get out today." He shrugged. "So no, not every day."

Had he really said church? "You went to church?"

He nodded absently, tearing open a sugar packet.

"Do you go every Sunday?"

Greg looked up from his coffee. "No, but at least once a month, usually more. Why are you so curious? Don't you go?"

"At Christmas. Weddings, funerals and baptisms, too. You know, the usual," she said with a faint laugh, thinking for the first time that for some people, that wasn't "the usual."

"But you believe in God?" he asked.

His intensity made her uneasy. Would he try to persuade her to join a cult? Then she laughed at herself, imaging a cult of crazed God-fearing accountants with Greg as their leader. She said, "Yes, I do. It's organized religion I'm not so wild about."

"That's fair," he conceded. "I struggled with that myself for a time." He glanced at his watch and said, "Come on, let's go. We still have to see the penguins."

So much for the cult! "I'll be right back, okay?" She pointed to the small building at the edge of the table area.

Washing her hands, she tried to conceive of going to church when the sole reason to go was that you wanted to go. As far as she was concerned, Sunday mornings were for sleeping in and drinking too much coffee over the newspaper in a café.

Another woman came in, and Nicola recognized the skinny redhead.

"Your brother is hot!" exclaimed the other woman.

Did this woman know Bill? But how would she know who Nicola was? And not even Bill's own wife would ever describe him as "hot." "Excuse me?"

The redhead pointed in the direction of the tables. "Isn't he your brother, that man you're with? You look like twins."

"No, he's not. My brother has red hair, actually, like you," said Nicola with a smile. But the woman's words reminded her that Kylie, when describing Greg, had said he resembled Nicola. She looked at Greg thoughtfully as she walked towards him. They couldn't possibly be as alike as that woman had said, could they?

When they reached Penguin Island, and the baby penguin enclosure, all other thoughts flew out of her head. "Oh, you were right! Completely adorable." She leaned down, her eyes misty at the sight of the small balls of fluff.

Greg smiled at her. "They'll lose that adorableness soon, but we should come back when they go to Fish School. I hear it's a laugh, watching the keepers teach the young penguins how to swim!"

She looked up at him. "It's a date!" she declared, then caught herself. "I mean, I'd love to see that."

His smile grew broader, and he pulled her up. Outside, they strolled along the path, dodging running children and watching the antics of the adult penguins.

"What's up?" he asked. "Why are you peeking at me from the corner of your eyes? Have I got something on my face?"

"It's nothing," she replied with a laugh, waving a hand in dismissal. "A woman told me we look like twins. She thought you were my brother."

"You're prettier than I am," he joked. He put his hands on his hips, and looked at her. "Maybe. We both have dark hair, though yours is almost straight. Blue eyes, though a different shade of blue." Greg ran a finger down her nose, making her laugh. "And your nose tilts up at the tip, delightfully. Mine doesn't."

Their eyes held, and a breathless, giddy feeling rose in her.

"I'm glad I'm not your brother," he said softly.

"Any particular reason?"

"If I was your brother, I'd have to kiss you like this." Greg deposited a chaste peck on her cheek. "Rather than like this."

His lips against hers were soft, and his hands rested on her shoulders. It was a light kiss, one she could pull back from easily if that was what she wanted. Instead, Nicola slipped her arms around his waist. She felt his own arms go around her, pulling her to him, and his lips pressed more firmly.

Nicola had always dated men much taller than she was, and if anyone had asked she would have insisted that was important. However, the feel of Greg in her arms, his body hard and muscular but only three inches taller than her own, was strangely arousing in its novelty, she was finding.

And Kylie had lied: he was definitely not a lousy kisser.

Chapter 3

"WATCH IT!" cried a man, as Nicola pushed open the heavy door to the fire stairs. She heard a quick scuffle of shoes on the small landing as someone jumped out of the way.

"I'm sorry!" she exclaimed, then saw who it was. "Greg!"

He took one step down and looked up at her, his expression changing with comical speed from annoyance to pleasure. She couldn't deny that she was just as pleased to see him.

"Hi," he said, smiling.

"Hi."

Voices and the thump of feet from the floor above propelled them down the stairs to street level.

"Where are you going?" he asked.

She pointed in the general direction of the bay, a few blocks away. "Just for a walk. I try to get outside at lunch whenever I can. Where are you going?"

"Just for a walk," he said. "My mind turns to mush if I spend all day staring at numbers. Can I join you?"

Nicola smiled. "Yes." Oh, yes. She wasn't going to question the coincidence that put him on that landing the moment she opened the door.

"Did you get home okay yesterday?"

"Fine, once I got out of the zoo parking lot. How about you?" she asked.

He nodded. "Fine."

They walked in silence. Not really awkward silence, but certainly not easy silence. It was impossible to forget that kiss yesterday, the feel of his arms around her and his body against her.

"Uh, when's your next zoo shift?" she asked.

"In a couple of weeks."

Curious, she asked, "How did you get into that, anyway?"

Greg laughed. "My mother. She's a great one for volunteering. 'In this life, we must give back part of what we are given'; if I've heard her say that once, I've heard her say it a hundred times. I guess it sunk in. I taught sailing to kids in Seattle, but I thought I'd try something different here."

Nicola glanced at him, and when she saw that he was looking away from her, watching a ferry, she let her gaze linger on him. Not especially tall, but big and solid, like a man who made his living from heavy manual labor; yet he was a CPA, and he did volunteer work. No one she had ever known, man or woman, did volunteer work. It would never have occurred to her.

"Let's go over there," he said, pointing, and she followed him across the Embarcadero to the railing that ran along the water.

They rested their forearms on the rail, looking out at the water that sparkled on this warm, sunny day and across to Oakland rising on the opposite shore. Their shoulders almost – almost – touched. His shirtsleeve brushed her bare arm.

"Thank you for yesterday," Greg said. "I wasn't sure you would really turn up."

"Why?"

He shrugged, and she felt the fabric of his sleeve slide along her arm. "Your rule. I was afraid you might think it was a date, after all, and change your mind."

"It was a date," Nicola said. "You were sneaky about it, but it was."

Greg turned, one arm still on the rail but his left hand now on her shoulder. "But you came anyway."

She turned, too, and somehow her right hand was on his waist. "Yes."

"I'm so glad you did," he said, his voice warm.

Nicola leaned closer. "So am I."

* *

"So it's graffiti, right?" asked Greg as they got out of his car. "Big graffiti?"

They had come to the Mission District straight from work. The day was still warm, the light still bright but edging towards the gold of early evening. Greg paused to remove his jacket and pull off his tie, tossing both into the back seat.

"Murals, not graffiti!" insisted Nicola, as she walked around the car to join him. "I can't believe you've never heard of Balmy Alley in the year you've been here."

He shrugged lightly. "Where I come from, painting things on walls is called graffiti, not art. We don't make a special trip halfway across town to look at it."

Greg tugged on her arm to stop her walking off, and with a slight pressure he pulled her closer; it was slight enough that she could ignore it, if she wanted. But as he had hoped, Nicola turned back and took a step towards him.

"Whatever they're called," he said, holding her eyes with his own, "I want to thank you for asking me to see them with you."

This was date number two. He didn't count that walk to the bay at lunch yesterday as a date, no matter how wonderful that kiss had been. During their slow stroll back to the office, she had asked him if he would like to join her on her semiannual visit to Balmy Alley. So here he was, giving up the sweetest Wednesday evening of sailing imaginable, to look at graffiti. And Greg didn't mind in the least.

They walked along tree-shaded 24th Street, one block from the car to the alley. Store signs here were in Spanish as well as English, and a small boy, running towards them so fast that Greg feared he would trip and fall, flashed an exuberant grin and cried "Hola!" as he passed.

Neither of them had an unthinking feel yet for where the other was; their elbows would knock together and they would veer away, or he would turn to point at something and she would walk into him. "Sorry," one would say, with a sheepish smile, or "Oops." The same thing had happened at the zoo. Finally, when the back of her hand brushed against his as she moved aside to make room for a woman pushing a baby stroller, Greg threaded his fingers through hers.

Nicola gave him a swift look of surprise, and a smile. Their fingers tightened at the same time.

"Okay," said Greg. "If I'm going to admire graffiti, you had better tell me why."

Another swift look from those brilliant blue eyes, but this one was laughing at him. "Murals! It started in the 1980s, as a way of protesting against what was happening in Central America then. Human rights abuses, you know? There's still a political theme to a lot of them, but now there are also local scenes and things that are there because they're beautiful or they make you laugh. Oh!" Nicola said, with a sudden smile. "I just remembered, there's one with a sailboat! You'll like that one. If it's still there. They change all the time."

"That's why you come twice a year," suggested Greg.

She nodded. "That's why." She steered him into the alley.

It wasn't very long, Greg saw, one block running from 24th to 25th Streets. And it was an alley, no doubt there. Narrow, and lined with garage doors and houses or the walls of buildings. Every surface was an artist's canvas. An explosion of vibrant color met his eye, big bold shapes and tiny delicate figures, and moss-edged brickwork forming a walkway from one end to the other. Nature vied for his attention in the form of vibrant spills of hot pink bougainvillea, or purple wisteria that cascaded over walls. He didn't know what to look at first.

"Still graffiti?" she asked.

"No way."

"Come on, I'll show you my favorite," Nicola said, and hand-in-hand they strolled between the murals. "There." She pointed up, above two mural-covered garage doors, to the side of a building: two narrow eyes stared down, and below them the word "Rejoice" in pale blue letters the color of the sky. "It's good advice, I think. It's so easy to go through life thinking only of what's wrong. Sometimes we need to stop and remember what's good, and be happy about that."

Greg's hand, still holding hers, slipped behind her waist and pulled her against him. "I couldn't agree more," he said, and rejoiced at the feel of her lips against his.

Her free hand slid along his bare forearm and then his sleeve, rolled back to the elbow. Her hand was warm on the back of his neck, her fingertips playing in his hair. He released her hand and tightened both arms around her as her lips opened to the darting pressure of his tongue.

Part of him whispered that this busy alley full of people was not the right place for a kiss like this, but the rest of him ignored it. On this delicious evening in late spring, or early summer, wrapped in Nicola's arms, nowhere could be more right than this.

"Hey," Greg whispered, when they drew apart. "That was more than I planned. Sorry."

Nicola laughed softly, and her hands skimmed down his back, then fell away. He missed her touch already.

"It takes two to kiss like that," she pointed out. "You've got nothing to be sorry for."

He brushed her hair back from her face.

"You hungry?" she asked, as they turned and headed back down the alley.

"Yes! I've been hungry since we walked past those Mexican restaurants by the car," he replied. "I'm surprised you haven't heard the gurgles." He patted one hand against his stomach.

Nicola said with dismay, "Does it have to be Mexican?"

He looked at her with curiosity. "No. Why? Don't you like it?"

"Oh I do!" she said. "I'm allergic to tomatoes, though, and so much Mexican food has them. It's easier to avoid it all than to force myself not to eat the salsa. I love salsa." She sounded forlorn.

Greg stopped, and stared, and then began to laugh. "I'll be damned!"

"What?" She frowned.

"I thought my mother was the only person who was allergic to tomatoes," he explained, still smiling. "I've never met anyone else. She'll be thrilled to know there's another sufferer."

Nicola sniffed. "I wouldn't call that a cause for celebration," she said tartly.

"Actually," Greg said, looking at her from the new perspective that this comparison with his mother had given him, "you look like my mother, too. I hadn't noticed that before." It was a disconcerting discovery.

She shrugged, and resumed walking. "That's hardly a surprise! That woman at the zoo said you and I look like twins, so it stands to reason I'd also look like your mother."

"Don't you think it's kind of weird?" he persisted.

"That I look like your mother?"

"That I'm attracted to someone who looks like my mother!" he exclaimed.

Nicola stopped again, and regarded him with an expression that he could only think of as indulgent skepticism. "No. If you were attracted to your mother, yes! I'm just me." She flicked a glance at him, then away, and smiled. "But I like that you're attracted to me."

She hesitated, and then with much less assurance she asked, "Um…do you like French food?"

"I like all food. Never yet met a nationality I didn't like."

"The thing is…." She paused again, looking uncertain, then plunged on with, "My friend Hélène's husband Antoine is a fantastic cook. I had supper at their apartment last night and he always makes too much, on purpose, so I can take it home. So I've got a pot of beef *bourguignon* plus some potatoes *dauphinoise* in the fridge that just need heating up. What I mean is, if you want, you can join me. It's very good!" she added hastily.

Greg had gone from polite yet puzzled at the beginning of her explanation to pleased at the end. "I'm sure it is. Real French food cooked by a real French man! I would love to join you, Nicola. Thank you for the invitation." He was pleased as much by the idea of the food as he was that she had invited him to her apartment, despite having had obvious doubts about the wisdom of doing such a thing on the second date. And," he added with a smile, "I know the invitation is only for supper, so relax."

Her own smile was part relief and part embarrassment. "Was it that plain? Sorry. I haven't been in this early dating stage in a while. I'm rusty."

He hesitated, but decided he had to tell her. "I lived with a woman in Seattle for three years. When it ended, I was…upset, and I took that year off that I told you about. I haven't been serious about anyone since then." He lifted her hand and kissed it. "So I'm rusty, too. But I'm sure we'll figure this out."

Her hand stroked his cheek, so soft. "I had wondered if it was something like that," she said, and the sympathy in her eyes was clear. "I guess we're two of the walking wounded, with bad relationships behind us."

There were at the car now and Greg opened the door for her. He put a hand on her arm. "A good one ahead, though, I hope."

"So do I."

She lived, as she had told him that first evening at Casey's, in Polk Gulch, near Lafayette Park. The building was brown brick, well kept, with stone steps flanked by potted shrubs leading under an archway to recessed wooden doors. Nicola's one-bedroom apartment was on the fifth floor.

"This is a nice building," Greg said, as he followed her down the hallway to her door. "I like these older ones. They have more character, I think. How long have you lived here?"

"About 10 years," she said, unlocking the door. "I like it, too. And it's close to everything, plus the park is nearby."

"That long?" he asked in surprise. He hadn't realized that the guy who ran off with her boss a year ago had lived here, too.

"Bathroom's there." She pointed to one of two closed doors on the right. "The other door is a closet. My bedroom," she added, as they walked down the hallway past an open door on the left.

Greg snatched a quick look, but couldn't see much – a glimpse of a bed with a white cover and bright cushions, a window, a dresser. At the far end, the hallway branched like a T, to the kitchen on the right and the living room on the left. He would never describe her apartment as spacious, but it was bright and airy with little architectural touches such as molded ceilings and art deco light fittings.

"Interesting curtains," he commented.

She looked confused, and then laughed. "Oh, the plants! Well, they need the light. I can't bring myself to get rid of any."

He followed her into the kitchen, where the window was also hidden behind foliage.

"Hélène and Antoine have huge, wrap-around balconies," Nicola said as she opened the fridge. "They get the sun almost all day long. And what do you think she grows out there? Cactus!"

Greg laughed at her look of disgust.

Nicola smiled. "I know, I could move. Do you like lemonade?"

"Love it," he said robustly. If he had been honest, Greg would have admitted that lemonade came far down on his list of favorite beverages, but he was so thrilled and intrigued to be in her home that he would happily drink the stuff all night if needed. He took his glass with a smile and sat at the table to watch while she pulled containers from the fridge. "Your friends are French, I take it?"

"Yes. They came here three years ago when Hélène was offered the position of West Coast sales manager for a French luxury goods group. Antoine is a software developer. His English isn't as good as hers, but, as he says himself, the code understands him perfectly well!" Nicola emptied the beef into a pan and put the potatoes in the microwave. "They have a son, Philippe, who's almost 13. He's in France right now. Antoine is afraid he's becoming too American and wants him to go to school back home. Hélène has other ideas!" she said with a laugh.

"How did you meet?"

"At Pilates. They live a couple of blocks from me, and Hélène and I go to the same class. We got along from the start, and became friends," she said.

Greg rose, and asked, "Can I help? Set the table maybe? I feel like an oaf sitting there while you do all the work."

Nicola laughed. "I'm stirring stew, which someone else made, so I wouldn't really describe that as work! But sure, thanks." She pointed out cupboards and drawers to him. "I suppose all your friends are back in Seattle," she said after a moment. "That must be lonely."

He shook his head, and shoved some bushy green thing out of the way. It bounced back. "No, actually, my best friends have lived in San Francisco for quite a while."

"Oh, you mentioned them!" she exclaimed. "They were why you stopped here on the way back from Mexico."

"Yes. Sam and Debbie. They have a son, too, Peter. He's nine. I'm his godfather," he added, rummaging for forks. "Sam and I had classes together at university, and Debbie is the sister of my roommate in second year. He set us up on a date. Boy, did that not work out!" Greg laughed, remembering that brightly lit pizza parlor and the way they had argued about politics all night, Debbie stabbing her fork towards him each time she made a point. "I liked her, but there was nothing between us. Not a spark of anything. She could have been my sister, not my roommate's. But I thought she and Sam would hit it off. So I introduced them, and I was best man at their wedding a year later."

They carried their plates to the table, and Greg pushed a straggling vine out of the way, hoping she wouldn't notice. "This is fantastic," he said, after the first mouthful.

Nicola nodded. "Antoine says there should be tomato paste in the beef, but he left it out because of me. You should taste his chocolate croissants!"

"He makes croissants?" Greg's fork paused halfway to his mouth. "What, by hand? From scratch?"

"Yes. Incredible, isn't it?"

"I hope that's not the sort of thing you're looking for," Greg commented with a smile. "A man who can make French pastries, I mean. I'm in big trouble if you are."

She rested her chin in her hand, as if considering the idea. "It would be a definite bonus if you could," she said, sounding serious, although the twitch of her lips was a giveaway. "They wouldn't have to be chocolate. You could start with the plain ones. Maybe Antoine could teach you."

Greg laughed. "Oh yes, I can see us in the kitchen, flour everywhere, while you and your friend relax on the balcony, drinking champagne and admiring the cactus!"

"Sounds like a good plan to me," she replied, eyes twinkling. "What about you? What sort of a woman are you looking for? Not a sailor, I hope!"

He regarded her, the laugh lingering. "That would be a definite bonus," he said, as seriously as she had. "But I'd settle for one with long dark hair and big blue eyes, who thinks a jungle is an adequate substitute for a curtain." He brushed the damned vine away, again.

"Oh."

Greg ran one hand over her shoulder, into that mass of dark hair, to bring her closer. "Just like you, in fact," he said.

Her mouth tasted of beef and wine and potatoes and lemons, and of her. Their tongues darted and jousted, teasing and playing.

Both of them were on the edges of their chairs, precariously balanced, lips and arms entwined. Greg leaned that little bit more and got both arms around her.

She gave a squeak of surprise when he pulled her off her chair and onto his lap, but didn't appear to object to finding herself there. Rather, she twisted to face him and wrapped her arms around his neck. Greg trailed his mouth down her neck, nibbling and kissing. One hand slipped under her blouse and stroked the soft, bare skin above her waist.

Greg gave one last, slow kiss to that enticing hollow at the base of her throat, telling himself not to go any lower. This was getting out of hand and he was in great danger of doing something he didn't want to do. Christ, yes, he wanted to, but what would she think of him, coming on so strong, so soon? Especially after assuring her that he knew supper was the only thing on offer. But her breasts were pressed against his chest, and with only his shirt and her blouse between them, he could feel their rise and fall as she breathed, feel the quick beat of her heart. The gentlest upward slide and he could, he could….

With extreme reluctance, Greg moved his hand from her bare waist to the less dangerous region of her back, and he pulled Nicola against him in a hug, safe and brotherly.

* *

"Ahoy, *Drifter*!"

Greg poked his head up through the deck, out of the hatch at the front. On the pontoon stood Sam and Debbie, a small heap of bags and a case of beer at their feet. Beside them, Peter was hopping from one foot to the other in excitement. "Come aboard!" Greg invited.

It was 7am on Saturday morning, the sun was shining and the air was clear and cool. A light breeze played in the bay, but Greg knew that once they cleared the Golden Gate the wind would pick up – perfect for sailing south along the coast.

"Ahoy, Greg!" shrilled the boy, as Greg reached across to hoist him over the rail and set him down in the cockpit.

"Hey, sport," said Greg, ruffling the boy's hair. "All set?"

Peter nodded enthusiastically. He had taken to sailing as naturally as Greg himself had at that age, and could competently handle his own small dinghy. Where this talent came from was a mystery to his landlubber parents.

"Stow your gear in the usual spot, put that beer in the cooler, and let's go," Greg said to them by way of greeting. "It's too nice a day for hanging around the marina!"

Ten minutes later, he backed the boat slowly out of its slip. Sam was sitting in the cockpit, legs stretched out and arms splayed along the rail, and Debbie was unpacking in the berth wedged into the front of the boat. Peter's head appeared as he started up the stairs from the cabin, but Greg's stern voice stopped him halfway up.

"Get your lifejacket on," he commanded. "You know the rules."

The boy's face was a mix of disappointment and disobedience. "Dad and you don't have one," he muttered.

"Your dad and I can swim. Very well. In an ocean. You can barely manage one length in a swimming pool," Greg pointed out, with some ruthlessness. He wasn't about to endanger the boy in order to avoid a tantrum. Then he added, with the beginning of a grin, "And don't forget that as well as we can swim, the sharks can swim even better. If you go overboard and sink, they'll get to you before we will."

Peter eyed him with suspicion, clearly weighing his chances with the sharks, and then backed down into the cabin.

* *

Nicola came to a gasping halt at the top of the stairs. If ever the day came when she could do this whole four-mile run in the Presidio without stopping at the top of these stairs, she intended to celebrate by hanging up her running shoes for good. To her left stretched the vast Pacific, its rollers crashing and booming onto the beach below, and ahead of her the Golden Gate Bridge pierced the sky in slender elegance. Behind her, Hélène dropped noisily to the grass.

"*Merde*, but I hate those stairs," declared Hélène. "Why do we do this to ourselves, eh?"

"Because we're masochistic suckers for punishment?" suggested Nicola. "No, wait, I think it's because both of us want to fit into the same swimsuits we wore last year."

Hélène laughed shortly. "Right now, I am happy to buy another one." She ran her fingers through her short blonde hair, which, Nicola noticed with envy, looked neat and perfectly coifed even after two miles of running. Nicola's own hair was straggling out of its ponytail and sticking to the sweat on her forehead.

She took her friend's extended hand and hauled her up. "How was Philippe when you phoned him?" inquired Nicola.

Hélène's face lit up. "Good. I miss my baby! But he will be home again soon."

"Philippe is 12! Hardly a baby," protested Nicola with a laugh.

"He will always be my baby. Sending him to France for this year of school was Antoine's idea, as you know, not mine. This summer," said Hélène, with a look that boded ill for domestic peace in their household, "we will discuss again this plan of Antoine."

Over Hélène's shoulder, Nicola saw a small boat making its way along the coast, its sails blazing white in the sun. The front bashed up and down, and spray flew every time it smacked into the water.

"How long do you think that boat is?"

Hélène shaded her eyes with one hand. "How long? You mean how short, I think! Nine meters?" She paused, doing the conversion in her head. "Thirty feet, I mean. Why do you ask?"

"Oh, no particular reason," said Nicola lightly.

Hélène looked at her closely. "No?"

"I met a man a couple of weeks ago who said he has a 30-foot sailboat, and he offered to take me sailing some time. Look at that!" she exclaimed. "Who in their right mind would go on the ocean in that little tub?"

Hélène smiled. "*Oh là là!*"

Nicola stared at her. "*Oh là là!?*" she repeated in disbelief. "I have never heard you say that!"

"I believe it is the man, not the boat, that you are thinking of right now, no? Which means this is about affairs of the heart, and the only language for discussing affairs of the heart is French. But since you speak no more than four words of French, all of them badly, I shall content myself with an '*Oh là là!*,'" explained Hélène. "So, who is he?"

"No one special," said Nicola, trying to sound casual. She failed. "Just someone from work."

"From work?" repeated Hélène in surprise. "But you refuse to have anything to do with men from your work. Or has that changed?"

In a low voice, Nicola admitted, "I guess we went out once. Okay, twice. Oh, and he bought me lunch yesterday, does that count?"

Hélène nodded with mock solemnity, and said, "I think we must include it. Three dates in how long?"

"Um, the first was last Sunday."

"Not even one week! He must be something!" exclaimed Hélène.

Nicola winked, and said, "*Oh là là!*"

* *

It had been an exhilarating sail south, *Drifter* leaning into the waves and cutting her way effortlessly through the water. Exhilarating, that is, for Greg and for Peter, who hadn't even objected to being tethered to the rail to ensure he didn't slide overboard as the boat heeled and rolled. For Debbie, it had been hours of lying on Greg's bed, which being at the back of the boat was marginally more stable than the berth at the front, one hand clutching a cool wet cloth to her forehead and the other clutching her stomach. Sam had toughed it out on deck, marveling at his crazy kid who loved the way the boat was bouncing around.

But now they were at a calm anchor in the sheltered bay, the men had gone for a swim and cracked open the beers, and Greg was relieved to see that Debbie began to take an interest in life again. The two of them were in the cabin, making a salad while the potatoes baked in the microwave. On deck, Sam and Peter were firing up the barbecue for hot dogs and hamburgers.

Without looking up from the tomato she was chopping, Debbie said, "There's a woman in my office I think you'd really like. Why don't we all go out for supper one night, and you can meet her?"

"Debbie!" laughed Greg. "That's the third woman you've tried to fix me up with!"

"You shouldn't be single, Greg. If ever a man was meant to be married and have children, it's you," said Debbie earnestly. "You're great with Peter."

He rinsed a cucumber and patted it dry, but didn't say anything, and she went on with, "Hey, I know you needed time after you and Jackie split. You can tell everyone else that story about dropping out of the rat race, but you can't fool me."

A wry smile, and Greg said, "I never could."

Like everyone else, Greg had fallen for all of Jackie's reasons for postponing marriage. He still found it nearly impossible to believe, though, that Jackie could have lied like she had about wanting to start a family and no longer taking contraception. The truth had devastated him.

"Have you gone out with anyone since you moved here?" Debbie demanded.

He looked at her with amusement. "I'm not a hermit. Of course I have."

Her expression was doubtful.

"I met someone at the yacht club not long after I settled in," he explained patiently. "We went out a few times. It didn't lead to anything."

"Why didn't she snatch you up?"

"Maybe because I didn't want her to snatch me up," he laughed. "Or maybe not every woman thinks I'm as much of a prize as you do! You see nothing but my good side, you know."

She snorted. "Right. Thirteen years of seeing nothing but your good side. What about your new job? Is there really no one there good enough for you?" she asked.

He said nothing, and she looked at him again, and began to smile. "Or is there?"

Greg shrugged lightly. "There might be." Not even to Debbie

would he admit how hard he had fallen for Nicola, and how fast. "I only met her a couple of weeks ago. And she has a rule against dating colleagues."

Debbie scoffed. "And you're going to let that stop you?"

Greg looked up from the cucumber, and grinned. "Three dates so far, so I guess not."

* *

Kylie plunked herself onto the edge of Nicola's desk, arms folded. "That Greg! Can you believe the nerve? After the way he treated me, now all of a sudden he's got nothing better to do than hang around the third floor and pretend to talk to you. All he's trying to do is make me jealous!"

"Uh, Kylie—"

"I'm sorry, Nicky. It's nice of you to pretend to be happy to see him, but he's wasting his time. Oh, and yours too," Kylie added, in what was obviously an afterthought.

"Kylie, I should tell you—"

One leg crossed over the other. "If he thinks I'm going to give him another chance, well, it won't—"

"Kylie!" exclaimed Nicola in sharp exasperation. "Stop! And lower your voice." The other woman had no problem with everyone within 20 feet knowing many of the details of her love life, but Nicola drew the line when it involved her personally. "Greg really is coming here to see me. We've, um, gone out a few times."

Kylie stared at Nicola in stupefaction, trying on expressions of disbelief and anger and outrage before settling on glee. "Nicky, you broke your dumb rule!" she crowed, and everyone within 20 feet looked up. "About damned time, too!"

She held out her hand, and Nicola, amused, shook it. "No hard feelings, right?" asked Kylie anxiously. "I mean, you're not sore because he liked me first?"

Nicola shook her head solemnly, biting her lip to keep the laugh inside. "These things happen. I see no reason why we can't all be adults about it."

Kylie jumped to her feet and clapped her hands, laughing.

"I am so happy for you, Nicky! And if he breaks your heart, I'll cut the bastard's balls off."

She smiled as she watched Kylie walk away, touched by the younger woman's genuine pleasure. Then she frowned, seeing how Kylie's bikini-cut panties dug into her generous curves and how the tight green pencil skirt clung to every bulge of skin and wrinkle of underwear. Did Kylie never check the rear view in a mirror?

Nicola turned back, and met the eyes of Max, looking at her with faint disappointment.

"You broke your rule, huh?"

In all the dizzy exhilaration of this budding relationship with Greg, she hadn't given a thought to how her colleagues might react, particularly those men whose offers had been firmly declined.

"Oh, Max," she said with consternation. "It's not…I mean, I…." Nicola had no idea what she did mean, beyond the bare truth that Max did not fascinate and excite her, and Greg did. She could not possibly say that.

"It's okay, Nicky. My heart's not broken and my ego's not crushed," he assured her with a wide smile. "I feel kind of stupid, that's all, telling Greg he was wasting his time with you."

She leaned over and touched his hand. "You sure, Max?"

He nodded, messy hazel hair flopping into his eyes. "Tell you what, if he does break your heart, I'll help Kylie cut his balls off. How's that?"

Nicola laughed. "Deal!"

* *

Nicola and Hélène had returned in mud-splattered weariness this Saturday morning from their assault on the rain-soaked running tracks of the Presidio. The cool, cloudy early morning was giving way to sun, and they were sprawled on cushioned loungers on Hélène's balcony with its view of the bay.

Hélène pushed the plate of warm croissants towards Nicola. "Have another, please. We assuredly burned off all of the calories for a dozen croissants this morning, and Antoine will be desolate if you have only one. He made them because I told him I would invite you."

Nicola hesitated for no more than a second. "I still can't believe your husband can actually make these things! He could give up the software business and become San Francisco's most sought-after baker," she commented, pulling apart the flaky, buttery pastry and dipping one end into her café au lait. Post-run breakfasts at Hélène's apartment had a delightful feel of Paris to them, but they did undo everything the two of them had recently sweated over.

"I believe not! He enjoys making them from time to time, but to get up at 3am to make them for customers every day? My Antoine is too lazy for that," she said crisply. And then smiled. "And can you imagine me in the front of the store, selling them?"

"I think poor Antoine would get no sleep at all, trying to make all the croissants that you could persuade people to buy," replied Nicola. "If you can do it with cognac and handbags, you can do it with pastry."

Hélène shrugged, and said complacently, "This is true."

Nicola's attention was diverted by the squat, elderly woman who had appeared on a balcony of the building across the road. Dressed in a fluffy blue bathrobe and wearing scruffy slippers, she was stumping purposefully from one end of her balcony to the other. She would touch the rail, turn, and repeat. A sleek black cat sat on a table in the middle of the balcony, head turning to watch her go first one way, then the other.

"Ah, it's Madame La Marche!" exclaimed Hélène.

"Who?"

Hélène laughed. "That's what Philippe has named her. Mrs Walk, you would say. She does that every day."

Nicola said thoughtfully, "And who's to say that she doesn't have the right idea? That looks better than killing ourselves on the Presidio stairs."

Hélène grinned wickedly. "And I'm sure your Greg would admire you just as much if you wore such a lovely gown rather than last summer's bikini. It is the one with polka dots, no?"

"Yes." Nicola eyed the plate of croissants. What harm could one more do?

"What delightful pastime has Greg planned for you this

weekend? There has been the zoo, live jazz and supper at the Grand Café, walking on the beach at sunset, a Spanish tapas cooking class and admiring the murals along Balmy Alley, in addition to those things you have not told me; what could be left?" Hélène asked. "Nicola, he is too good to be true! You say he is handsome, he makes you laugh, he kisses you so that your toes tingle, he volunteers at the zoo and he likes children! For he must like them; think of the noisy little brutes that overrun the zoo. Surely he must be hiding a terrible flaw."

Nicola laughed. "A terrible flaw?"

"Or perhaps a terrible secret? Yes, that is it!" Hélène threw herself into her theory. "There is a deep, dark secret that will prevent you from ever finding true happiness with this man."

"Hélène! What could he possibly be hiding?" demanded Nicola, still laughing.

She shrugged again. "I don't know. Perhaps…perhaps he wears women's underwear?"

"What!" exclaimed Nicola in astonishment. "Why would that be the first deep, dark secret you would think of?"

Hélène sipped her café au lait. "I am a Frenchwoman, after all. We know these things."

Chapter 4

THIS WAS IT. She had known Greg for four weeks now, and had run out of excuses. Even the weather had let her down. It was a beautiful Sunday in June, the sky was blue and the sun was warm, and delightful breezes played over the water; and, God help her, she was about to go sailing.

Hélène had shrieked with laughter yesterday when Nicola had told her the nature of Greg's planned "delightful pastime." "Oh, *chérie*," she had said, "this must be love!"

Nicola fell in with the stream of passengers leaving the train station. In the car park, she spotted Greg waving, and hitched the beach bag's strap higher over her shoulder as she headed his way. She had followed his suggestion that she bring her swimsuit and a change of clothes. And she had brought something else, too: tucked in a small pocket inside the bag were two condoms. Just in case. After three weeks of dating, and kissing, and cuddling, she was ready for more.

What worried her, though, was his reaction to Kylie and her casual approach to sex; would Greg consider nine dates in three weeks to still fall within the casual sex bracket? If Nicola made a move he wasn't ready for, would that be the end? She strongly hoped not, because apart from Greg being the sexiest damned man she had ever dated, it had been a long, passion-free year since Andrew had run off.

"Hello," they said at the same time, and laughed.

She leaned closer to kiss Greg, a brief touch of lips that gave away nothing of what she had just been contemplating. "I'm sorry to drag you to the station like this."

"It's not your fault someone backed into your car," Greg replied. "Did you take your seasickness pill?"

She nodded dutifully. Not only did she have no desire to get sick, but she couldn't imagine him having any interest in making love to her if she was pasty and nauseous. Nor, of course, would she be able to muster much enthusiasm for it herself.

It was only a few minutes in the car from the station to the marina. The forest of bare masts was a giveaway even to Nicola.

As they walked towards the security gate leading to the pontoon, she asked, "What's that noise?"

"What noise?"

"Don't you hear it? That sort of metallic tapping-knocking sound. It's everywhere." How could he not hear it?

Understanding dawned on Greg's face. "No, I don't hear it. I mean, not anymore. It's the bits of rigging flapping against the masts in the breeze. You'll hear it in every marina."

She looked at him pointedly. "I've never been in a marina before. How can you sleep with that racket?"

He shrugged. "I don't hear this, and I'll bet you don't hear that roar of traffic outside your apartment."

"What traffic?"

He laughed, and ushered her through the gate. "Exactly."

She followed him along the main pontoon, passing smaller ones stretching to right and left, each lined with small yachts. So many boats! And there was another cluster of pontoons and boats off to one side. At the end of the pontoon, he turned right and led her halfway along a row of boats, stopping at one on his left.

"Here she is!" he announced with a wide smile of pride.

Drifter was a sleek white shape with lots of shining metal and gleaming wood. It looked bigger than she was dreading, tied up in its own little U-shaped harbor. Two small walkways separated Greg's boat from the ones on either side.

"It's pretty," she said, with mild surprise, and felt a stirring of interest at the idea of being on the bay on it.

Greg stepped easily over the boat's wire rail. "Come aboard," he invited, and held out a hand to help her. "Be sure to hold on to something whenever you're moving around."

There was a slightly greater sense of movement on the boat than on the pontoon, but not enough to disturb her. Once down the narrow stairway to the cabin, Nicola was pleasantly surprised at how bright it was. The walls and ceiling were white, and all the cupboards and shelves were of a pale wood. Air and sunlight poured in through a number of small open windows and hatches.

"There's the bathroom," he pointed to a small door, "and

at the front is a berth, uh, a room, you can use. For changing clothes, I mean."

"Okay. Is that where you sleep?" she asked. She could see through its open door, and it was small. No, it wasn't big enough to be small; it was tiny. How could he possibly live here? she wondered. They were standing at the bottom of the stairs, and there was nothing but a minuscule kitchen, then padded benches on either side of a drop-down table in the center, and that small room no more than five steps away. That was it.

But he shook his head. "No, that's the 'spare room.' My cabin is there." He pointed to another small door, to the left of the kitchen.

She had to say it. "How can you possibly live here?"

Greg threw back his head and laughed. "I have low standards, I guess! And I don't have much stuff, so the space isn't a problem."

Nicola shook her head in amazement. She looked around the cabin again. So small!

"What's that?" she asked, pointing to something woven that stuck up over the top of a bench cushion.

He plucked the object from the shelf. "It's a floor mat," he explained. "Or rather, it will be when it's done."

She turned it over in her hands. It was rope, intricately knotted and woven to form a mat. "You must have a lot of patience to make this," she commented.

"Not a chance!" he exclaimed. "That's my godson's handiwork. Peter. He thinks I need a mat at the foot of the stairs. Every time he comes, he adds a bit to it. A very small bit!" Greg traced one finger along the knotting. "He did that yesterday." He tossed it back onto the shelf.

"You ready to go?" he asked her with a smile. "Last chance to jump ship!"

She shook her head. "I'll hang around."

"Good," Greg said, his voice gone soft and his gaze steady.

Nicola swallowed. What if I push him onto that bench and–

But he took her hand to lead her back outside, and with a sigh of resignation, Nicola followed.

In only a few minutes, they were motoring away from the

pontoon. Before they cleared the marina, Greg asked, "Do you want a lifejacket?" He stood behind the wheel, peering ahead.

She was sitting on the wooden decking around the cockpit, her back against the wire railing and actually enjoying herself, but now she looked up at him, startled. "Do I need one?"

"It's up to you. How well do you swim?" he asked with a smile of mischief. "In case you go over the side unexpectedly, I mean."

"I think I can manage to stay afloat until you turn this thing around and come back for me," she replied tartly. Then, with suspicion, "What are you laughing at?"

"Peter's a great kid, most of the time, but he's got a real thing about not wearing his lifejacket. I gave him a story about the sharks getting to him before I could if he wasn't floating on the surface. I debated trying it out on you, too, but I think you're harder to scare." Then he asked, with studied casualness, "Do you want children some day?"

"Yes. Very much. And given I'm almost 36 now, I should probably get started soon," she said lightly. Matching his casual tone, she added, "How about you?"

He looked down at her. "Yes."

Their eyes met, and held.

Desire flashed through Nicola, hot and fast. Oh yes, she wanted children, but what she really wanted right now was to do what made them.

Greg stepped out from behind the wheel and she pulled her legs up, out of the way of whatever he was about to do. How could anyone make sense of these ropes? she wondered.

"Am I in the way?" she asked.

"Never."

She paused, smiling at that. "Can I help?"

He spared her a glance as he wound a rope around a winch. "No, I'm fine on my own. And I think you're only being polite, aren't you?"

"Yes." She couldn't imagine herself ever being any use on this boat, except maybe making coffee.

Then Greg wrapped both hands around the winch handle and began to turn it furiously, his whole body swaying with the effort as he crouched over it, legs apart. A sail crept up the mast, flapping and rattling in the breeze. Nicola's eyes widened, but she wasn't looking at the sail. It wasn't only the gym that explained those muscles on his arms, and the breadth of his shoulders.

When he had finished, and also raised a sail at the front, he straightened up and looked around. He gave her a smile as he leaned over and tweaked the wheel, but Nicola thought his attention was more on the boat than on her. Sweat glistened on his forehead and darkened the back of his t-shirt. In one easy motion, Greg pulled the shirt over his head and tossed it onto the floor of the cockpit.

Oh. My. God. A breathless jolt shot through Nicola.

He was wearing only swim shorts, which hung low on his hips. Brown; his skin was tanned everywhere she could see, from forehead to toes. Did he sail in the nude? Under the shorts, what color was he? Her gaze traveled over the hair sprinkled lightly across his wide chest and down to the solid, defined muscles of his waist, and farther down to where the line of dark hair dipped into the shorts and led to– she looked hastily away.

Greg seemed unaware of her scrutiny, and her heightened color, as he turned in a circle, shading his eyes with one hand. He hoisted up the shorts in an absent gesture.

"Where…." Nicola cleared her throat. "Where are we going, by the way?" The Golden Gate Bridge and Sausalito were behind them and over to the left, and it looked to her as if they were heading towards San Pablo Bay.

Greg turned to her, and with a smile he sat beside her, one hand on the wheel and one hand on her knee.

"China Camp," he replied. "It should only take a couple of hours, max, with today's wind. I thought we could have a swim, and lunch. Then when we get back to the marina, we can have supper. I make a mean chicken stir-fry, I warn you! Is that okay?"

She slid closer and he lifted his arm to drape it around her shoulders. "Sounds great," Nicola said. "We used to go hiking there when I was a kid, but I've never seen it from the water." His skin, where she leaned against him, was warm from the sun and the exertion, warm and smooth.

After a while, she said, "I can't believe I've never been sailing before. This is great."

"Good," he said, and his lips pressed against her forehead. "Though I warn you that as sailing goes, what we're doing right now is pretty tame. More of a stroll than a sail."

A little while after that, she said, "Greg, have you seen that container ship?" She pointed tentatively to the massive vessel bearing straight for them; it wasn't worryingly close, but it moved significantly faster than they moved.

He nodded.

"Shouldn't we get out of its way?"

He shook his head. "No need. We're under sail, it's under engines. We have right of way."

Nicola turned to stare at him. "You're joking. You expect that thing to politely get out of our way?"

"Oh yeah, they always do. Well, sometimes it can be touch and go. Depends on the captain's mood, I guess. Some of them like to play chicken," he confided.

"You play chicken with that?" Her voice squeaked. "Greg, it's very close!"

She finally noticed the way his lips were pressed together, and the tilt of his head. "Oh!" Nicola slapped his arm.

"If it will make you happier, I'll tack," Greg laughed.

* *

Nicola made her way with care down the stairs into the cabin while Greg dropped the anchor and did mysterious things with the sails. She had been enthralled as the state park grew slowly larger with their approach, and pointed out to him where she and her family had hiked and camped. She hadn't been here in years, and felt nostalgic to see the familiar line of ramshackle wooden buildings straggling along the beach, the green wooded hills behind and the spindly dock stretching out over the mud flats.

She closed the door to the small cabin at the front of the boat. He had called this a V-berth, and she could certainly see why! She couldn't believe his friends, Peter's parents, both slept in this small bed, which was itself V-shaped to fit the walls.

Poor Debbie! Greg had related the tale of how sick she had been during that weekend sail. Nicola had not felt so much as a twinge of seasickness in the time it had taken them to get here, but she didn't know if that was because she was a naturally robust sailor (not likely!), or if the bay was much calmer than the ocean Debbie had experienced, or if Debbie had not taken any pills. She hoped she'd get a chance to meet Debbie and talk about it. Nicola knew Greg well enough by now to know that if they had any future together, this boat would be part of it.

But, Nicola vowed as she unzipped the beach bag, there is no way I will ever live on this thing!

* *

Greg pulled sharply on the anchor cable. It seemed firm. The bottom was sticky mud, he had been told, and could be unstable. He had never been here himself, but a neighbor at the marina had been full of helpful information. And there was only one other boat nearby, so even if the anchor slipped, it wouldn't be too bad.

His eyes fell on a dirty shoe print on the deck. Where had that come from? Yesterday, he and Peter had polished and scrubbed *Drifter* so that she looked her best for Nicola, and Greg would have sworn that print hadn't been there this morning. It couldn't be Nicola, for she was in smooth-soled deck shoes.

He grinned, remembering that first sight of her this morning in the crowd streaming from the station. She had been wearing white pants that stopped somewhere between her knees and her ankles – he knew women had a name for them, but he could never remember it – and a blue-and-white striped top, plus a white baseball cap on her head: it was as if she had stepped out of a sailing fashion photograph. At least she had dressed the part, even if, as he knew, she had agreed to go sailing only to please him.

And to please her, he had cleaned *Drifter*'s cabin as thoroughly as the deck and brightwork, putting fresh flowers on the table and fresh towels in the bathroom – and fresh sheets on his bed. Just in case. Today was three weeks since their first date at the zoo, three weeks of long walks and long talks, drinks and dinners, and increasingly intense kisses and caresses. Greg was ready for more, and he fervently hoped that Nicola was, too.

"What a great view," Nicola commented behind him, and he turned.

Holy Christ, talk about great views. She was wearing a sky blue bikini with big white polka dots, and nothing else. He had never seen her in anything that could be called revealing, no low necklines or high hems, so he had been expecting a more modest swimsuit, probably a one-piece.

This polka-dotted thing was not modest, and as the blood rushed south of his navel Greg wondered what else about Nicola might not be as modest as he had thought. He was thankful that his sunglasses prevented her from seeing how his gaze lingered on her full breasts, their curve highlighted by a scallop of ruffle below. The straps rose over her shoulders, which were as straight and as level as the horizon at sea. Below the bikini top, she tapered in like an hourglass, and then swelled out again, the pale skin of her hips disappearing into the bikini bottom. Her legs were shapely and long, like those of a dancer. Must be all that running she does, he thought absently. She turned to look at the beach and revealed an absurd flounce of polka-dotted ruffles sticking out behind.

He wanted to fling her onto the deck, rip off those polka dots and ruffles, and discover what lay beneath them.

"Nice bikini," Greg managed to say.

His eyes followed her hand as she ran it along the curve of her waist. He licked his lips.

"Thanks! I was such a slob all winter I wasn't certain it would still fit."

"Oh, it fits," he assured her.

Nicola flashed a smile at him, stood poised for a moment on the stern and then dove neatly into the water, making only the smallest of splashes. The water was murky with mud particles and Greg soon lost sight of her. He wasn't really worried, but he wasn't entirely at ease, either.

She surfaced, much farther from the boat than he had been

looking, took a few breaths and then calmly treaded water, looking around with a smile. Yes, Greg thought, she'd have no trouble staying afloat if she ever went over the side.

"How's the water?" he called.

"Freezing!" she yelled back cheerfully. "Get in here, unless you're a coward!"

His dive was not as elegant as hers, but his strokes were much stronger. He came to a halt as she disappeared under the water, that ridiculous bunch of ruffles sticking up as she doubled over. With only his head above the water he had even less chance of spotting her than he had from the boat, so he floated and waited. She'd have to come up for air at some time.

She did, shooting up right in front of him and blowing a spray of salty water into his face, then laughing. Greg grabbed for her. Her arms crossed behind his neck and he ran his hands down her back.

"You're like a seal," he said. "Smooth and sleek."

The kiss ended abruptly when they forgot to keep moving their legs, and their chins began to sink below the water. They broke apart, spluttering.

"Race you back to the boat," she dared.

He was off, churning through the water. When he climbed up the ladder at the stern and looked back, she was stroking lazily towards the boat.

"Since you're there anyway," she said, and held up a hand, "you can help me up."

He helped her up and drew her nearer. "You set me up, didn't you?"

She laughed, her hands against his chest, and pushed him away.

Greg lay on his back on the sun-warmed wood along the wide flat edge of the cockpit, watching as she wrung water from her hair. He'd guessed those curves were hiding under the pantsuits and blouses she wore to work; he had caressed her and stroked her, but never undressed her. To finally see her like this...Christ. The boat swung easily on the anchor and the sun fell full in his eyes. He closed them, enjoying the feel of the gentle movement and the warmth of the sun after the cold of the water, and wondering what all that skin would feel like against his skin. His fantasy ended abruptly with a patter of cold water on his chest and he jerked half up, to find Nicola leaning over him, laughing and squeezing her hair.

"You'll pay for that," he laughed, and pulled her down to him.

She sprawled partly on him and partly on the deck. Greg slid one hand slowly along her back, tracing the bumps of her spine, until his hand rose with the swell of her bottom – where he ended up with a handful of ruffles.

"This is the silliest bikini," he murmured, lips trailing down her neck.

"Don't you like it?" she asked.

"I love it. But it is silly."

Her tongue, warm and moist, traced around the curve of his ear.

"Agh!" He sat up suddenly, almost dumping her into the cockpit.

"What? What is it?" she asked wildly, looking around in alarm.

Rubbing his ear, he said, "Don't ever do that!"

She started to laugh. "Oh dear. Not an erogenous zone for you, is it?"

Greg shook his head. His reaction had been completely beyond his control, but she was right: what he had felt was the physical equivalent of nails on a blackboard. "I do have others," he told her. She cocked her head to one side and regarded him, eyebrows tilted up and blue eyes moving over him as if expecting to see signs reading "erogenous zone here!".

The sound of an engine drew his attention from her to the motor cruiser that slowly approached. Another sailboat had also anchored while they had been swimming, and he decided, reluctantly, that this wasn't the best place for what they had been doing.

"You ready for lunch?" he asked. "I've got cheese and fruit and a baguette."

She nodded. "I'm famished. Is there a shower? I hate the feel of dried salt water."

"Come on, I'll show you."

The bathroom was tucked along one hull. A toilet, a counter with a sink, and cupboards fitted over the counter. A square of floor with a large drain hole in the middle, and a small window. There was no shower, or none that a landlubber like Nicola would recognize.

Greg pulled the faucet up, revealing a long flexible hose. "Spray it over yourself. Try not to get the towels wet, okay?"

She pulled a face at him, and pushed him out.

Greg stood in the galley and reached out his hand for a knife to slice the baguette. But his mind was in the bathroom: she was in there, nude, a few feet away. He imagined running soapy hands over her, up those long legs and the curve of her hips, the roundness of her breasts, his hands gliding on her smooth, warm, wet skin. Greg twitched at the damp swim shorts that clung to him uncomfortably. Lunch, he told himself, think of lunch!

"Greg? Can you give me a hand?" she called.

He frowned, wondering what she could need a hand with. Turn on tap, spray water. That was it. He twitched again at the shorts, hoping nothing was noticeable, and went back to the bathroom.

She was still in her bikini, her arms raised, leaning against the counter. "The clasp seems to be stuck. Would you try?"

His breath stopped. "Turn around," he said hoarsely.

"It's at the front."

He swallowed. He would have to put one hand inside the top in order to get hold of the clasp. Her skin was cool and stippled with goose bumps, but, oh, so wonderful against the back of his fingers.

The clasp opened easily.

"I guess I loosened it," she said with a straight face, and put her arms around him.

Greg shuddered, with no hope now of any restraint. His hands cupped her breasts and he lowered his head to them. He felt the shiver run through her as his lips brushed her, and he tasted the salt. Nicola's hands were on his back and down into his shorts, cool and soft, closing around his backside and then pulling him hard against her. Oh Christ, how he wanted her! The air brushed cold against his damp skin as she tugged the shorts down.

Greg kicked them to one side and reached over her shoulder, wrenching open a cupboard. He fumbled a condom from the package, fingers clumsy in his urgency, and ripped it open. She had shrugged off her top and was wriggling out of the wet bikini bottom. He moved against Nicola and she lifted one leg, wrapping it around his hips and bracing her foot against the wall behind him. She was liquid fire in his arms, scorching him and burning him, and there was nothing in the world but the feel of her body moving with his.

Nicola fell against him with a sigh, and her foot slid slowly back to the floor.

Greg rested his forehead against hers, breathing hard. "That was not how I had imagined our first time," he whispered.

"Me, either," she whispered back, then added, "But damn, it was good." The boat lurched and she clutched his arms for balance. "See, the earth moved!" she joked.

He started to reply, a glib comment about San Francisco and earthquakes, and then realized what had happened at the same time as he heard the shouts of alarm from outside. "The anchor's come free!" He was out the door and up the stairs.

The warning calls turned to shrieks of laughter as Greg, stark naked, lunged for the engine controls at the side of the cockpit. As *Drifter* backed slowly away from the cruiser she had seemed intent on ramming, Greg became aware that at least a dozen people in three boats were laughing and clapping, and pointing at him. Well, there wasn't a lot he could do but brazen this out. Then he saw Nicola coming up from the cabin, a large red towel wrapped around her, and in a moment she had whipped another one around his hips and tucked it in.

Cheers rang out, and someone called, "There's quick thinking!"

He put an arm around her and pulled her to him, and kissed her, to the delight of their audience.

"Do you think we'll be on YouTube tomorrow?" she asked, with a teasing smile.

"Probably," Greg said glumly.

* *

Nicola reclined on one of the padded benches, her back against the wall of the V-berth. Greg had declined her offer of help, so she sipped her wine and watched him make supper. One part of her mind was thinking that she had never dated a man so at ease in the kitchen, and no previous boyfriend would have spent an evening happily making tapas, as Greg had done, nor have suggested it in the first place. Tonight he was cooking only a stir-fry, but it might have been a five-course gourmet meal as far as she was concerned. Her stomach rumbled as the smells of chicken sautéing with onions and garlic filled the cabin.

Another part of her mind, however, was remembering what had happened in the bathroom and wondering when it could be repeated, preferably somewhere more comfortable. His jeans were old and had molded themselves to his thighs and backside, the t-shirt stretched across his shoulders and chest, and as much as she enjoyed looking at him, Nicola found it difficult to sit still. She knew now what was under the clothes, and she longed to touch him, to have him touch her, to feel him inside her again.

She took a deep breath, and told herself to slow down. To let it happen. To not leap up, push him to the floor and ravish him. Although, she admitted, given that he was many times stronger than she was, the only way she was going to ravish him was if he let her. Nicola smiled, and sipped her wine.

Greg looked up and caught her watching him, and raised his glass in salute.

"You don't drink much, do you?" she remarked, noticing that his wine had barely been touched.

"Alcohol? No. Not at all if I'm sailing or driving, and I do one or the other most days. I can't remember the last time I was really drunk," he added thoughtfully. "University, probably."

Nicola worked out the logic of the no-drinking-at-all-if-driving rule. "So am I walking back to the station tonight?" she asked.

"You can, if you want. Or you can get a taxi from the yacht club. Or," he added, and walked around the table to lean over her so that his face was inches from hers, "you can stay here.

That's what I'm hoping you'll do. I can drive you home early tomorrow, so you can change for work. I'd hate to think I put clean sheets on the bed for nothing." He leaned the small extra distance, and kissed her, long and slow, touching her only where their lips met and sending fire dancing along her nerves.

Greg pulled away and looked at her, eyebrows raised.

"If you went to all that trouble, it would be discourteous not to stay." Courtesy had nothing to do with it; desire quivered through her at the thought of staying. Sex in the bathroom, so brief and so intense, had been the release of the tension that had been building between them. But a whole night of loving each other, playing and discovering, in his bed…oh, that would be something very different.

He went back to his cooking, and her eyes devoured him.

The setting sun bathed the cabin in gold while they ate, and seagulls cried harsh and strident over the ever-present flap of rigging on masts.

"This is really good," Nicola said. "What other specialties do you have?"

"I'll show you later," he said with a leer, then with assumed innocence, "Oh, did you mean cooking?"

She eyed him with a leer of her own. "Not necessarily."

He laughed, and forked up a chunk of celery. "It's your birthday soon, isn't it?"

"That's an interesting change of topic. What made you think of that?" she asked.

"I remembered you told me your sister is five weeks older than you, so I figured it had to be coming up," he explained. "And I wondered if you're one of those women who refuse to have birthdays and don't want anyone to acknowledge them, or if I'm expected to shower you with presents and take you out for an expensive dinner. I'd like a warning, either way, so I get it right."

"Oh, showers of presents and expensive dinners, definitely," she said with great seriousness. Then, "You don't have to do anything, Greg! I get enough of that at home. Next Sunday I'll have to go to Sausalito and do the whole family thing. You and *Drifter* can have a proper sail!"

He glanced at her but was silent, toying with a piece of chicken.

"Unless," she began hesitantly, "I mean, you can come with me. If you want. I'd like that. I wouldn't expect you to want to, though."

"I'll have to meet them all at some point. There would be less pressure at something like a birthday party," he replied. "Or don't they know about me?"

"I had to explain the sudden increase in my social activities somehow," she laughed. "The truth seemed easiest. Does your family know about me?"

"You may have crept into an email or two," he admitted. "And a text message. Maybe a phone call, too."

They looked at each other, blue eyes into blue eyes, admitting for the first time, even in this roundabout way, that what was going on was important enough to share with their families. Greg traced one finger down her cheek, and smiled. "I think it's time you saw the only room in the boat you haven't seen already. And I don't mean the sail locker."

When he opened his cabin door, she stood in the galley and peered over his shoulder. It wasn't square, it wasn't triangular, it wasn't any shape she could name. Nor was it much bigger than that squashed berth at the front. And most of it was the bed, a mattress fitted into the strange shape at knee height, plus a drawer unit to one side and a closet to the other. One window high up let in air and light.

"The master bedroom?" she asked.

"And yours, for tonight at least," Greg replied softly. "Although I hope it's not the only time. Put your arms up." She did, and he pulled her striped top over her head, then reached behind to unfasten her bra. "This one doesn't seem to be stuck, either," he said with a smile. "I couldn't believe you did that. I was afraid I was reading it wrong, and you would slap my face or something."

She laughed, low in her throat, and lifted first one foot and then the other as he slid her pants down. Then she pulled off his t-shirt and threw it onto the small pile of clothes building up on top of the drawer unit. She ran her hands over the hard muscles of his chest, and down to the zipper of his jeans. "And I was afraid you would think I was only after casual sex, and throw me out."

The jeans didn't slide as easily as her pants, and he had to tug them down. He stood before her in the dimly lit cabin in only his underwear.

I must remember to tell Hélène it's boxer shorts, she thought, absurdly, and bit back the giggle.

His shorts and her panties joined the rest of their clothes, and Greg eased her down onto the bed with him.

"Oh, Nicola," he whispered, as her body rose to meet the rhythm of his own, "what's between us is anything but casual."

Chapter 5

Five months later

"THIS IS RIDICULOUS," groaned Greg. He folded his hands under his head on the pillow, and frowned.

"What is?" Nicola asked, her fingers tracing over his chest. *Drifter* rocked gently in the wash from a passing boat. To her surprise, she had found that she enjoyed the motion once she became accustomed to it.

"My gray suit is at the cleaners, and the pinstriped one is at your place," he explained. "I'm going to have to get dressed for work at your apartment tomorrow."

She laughed softly. "Or you could buy another one in the morning."

"Very funny," he said, and turned his head to kiss her forehead. "If we were married, everything would be in one place and neither of us would have to get up early and drive halfway across the city on the way to work."

"That's a practical, if not very romantic, reason for getting married," she remarked.

"Well, there's the love thing, too, and the kids," he pointed out.

"What kids?"

He sighed. "Ours, of course! But mostly I think we should do it for the sake of an extra hour in bed each morning."

Nicola pushed herself up to look at him, joy and delight fizzing through her veins as she began to suspect that he was serious. "Greg, is this a proposal? It doesn't sound like I had imagined one would sound, but I could be wrong."

He looked startled. "Christ, I made a mess of that, didn't I?" Greg scrambled up to kneel on the bed beside her, legs wide for balance, and flung out his arms in supplication.

Interesting view, thought Nicola, as her eyes traced along one hairy leg to where it met the other hairy leg.

"Nicola my darling, will you marry me? Will you make me the happiest man in the world? Will you consent to be my wife?

Bear my children? Will–" He broke off as her fingers slid up his thigh.

She pulled him down into her arms with a laugh of pure elation. "Of course I will! All of the above. But I refuse to move onto this boat," Nicola declared, slapping one palm against *Drifter*'s side for emphasis. The bed was so small she could reach the side easily.

"No, of course not," he laughed. "I'll move in with you while we look for a house. Your apartment is nice enough, but I want my kids to have somewhere outside to play."

"Your kids?" she asked.

"Our kids," he replied softly. Arms around her, he rolled so that she lay on top on him, and slid his hands down to fasten onto her bottom. "Let's make one now, what do you say?"

She laughed. "I'm on the pill, remember?"

"Then we'll just practice."

* *

"Engaged?" repeated Gwen.

Silence fell in the living room as her parents and sister turned to Nicola, identical expressions of surprise on their faces. Only her niece looked pleased.

"Wow!" enthused the girl. "To Greg?"

Nicola laughed. "Who else would I marry, Tiffany? How many men do you suppose I'm seeing at the same time?"

Tiffany shrugged, dismissing the question with all the world-weary aplomb of a 14-year-old. She snatched a pecan tart from the dessert tray on the coffee table and stood up, saying, "I'm going to tell Thomas!"

"Take one for your brother," commanded Alison automatically, still regarding Nicola with doubt.

When the girl had left, Nicola said, "I don't think Tommy will be any more thrilled with my news than you three are. I thought you'd be happy for me!"

Gwen settled herself into her armchair and said, "Of course we are. It's just that it's so sudden! You only met in May, and now in October you get engaged."

"I thought you liked Greg?"

"I do like him! What little I know about him, that is," she added pointedly. "How can you be sure you want to marry someone you hardly know?"

Arthur leaned forward, nodding. "You haven't even met his family."

"I don't want to marry his family!" exclaimed Nicola. "I want to marry Greg."

"In-laws are part of the package," said Alison, her mouth puckered as if she was chewing sour cherries rather than a brownie. "You're stuck with them. Just ask me."

"Bob's parents live two blocks from you," Nicola pointed out. "Greg's parents are in Seattle. Even if they turn out to be the in-laws from hell, I'll rarely see them."

Gwen placed her teacup in its saucer with an emphatic clink of china on china. "But you hardly know him!" she repeated.

"Mom! You can't seriously believe that Greg is hiding something from me? That he has an unsavory, mysterious past that will come back to haunt him? He's an accountant, for God's sake! Not a drug smuggler or a spy. How many times have you met him so far?" Nicola demanded, but smiling at the idea of Greg as a spy. "At least twice a month since we met. Let's say 15 times. Suppers and birthday parties and whatnot. And has he ever done anything to make you suspicious? He even fixed the broken leg on that old chair you won't let anyone throw away."

Her mother stroked one hand over the threadbare, rose-patterned cover of her favorite chair. "True," she admitted.

Arthur pushed the lever to bring his recliner upright, and struggled up from its padded depths. "Come here, sweetheart," he said to Nicola, and when she approached, he put his arm around her and steered her to the large window overlooking the back yard.

"Are you positive, Nicola?" he asked, searching her face in the strong sunlight as if expecting to see something there that would give the lie to her words. "Do you truly want to make such a commitment to a man you've known for only six months?"

"Oh, Dad," she sighed, torn between frustration at her family's unwillingness to understand and appreciation of their concern. "Six months or six years, our feelings won't change!"

"Perhaps not," he conceded. "But I was thinking of Andrew. Look what he was hiding."

Nicola dismissed her former lover with one curt gesture. "Andrew was nothing like Greg. He never even pretended to want a family, or to get our own place. He never made me think that I was more important than anything else in the world to him, never made me feel that he would die without me."

Arthur looked embarrassed yet pleased to hear this. "And Greg does?"

She nodded. Something else that Greg made her feel, which Andrew never had, was a seemingly insatiable desire for his body. She had seen Greg this morning, would see him again in a few hours when his shift at the zoo was finished – and at the back of her mind all day, even now, was this physical need for him, this yearning to touch him and be touched by him. But that, she decided, probably wasn't something her father wanted to know.

"Well, then," said Arthur, like a man who has come to a decision. "Gwen!"

From across the room, her mother had been watching them with a look of satisfaction, apparently sure that Arthur would make their wayward daughter see sense.

"Do we have plans for next Sunday?" Arthur asked.

Gwen frowned, and shook her head.

His round, wrinkled face broke into a smile. "Then phone everyone we know! We're having a party for our daughter and her fiancé," declared Arthur. He pointed out the window, to the lawn behind the house. "Right there."

"A party!" Gwen gaped at them. Then a smile spread across her own face, and she pushed herself out of the armchair. With a laugh, she said, "If you can't beat 'em, join 'em, huh?"

Her mother flung her arms around Nicola, who hugged her tightly, the soft body so familiar. "You sure you're okay with this, Mom?"

"Oh sweetie, I do like Greg, you know that. I just don't want you to get hurt again, or make a mistake," Gwen said.

Nicola smiled. "Loving Greg could never be a mistake."

Alison leaned back against the sofa, eyeing the pastry in her hand. "A party, huh? Good. I need a new dress."

* *

"Engaged?" repeated Hélène.

She stopped running so abruptly that Nicola had gone 20 feet before she realized that she was talking to herself. "Are you so surprised?" she asked, coming back.

"No," said Hélène slowly. "Not entirely, not after seeing you together. But it seems very soon. You know so little about each other! Perhaps you should wait some time before marriage? Have a long engagement?"

They sank onto a bench and looked out over the ocean, sparkling and glittering in the morning sun.

"That's what Mom suggested," Nicola admitted. "And Alison, and Kylie, and, oh, practically everyone else! But why should we wait, when we both know it's right? Hélène, I've been waiting for Greg all my life without knowing it. When I'm with him, everything is right. It's like a hole I never knew I had inside me has been filled. And I'll tell you," she added, lowering her voice, and feeling the warmth rise in her cheeks, "I never knew sex could be like it is with Greg. I had no idea I could want it so much. It's like a fire, one that springs right back into life a moment after it's been quenched." The blush grew hotter, partly now in embarrassment at such words.

But Hélène didn't laugh at her, she just smiled in a knowing way and said, "It is more than your toes that tingle now, no?" Then she asked, carefully, "Does this rush into marriage have anything to do with your age, and children?"

Nicola laughed. "It may do. I'm not getting any younger! You know I want to have children, and so does Greg. We both want a family. I want to be able to keep up with them!"

"The way you sprinted up those stairs today, I think you will be fine," Hélène remarked dryly. "But...must it be marriage, now? You could live together."

"We could. And we will, the day we get married! We practically live together now, at my place and on *Drifter*. You know," she added with a smile, "that's definitely a big advantage to getting married, or officially living together."

"What is?"

"I won't have to spend any more nights on that damned boat!"

Hélène laughed, then she put her arms around Nicola and hugged her. "Many congratulations, *chérie*! I believe Greg is a fine man, and I wish you both every happiness in the world."

"Thank you so much! We're going ring shopping this afternoon. My parents are having a big party tomorrow, and Mom says it won't look right unless there's a chunk of diamond on my finger." She studied her bare left hand. "Maybe a small chunk.

"Can you and Antoine and Philippe come? Greg knows my immediate family, but I think he's going to be overwhelmed by the whole lot and I know he would appreciate seeing some friends. Do you remember Sam and Debbie, you met them when we all went sailing that day? They'll be there too, but they won't know anyone either. I'm sorry it's last minute," she apologized. "I should have asked you earlier. I seem to be dopey these days."

Hélène smiled. "I believe it is called 'in love' rather than dopey. Of course we can come."

* *

Greg clutched his beer, pasted a smile onto his face, and looked with a sinking heart at the hundred or so people crowded into Nicola's parents' back yard. A hundred or so people who all wanted to meet him. More appeared every minute, coming out the kitchen door from the sprawling, older-style house or walking around the house on the brick path. He'd had no idea that Nicola's family was so large. Still no sign of Sam, Debbie and Peter.

A small white party tent tucked under the trees at one side of the lawn housed the bar and provided shelter from the cool wind blowing off the bay. Most people braved the elements, however, milling and mingling in a happy, noisy throng. Waiters circulated with trays of canapés and drinks.

"So she's finally getting married," said a woman behind him.

"It's about time, too. My husband and I were beginning to wonder, you know."

No need to wonder about that, thought Greg with amusement.

Another woman replied, "I'm surprised Arthur and Gwen are making such a fuss. It's not as if Nicola is really their daughter."

Greg clenched a fist at his side, and told himself not to turn around, not to get involved. The memory of schoolyard taunts rushed back, other kids calling him names because Edward wasn't his real father, and where was his real father, huh? It shook him to think that Nicola must have endured the same thing.

He slipped his arm around her slender waist, and she leaned lightly against him for a moment; she didn't break off the conversation with the aunt or cousin-twice-removed or whoever this was, but that slight movement was enough to say to him "I'm here."

At last, someone he knew! Around the corner of the house came Hélène, Antoine and Philippe. Greg grinned at the sight of the boy. He was a remarkably well mannered almost-13-year-old, brought up to respect his parents and be polite to strangers, but even Philippe made clear his resentment at having to forego his Sunday soccer practice. He lagged behind his parents.

Hélène said something to the boy over her shoulder, and Greg could almost hear the sigh Philippe dredged up from his plodding feet. He would have liked to have gone to them, but another group of relatives or friends had claimed him. Out of one eye, he could see Nicola's sister Alison heading towards the French family.

Air kissing between the women, and Hélène introduced Alison to her family. Alison's pale face flushed when Antoine kissed her on both cheeks. Hélène said something, and Nicola's sister smoothed the purple dress over her bony hip. Was it just him, or did that color really not go with her red hair?

Hélène, in return, touched one hand to the silk scarf tucked into the neck of the cream-colored skirt suit she wore. Even to Greg, the difference between the two women was startling: designer versus discount.

"Hélène!" called Nicola, who had seen them, too. She waved. "We'll be over in a second!"

The second was closer to five minutes, during which time Alison wandered off and Philippe escaped.

"I'm glad to see a familiar face, Antoine," confessed Greg, shaking hands. "Did you have to go through all this when you and Hélène got engaged?"

Antoine nodded. "Oh yes. And the wedding, that is worse." He shrugged. "It is the price a man must pay, *mon ami.*"

It was a source of amazement to Greg that Antoine, slight and stooped, thin hair combed across his head to cover the bald crown, was the husband of a woman as elegant and self-possessed as Hélène. The unlikeliness of it was greater today, seeing Hélène so assured and perfectly groomed beside Antoine in his old suit, ill at ease in this large gathering of Americans. These French men must know a thing or two, Greg thought, and about more than making croissants. "My family is nowhere near this big, nor all in the same place," he said. "Nicola will only have to meet my parents and sister next weekend."

Antoine tasted the wine he had accepted from a waiter, and pulled a face.

"Not good?" asked Greg, hiding a smile. He suspected what the problem was.

"It is Californian," shrugged Antoine. "It is what it is. So, you go to Seattle?"

"Yes, Friday afternoon. Back on Sunday. She's never met them, and I think it might be good if they all at least recognized each other at the wedding," said Greg.

"I had not noticed before how alike you are," remarked Antoine. "Until now, seeing you both come towards us. Such dark hair and blue eyes, and a certain way of standing. You are a fine-looking couple."

Greg laughed. "I think Nicola supplies most of the looks! She is so beautiful."

Antoine's eyes rested on Nicola with fondness. "Especially today. She loves you very much, my friend. You are a lucky man."

"I know I am," said Greg softly.

He and Antoine turned to join the women.

"*Chérie*, you look stunning," Hélène was saying, fingering the sleeve of Nicola's emerald silk blouse and looking with approval at her skirt and shoes.

Nicola said wryly. "I should, you persuaded me to buy all this that day in July, remember? 'Never mind the cost,' you said, 'they are good quality and well cut, and will last years.'"

"That does sound like something I would say," agreed Hélène, then her eyes gleamed. "And the wedding gown? I know two fabulous designers here in San Francisco."

There was a pause, and Nicola said, "My mother has some ideas, too."

The four of them looked across the lawn to Nicola's mother, for whom fashion had never held the slightest interest. Gwen had retired from teaching high school biology five years ago, at the age of 60, and professed to see little reason to buy new clothes now. Today's jacket and pants had seen her through many years of teaching, and had not flattered her plump frame even when new.

As if she felt their eyes on her, Gwen turned, and smiled as she negotiated her way around clusters of people to join them.

"Hello, Hélène! How nice to see you again," she said warmly. "You know, what Nicola needs is someone like you to advise her on her wedding gown. You're always dressed so nice."

Both Nicola and Hélène looked startled, but the French-woman rallied quickly. "I was saying to Nicola that we three should make a day of looking at gowns – visit designers I know, have lunch, get our hair and nails done. Perhaps finish off with a cocktail at a little bar?"

Greg, who knew she had been saying nothing of the sort, raised his beer in silent salute to her quick thinking.

Gwen's lined face creased into a smile and her eyes shone. "A girls' day out? How fantastic!"

"Um," began Nicola, but her mother and her friend were deep in discussion about bias cut and satin and tulle, white versus off-white, the advantages of an embroidered bodice over one with seed pearls. She cast a helpless glance at Greg, who grinned and shrugged, and wondered what the hell "bias cut" meant.

"Of course, the gown will take some months to finish to per-fection, but it will be worth the wait," said Hélène.

"Oh yes!" agreed Gwen.

"Oh no!" declared Nicola.

They turned to her, faces wearing polite surprise.

"We are not waiting months while a dress is made," stated Nicola. "We were thinking of a small, quiet wedding in November. Something easy to arrange."

Stunned silence had fallen in their immediate area.

"In one month?" asked Gwen, shocked.

Hélène leaned closer and said quietly, "Ah, you are pregnant, no?"

"No!" laughed Nicola. "I'm not."

She gave him another helpless look, and he came to her rescue. "It's that we don't want to wait. We've each finally found the person we want to spend our life with. And we want to start doing it as soon as possible. Nicola will look as beautiful in a dress off the rack as she would in one that takes three months to sew by hand." He put his arm around her shoulder and pulled her to him.

She was exactly his height today, given she was wearing those crazy heels Hélène had talked her into buying. She looked across at him, her face radiant and her blue eyes glowing with love, and Greg wanted badly to kiss her, long and hard. Hell, he thought, this is my engagement party – so he did.

Chapter 6

NICOLA ROOTED among the brochures and pamphlets she had spread on the tray table, folded down from the back of the seat in front. "Here. I liked this one," she said, handing a glossy paper to Greg. "It's fairly easy to get to, and Mom said they can take us on that day. I told her to put a deposit on it. I'm glad she volunteered to find a venue. I had no idea how crazy this would be. Do you know there are people who book their reception a whole year in advance?" She leaned against his arm as he studied the pamphlet.

"Can't we just have a few people over for drinks on *Drifter*, and when we've had enough we can put them ashore and sail away?" Greg asked, sounding plaintive. He ran a hand through his hair and glanced past her, through the plane's small window.

She laughed. "A very few!"

"Or Vegas," he suggested. "You and I can sneak off, and tell everyone after the fact."

"My family would never speak to me again," she said.

"Mine either," he admitted. "Mom is dying to meet you. Janine even gave up free tickets to a Blackhawks hockey game to fly home from Chicago this weekend. She says as her big brother, I owe her."

Sneaking off to Las Vegas was not entirely a bad idea, Nicola thought, because it would get her out of meeting Greg's family. She knew her nervousness was ridiculous, but she was worried she would get something wrong or, worse, forget a name at a crucial moment. She went through everything Greg had told her, again, like a mantra. Father Edward, 63, is an executive at a large pharmaceuticals company, which he joined when he and his wife Desdemona (Mona, she prefers Mona, Nicola reminded herself) arrived in Seattle soon after Greg was born. His mother is 10 years younger than Edward, was a stay-at-home mom while Greg and Janine were in school but has worked part-time in local government for the past 15 years. She's heavily involved in the church (So that's where he gets it from! Nicola had thought when she heard this) and does volunteer work with street people;

this impressed Nicola, although she doubted she could ever do such a thing herself. Finally, Janice, five years Greg's junior, living in Chicago and working as a travel agent.

Janine! Not Janice, Janine! He said her name five seconds ago, you idiot! Nicola berated herself.

"What on earth are you thinking about?" asked Greg, peering at her and beginning to smile. "Cornering the stock market in a particularly daring manner? Global domination? Or do you just have wind?"

She was so startled by these options that she laughed. "I was trying to get your family straight in my head. We'll be there in an hour."

Greg leaned closer and kissed her. "Stop worrying. There are only three of them. I had hundreds last Sunday, and I survived."

"Yeah, and you called all the men 'sir' and all the women 'ma'am'!" she retorted. "No wonder they all loved you."

He looked smug. "It worked, didn't it? Though I don't recommend you call my mother 'ma'am,'" he advised with a grin. "She's only 17 years older than you, and it might not go down well."

* *

It was only Janine who met them at Seattle's airport, to Nicola's relief. Greg's sister was outgoing and chatty, and she teased him mercilessly on the drive to their parents' house.

"Oh chill, Greg!" she said disparagingly, when he remonstrated with her from the back seat for taking a corner too fast. "Who was it who failed their driving test the first time, huh? You or me?"

Nicola grinned. "Did he really?" She had not considered until right now that Greg's family would be a wealth of information about things that he might prefer not to share.

"Yup. Wrong way down a one-way street, can you believe it? I mean, how can anyone not see those arrows, right?"

"Janine," came Greg's pained voice from behind them, "if you're going to rip my character to shreds for Nicola, can you at least wait until after the wedding?"

Nicola laughed, but she reached her right hand over the seat back and, after a moment, she felt him take it in his own hand, big and warm, and kiss her palm.

It wasn't a long drive to his parents' house in Blue Ridge. The house was separated from Puget Sound only by a railway line, Greg said.

"And of course, Greg never crossed that railway line," Janine added sweetly. "Never sneaked across with his friends to swim in the Sound, despite us having a perfectly good pool in the back yard."

"And you never told on him?" asked Nicola.

Greg laughed. "No, she didn't. She could be an annoying little sister sometimes, but she was never a snitch."

The house was set back from the road and not visible from the wrought metal gates, already open in anticipation of their arrival. It was larger than her own family's house, two white-painted stories nestling among spreading elm trees on an expansive lot. His father appeared on the covered porch even before the car had stopped, his mother hovering in the wide doorway behind him. Nicola took a deep breath and reached for the door handle, but Edward was already there and he extended a hand to help her out.

"Nicola, my dear, how wonderful to meet you at last!" he exclaimed, and pulled her into a hug. He was tall and stooped, and felt bony to Nicola in even this light embrace.

His mother was not as effusive, but she squeezed Nicola's hand. "I'm so pleased to meet you," she said warmly.

They certainly seem nice, Nicola thought as they all walked towards the house. Her eyes skipped over the house itself, for she was more interested in the many flowerbeds and the paths meandering between them. "Is that a peony?" she asked, pointing to one of the shrubs with withered, mottled leaves that stood guard on either side of the door. "That's my favorite flower!"

Mona nodded with enthusiasm. "Yes, it is! It's really time to cut them back for the winter. Are you a gardener too, Nicola?"

Greg laughed. "Don't get her started on plants, Mom! You should see Nicola's apartment. You can't get near the windows for all the plants she's got crammed against them."

"They need the light," protested Nicola and Mona simultaneously. She glanced at his mother, to see that she looked as pleasantly surprised as Nicola felt to discover this shared interest.

"I'm sure that's the only reason she agreed to marry me," commented Greg. "She's more excited about us getting a house, and therefore her getting a real garden, than she is about spending the rest of her life with me."

"You only figured that out now, huh?" teased Nicola. "You'd better take care our kids don't trample my flowerbeds!"

Mona asked, "Before it gets too dark, would you like to see the back garden, Nicola?"

"Oh, yes please!"

Greg rolled his eyes. "The two of them will be out there for hours now. We'll have to send out flashlights and hot drinks," he said to his father.

Edward clapped a hand onto his son's shoulder. "Come along, you can help me in the kitchen. Janine, are you doing gardens or setting the table?"

She pulled a face. "What a choice. Why do I suddenly feel 13 again? The table, I guess."

Greg dropped a quick kiss on Nicola's cheek. "Don't stay out here all night," he warned, then followed the others inside.

The sun had set but twilight lingered, and Mona led the way around to the back of the house. "We bought this house when Greg was 10, so we've been here for 23 years. Plenty of time for me to get the gardens into shape. At least, you'd think it would be plenty of time," she laughed, "but I never seem to get it finished. You'll find that yourself."

"I'm really looking forward to it," said Nicola, then added, "What you said about being here for 23 years? It's hard to believe you could be Greg's mother. You look too young."

"Why, thank you!" said Mona, and tiny lines sprang up her around her eyes as she laughed. She was Nicola's own height, slender and straight. Her dark hair, ear-length and swept back from her face, showed no telltale gray at the temples. "I do try to look after myself, but I think the fact that I was only 20 when I had Greg has more to do with it. And, also, I do a lot of volunteer work, which keeps me too busy to wallow in self-indulgence."

Nicola nodded. "Greg mentioned that. Homeless people, I think he said? That's admirable."

Mona's gesture was slight, but impatient. "It's not admirable at all. It's necessary. We would be a poor society if people who can help those less fortunate than themselves simply turned their backs."

Shame stirred as Nicola acknowledged that she had never given anything back. To her, homeless people were little more than an obstruction on the sidewalk, faceless and nameless.

Mona pointed to a heap of bulbs on the grass. "Excuse the mess, I was planting tulips earlier. I thought I would finish before you arrived, but lost track of time."

"I'll help you tomorrow, if you like. It looks as if you still have dozens to plant!" Nicola offered.

"Thank you," said Mona, and she reached out to touch Nicola's arm lightly. "Yes, I bought 200 mixed exotics. It seemed like a good idea at the time!"

Their voices drifted into the kitchen through the open window, and Greg stopped slicing carrots to look outside at his mother and Nicola as they paused in front of a patch of what to him were bare sticks. His face softened as he watched them, interrupting each other in their enthusiasm. Both he and Nicola seemed to have come out ahead with mothers-in-law: he liked Gwen, and, from the look of things, Nicola and his mother would get along, too.

"She seems very nice," commented Edward from the other side of the sink. "Of course, I wouldn't expect you to marry someone who wasn't."

Greg glanced at his father, and said dryly, "Apart from Jackie."

"She doesn't count," replied Edward. "You didn't actually marry her."

"It wasn't for lack of trying."

Edward shrugged. "She seemed nice, too. Said all the right things, fooled all of us. You shouldn't blame yourself for any part of that." He chopped more parsley, the knife a blur of silver against the wooden board. "I saw her the other week."

"Jackie?" She flashed into his mind, petite and blonde, with green eyes that could sparkle with humor or freeze with disdain.

"At the gas station. She was as surprised as I was, I think. And about as pleased," Edward added.

Greg was silent. Curiosity itched, but he wouldn't ask. Part of him – a small, unworthy part – hoped she was destitute and homeless, miserable and repentant.

"She's in line for a partnership at your old firm. And she's bought a big new condo by the water. Oh, and a new car," said Edward. He shook his head in bafflement. "In the 30 seconds we spent together, that was all that was said. She didn't ask after you, or any of us. I didn't get a word in. You had a lucky escape there, my boy."

Greg's mouth twitched in what might have been a smile. "But Dad, think how much better off I would have been if I had stayed with her."

His father scraped the parsley into the soup, banging the knife against the board with more force than needed. "Materially, maybe. But think of the price you would have paid."

"Peace of mind? Self respect?"

"Yes, but what I meant was that you would never have met Nicola."

Greg looked outside again, at his mother and Nicola squatting down by a mound of dirt, the two of them pointing and laughing. It was full dark now, but they were visible in the rectangle of light shining from the kitchen window, their faces and hands glowing pale against the night.

"Why are you always right, Dad?" he asked.

"Because I'm the father," Edward replied. He sounded serious, but he looked amused. "Wait until you and Nicola have children. Then it will be your turn to be right."

* *

Ensconced on a sleek leather sofa beside Greg, a glass of red wine in her hand, Nicola began to relax. She had got none of the names wrong, and all of Greg's family had been nothing but welcoming. Even being unexpectedly alone with his mother had been enjoyable. They were all sitting in the high-ceilinged living room now, and she could see their reflections in the sliding glass doors that led to a deck overlooking the back garden and Puget Sound. In the fireplace, a log collapsed in a shower of sparks.

"Greg said you're the travel editor at his newspaper," said Janine, cupping both hands around her glass. "How amazing that we're in the same field! I mean, people read what you write about somewhere and then they come to me to help them get there."

Edward commented, "I had always imagined newspaper editors as tough, grizzled men in their 60s. I'm sorry, my dear, but you fail on every count!" Mona, beside him on a sofa, kicked him discreetly on the ankle and he hastened on with, "Although I'm sure you are an excellent editor!"

Nicola laughed. "I hope so. They haven't got rid of me yet, so I guess I'm doing something right. The job became unexpectedly vacant a year ago," she said lightly, with no intention of explaining why it became vacant, "and they gave it to me on a provisional basis, then made it official six months later. I'm not very tough, or grizzled, but I'm only 36 so I can practice!"

"Thirty-six?" repeated Mona. "I assumed you were Greg's age."

"Yeah," said Greg with a grin, "I was surprised when she confessed how old she was, too. I've never been the younger man before!"

"Confessed!" said Nicola with indignation. "I told you straight up that first lunch in the park, when I showed you my family's pictures on my phone."

Mother and daughter looked interested at this. "Do you have it with you now? Can we see the pictures?" asked Janine.

"Yes, I would like to know what they look like before we all turn up at the church in three weeks' time," said Mona dryly.

"I'll check on supper," said Edward. "Greg, give me a hand, will you?"

As Janine and Mona sat down on either side of Nicola, she asked, "Is Edward making supper?"

Mona nodded. "Yes, we split it fairly evenly. He enjoys it, and says it helps him relax. Personally, I prefer yoga to cooking for relaxation."

That must be why Greg is so at home in the kitchen, Nicola thought. Another piece of her future husband slotted into place. "Here we are. This was last Christmas. Mother of the bride," she said with a smile as she pointed to her phone, "father, brother and sister." She relayed names.

"They all look different to you," commented Mona.

"Oops, I did it again!" exclaimed Nicola. "I'm adopted. I always forget to tell people that."

Janine turned to scrutinize her. "Actually, you look a lot like us. You could be my sister."

She had blue eyes like Greg and Mona, although Edward's were brown. All four of them had dark hair. Edward's wispy hair was more gray than anything, but Nicola could see in family photographs on the walls that it had been dark.

With a laugh, Nicola said, "You wouldn't believe how many people have thought Greg is my brother." She heard Mona, on her left, gasp sharply, and she turned to her.

The older woman's face had gone pale, her eyebrows two dark slashes above large blue eyes, the pupils dilated now in what looked like shock.

"What is it?" asked Nicola, worried. She grasped her hand. "Are you okay?" She looked up with relief as Greg and his father came back into the living room.

But when Nicola turned back to her, Mona smiled brightly and patted her hand. "Fine. So you're adopted, you said? Was that in San Francisco?"

Nicola nodded, but still regarded her with concern. Mona had looked more than shocked; she had stared at Nicola with something like horror. It had lasted for only a second, but Nicola was convinced she had seen it.

"What do you know about your real parents?" continued Mona, sounding casual.

"Absolutely nothing. All I know is that I was abandoned when I was a few days old. Someone left me outside a hospital. The doctors guessed at the date when I was born."

Greg, sitting now across the room, leaned forward. "Really? You didn't tell me that."

She shrugged. "It's not important. Not to me. They decided it was June 30th, so that's my birthday."

Mona gasped again, and Nicola whirled around to face her. Something weird was going on here. The woman could not be this disturbed just by the idea that Nicola was adopted.

"How could anyone possibly abandon a newborn baby?" demanded Janine in outrage.

There was scorn in Mona's voice when she said, "What would you know? You've had a safe, protected life. You have no idea what goes on out there."

Janine looked startled to have her mother speak like this to her.

Edward said, "My wife works with street people, Nicola. She's seen some terrible things."

Nicola nodded, unsure what to say.

"Now let's eat!" said Edward heartily, standing up. "My famous mushroom soup is getting cold."

* *

The guest room was Greg's old bedroom, but it had been redecorated years ago and had gained its own bathroom, and bore no trace of his time there. Nicola undressed slowly, her thoughts still on that strange episode with his mother.

"What's wrong?" asked Greg, from the queen-sized bed. "You're miles away."

Nicola asked, "Did your mother seem all right to you tonight?"

He looked puzzled. "Yes. What do you mean?"

She sat on the side of the bed. "She reacted strangely to the news that I was adopted. I really wondered if she was having an attack."

"An attack?" he repeated, and the bed shook with his laughter. "What, of the vapors? My mother? She's tough as nails. Dad's right, she has seen some terrible things in her volunteer work, but she keeps doing it. She caught me when I was 17, smoking a joint in this very room with two friends. Next day, she hauled me down to a drug rehab center and forced me to volunteer on the weekends. I tell you, after the things I saw there, and the stories I heard, I didn't touch anything stronger than beer for years. Nicola, it would take more than learning that you were abandoned to disturb her, believe me."

Greg flipped back the covers and folded his arms around her. "Although how anyone could ever abandon you, my darling, I can't imagine." He kissed her, deep and long, and ran one hand down to her bottom to pull her firmly against him.

"Not here!" hissed Nicola.

"It's here or the floor," he murmured, lips moving lower, "and I think this is more comfortable."

She stifled a laugh. "I mean, not in your parents' house. This is your old bedroom!"

"That's precisely why," he said, lifting his head so the words were clear. "I spent all my teenage years in this room, frustrated and frenzied, dreaming of all the things I'd do if I ever got a girl in here."

Nicola drew a sharp breath as his fingers joined his mouth.

He stopped long enough to say, sounding very pleased with himself, "Well, now I've got one."

She managed to ask, "Do you really plan to do all those things tonight?"

His hair brushed against her thighs as he shook his head, and Nicola heard him say indistinctly, "We've got tomorrow night, too."

* *

Rain fell steadily the next morning, turning what Nicola had been assured were glorious views of Puget Sound into dim, hazy shapes through the window. They were in the kitchen, eating breakfast. All except Mona; Edward apologized for her, and explained that she had a bad headache.

Greg frowned. "Mom doesn't usually have headaches. Is everything all right?"

His father nodded. "She didn't sleep well last night, I think that's all it is. Do you still want to go out today?" he asked, waving towards the direction of the water.

He shook his head. "In that? No." To Nicola, he explained that he and his father had considered taking the boat out for a while.

"But don't worry, I wouldn't have expected you to come," he told her with a smile.

"I take it you don't sail, Nicola?" asked Janine. She reached across the blue-checked tablecloth for the jam.

"A lot more than I did before Greg came along!" Nicola said, and cast him a teasing look.

"Yes, she's almost got port and starboard figured out now," commented Greg.

"What's that?" asked Janine innocently.

Greg rose to the bait, and started going on about how could Janine possibly not know what they were after all the years they'd gone sailing on that very Sound outside. Janine winked at her soon-to-be sister-in-law.

Nicola laughed with everyone else, feeling quite at home with this family. They were nice people, even if his mother had seemed slightly strange at one point last evening. But by the time supper was over, Mona had once again been pleasant and friendly, and this morning Nicola had decided that Greg was right and she had imagined it.

The laughter ended uncertainly as the door opened and Mona came in. She was barefoot and still in her bathrobe, and her hair, swept back so neatly last night, stuck up in disarray.

Edward seemed surprised. "My dear, are you better?" he asked, walking towards her.

She ignored his outstretched hand and sat at the table. "Sit down, Edward." Her eyes were bloodshot and her face drawn; she looked 10 years older than she had last evening.

"There is something I must tell you all."

Chapter 7

San Francisco, late June 1975

SNAKE PUNCHED the air. "We were hot tonight! We were on fire, man!" He propped his bass guitar against the stained wall of the dingy, airless room behind the stage. "Fuck me, we killed 'em!"

Scorpion threw himself onto a wooden chair, long leather-clad legs stretched out. "That's why we're called Killer Kreetures! And I ain't fuckin' you, man, no way!" He tilted his head back, laughing uproariously at his own joke. He opened a beer bottle with his teeth and swigged, then spat it out in a spray of foam. "Christ, it's warm as piss. Can't that bitch do nothin' right?" Scorpion flung the bottle at the girl lying on the couch, curled on her side away from them. Her long dark hair fell in a dull mass to the floor.

She twitched when the bottle bounced off her back, but nothing more. The beer puddled slowly on the floor.

"Out of it again," Snake said in disgust. "Who she done this time to pay for it, eh?"

"Not me, man!" insisted Scorpion. "I ain't goin' near the crazy bitch. Drunk one day, then wired on bennies or zonked on benzos."

"And how do you think she got that way, huh?" asked a woman sharply, from the doorway. "She was a stupid kid when she ran away from mommy and daddy, but you turned her into a drunk and a pill popper."

"Not me!" repeated Scorpion. "Snake here's the dumb mother what took up with her."

The woman stalked across the room, the stiletto heels of her black knee-high boots rapping on the concrete. She bent over to look at the girl. Still breathing. "She'll live."

Snake shrugged. "So?"

"So, you idiot, you want to talk to the cops if she doesn't?" She looked down at him with scorn.

Scorpion gave a bray of laughter, spittle flying. "This here's the Tenderloin, you dumb bitch. No one cares about one more druggie in the street, dead or alive."

The crack of the back of her hand against his face came an instant before his head slammed into the wall with the force of her blow.

"I warned you, don't ever call me that," she hissed. "I'm not a messed-up little girl like that one, and I'm not taking any shit from scum like you."

He sprang to his feet, fist raised and teeth bared, but a cold voice stopped him.

"Don't."

It was Shark. Small and intense, he stood just inside the door, guitar over one shoulder.

"She—" began Scorpion with a snarl.

Shark lifted one hand, and he shut up.

"Spider found a car. We're outta here in five," Shark said.

"What about her?" Scorpion muttered, pointing to the figure on the couch.

"Snake's problem. He wants her, he brings her. If not, she stays here."

Snake shook his head, matted hair flapping. "No way. Stupid slut's out of it most of the time. It's like screwing a corpse. And she's getting fat. Man, I hate fat chicks."

The woman turned sharply, but to look at the girl. Fat? The kid lived on booze and pills; she couldn't be fat. But...her long mauve skirt was tight around the bulge of her abdomen. Oh, you stupid kid, she thought, not without compassion. She wondered who the father was. Probably Snake, but maybe not, not if Dezzie had wanted a hit and traded it for sex.

"Hey." Shark jerked his head, and she followed as the band left the room. Yeah, she felt sorry for the kid, but not enough to do anything about it.

* *

Rough shaking woke Dezzie.

"Up, you get up!" insisted a shrill voice. "Up now. Go now!"

Slowly, she dragged herself to a sitting position, head heavy and body aching. Who the hell was this? Where was Snake?

"Go! Go!"

It was an elderly Chinese man. He dropped his mop and grabbed her arm, his thin fingers like pincers. She cried out, but he ignored her and dragged her out of the room, down the hallway. The blast of fresh air when he yanked open the door almost choked her, and then he thrust her out and slammed the door behind her.

The alley was dark, but not so dark she couldn't make out the figures of other people, sprawled on the ground.

"Hey, girlie girl, come here and see what I got," came a wheedling voice, and fingers brushed her ankle.

"Fuck off," Dezzie said, and kicked at the shape. She picked her way unsteadily down the alley, to the brighter lights and traffic of the street.

She felt like shit. She usually did. God, she wanted a drink. Where was the band? Even Shark's creepy girlfriend, who was too much like Dezzie's mother with all her "do this" and "don't do that," would be welcome. She stopped abruptly and put one hand to her side, gasping with the sudden pain. It passed, though, and she carried on.

The street was a kaleidoscope of lights, the red and white streaks of moving cars, the throbbing red- green-yellow of traffic lights, the garish neon of storefronts. The noise was an assault. Dark. She wanted dark. Somewhere dark and quiet, to lie down again and find oblivion. Dezzie wove and stumbled across the street, cars and trucks looming up as indistinct shapes and passing in a rush of wind.

"Get off the road, ya stupid bitch!" a harsh voice called.

She survived the crossing of Market Street, stumbled farther and crossed Mission Street, with little idea of where she was or where she was going.

Here, at last, was darkness, and almost quiet. It was cool beneath the trees, and like a wounded animal seeking shelter, Dezzie crawled through a thicket of shrubs to the damp earth beyond. She lay on her side, panting, head tilted back. Far overhead, stars trailed ribbons of light as they spun and whirled.

The pain took her again moments later, pulling her from the oblivion she craved. It was worse now, claws ripping at her insides, reaching up into her back and down into her legs. She'd had no idea giving birth would hurt this much.

Dezzie gagged at the sudden stench of cheap wine and stale urine that enveloped her.

"Dearie me, what's this?" drawled a cracked, hoarse voice. "What interloper has so rudely and thoughtlessly invaded my patch?"

Go to your room! You're nothing but a rude, thoughtless child! Her mother's voice, strident and furious, echoed in Dezzie's head, and the sound of the ringing slap against her cheek.

Was she dying? Was she dead? Was this hell?

Oh God the pain again. Dezzie curled up, and cried out.

"Ohhh," said the voice, but now it held a note of understanding. The stench grew stronger and against the star-filled sky loomed a bulky shape swathed in loose layers, and an aureole of frizzed hair. One hand grasped Dezzie's wrists and pulled her arms away from her torso, and the other felt firmly over her abdomen.

"Stop that noise, d'you hear!" commanded the voice. "You keep that up, everyone 'round here who preys on the weak will be down upon us. You're only having a baby, dearie. You're not dying."

"Help me!"

"Well, dearie, you come to the right place, at least," said the voice, sounding amused. "You might justa found the only street person in the Tenderloin who delivered a baby before."

"I need a drink!" begged Dezzie.

The gust of a wine-scented sigh. "Don't we all, dearie, don't we all."

Hours passed, or perhaps only minutes. Dezzie had no idea, caught up in waves of pain, her mind spinning and turning like the stars overhead. Release, at last, and she heard the crooning of her makeshift midwife, nonsense words of comfort. There was a thin, keening cry from somewhere.

"Well, my dearie, I think it's a girl, but it's too dark here to be sure." A moment's pause. "Yes, a girl. Poor thing."

The pain had stopped, oh dear God thank you. Dezzie rolled awkwardly onto her side and closed her eyes.

"My dearie, what are you going to do with her?"

Do with it?

She shook her head, tired beyond bearing, wanting only, somehow, to be anywhere but here.

"Nothing. I don't care. Take it away."

* *

It was still dark when she awoke. Or dark again. Dezzie had no idea how long she'd been lying on this dirt under this tree. She pushed herself up, wincing, wondering dazedly why her stomach hurt so much. No, not her stomach; lower. She could feel her skirt, wet and sticky, wrapped around her legs.

Baby.

Dezzie gasped as the memory crashed into her brain. There was more light in the sky now, the barest hint of the coming dawn, but enough for her to see the dark stain on the skirt, and the dark smear on her fingers when she tentatively wiped herself. To see, too, that she was alone in the small clearing, with no sign of the woman – or of the baby. It had been hard enough for Dezzie to believe that a baby was growing inside her; she had given no thought to what she would do when it was born, and felt only relief to be spared the need to make a decision now.

She dragged the strap of the large bag over her head. Fumbling it open, she rummaged inside for her other skirt. She managed to pull off the mauve one and wriggle into the black one, then lay back, too exhausted to care about the stone digging into her back.

Dezzie forced herself to her feet and slung the bag's strap over her head and shoulders. More light now, the colorless gray of very early dawn, and she pushed through the shrubs into the grassy center of the park. A fountain splashed into a carved stone bowl a few feet away, and she thrust her face into the water greedily, drinking until she thought she would burst.

Then she pulled the ruined skirt from her bag and soaked it in the water, and retreated back through the shrub. Black skirt rucked up and held in her teeth, she cleaned herself as best she could, biting her lip as the rough fabric scraped her tender flesh.

The panties in her bag were far from clean, but they were all she had. More importantly, there was also a handful of sanitary pads.

Now what?

Dezzie was 17, hundreds of miles from the home she had run away from 18 months ago, with little money, no friends, and no expectation of a miracle. She frowned. Where was the band's next gig? She knew, she'd heard them talking…Sacramento! That was it. Dezzie giggled softly. Man, would Snake be surprised when she turned up! She hoped to hell he had some bennies when she got there.

* *

She never found out if Snake had bennies, but the four college students who picked her up beside the Bayshore Freeway did. They offered her a pill and a beer to wash it down. All five of them sang along to a cassette tape, up for anything and on top of the world. They were two boys and two girls, none much older than Dezzie, and they agreed to drop her off wherever her band was.

They had no luck tracking down the band.

"Whatcha gonna do now?" asked one of the girls, named Carla.

"I don't know," admitted Dezzie, who had not considered the possibility of not finding them.

"Hang with us," suggested Gavin. He was the eldest of the four, good looking in a rough way. "We're on our way to Reno."

"Cool." She hesitated. "I don't have any money."

The boy laughed. "Me neither! But Carla's old man's got buckets of it."

Carla looked embarrassed to have a rich father. She nodded. "Yeah, money ain't a problem."

When they arrived in Reno, Dezzie was hungover and tired, and her lower back ached as if it had been hit with a sledgehammer. She squinted in the sharp light. "Shit, what a dump," she muttered when they found a motel, decorated in red, white and blue bunting and balloons.

Carla linked her arm through Dezzie's, and laughed as she

towed her across the parking lot. "Come on," Carla urged. "Have a sleep and you'll be fine. It's the 4th of July! Party time!"

The 4th of July was party time, and so were the days that followed. The days blurred into the nights, one long drink and drugs session funded by Carla's father. When they got tired of Reno, they drifted east along Highway 80 until they ended up in Salt Lake City. That was no place for five partying teenagers, and they stayed only one night.

Just past Boise, outside a town called Caldwell, Carla caught Dezzie making out with Gavin, who'd been coming on to Dezzie whenever Carla wasn't around. Gavin was given a choice: Carla or Dezzie. He shrugged apologetically at Dezzie but, hell, Carla had the dough. It was a no-brainer. The van roared off, leaving music and exhaust fumes – and Dezzie – in its wake.

She stood by the side of the road in the slanting early evening sun, and took stock. She had only the long black skirt and t-shirt she was wearing, a sweater in her bag, a couple of bennies to pep her up and a couple of benzos to chill her out, and the $20 she'd taken from Carla's bag while she'd been screaming at Gavin. Dezzie had no idea where she was, had only the vaguest idea of where Boise was on a map, and no idea which direction to go. One place was as good as the next; she'd go where whoever stopped to pick her up was going.

No one picked her up that day. Dezzie swore, and eyed the ragged trees behind her. She would have to sleep rough. She dragged the sweater over her head, and huddled at the base of a tree.

It rained before dawn. Dezzie was back at the side of the road as soon as it got light, wet and bedraggled. She got her first ride almost immediately, a middle-aged couple who felt sorry for her but could take her only as far as Baker City. Her second ride changed her life, although as the big transport pulled to a shuddering, chuffing halt and she ran along the roadside to catch up, it meant no more to her than relief from the rain.

Big and bluff, baseball cap firmly on his head and checked shirt straining against his belly, the driver extended a hand to help Dezzie climb up. He eyed her up and down, the way her father used to when she came home too late. "What's a bitty thing like you doing on the road by yourself?"

She shrugged. "Just traveling."

He snorted at that. Kevin, he said his name was, and he lived in Portland. "That's where we're headed. Ever been to Portland?"

"Nope." Couldn't have cared less about going there now, either, but she held back from telling him that.

Kevin continued talking, telling her about his wife Susie and his daughter Pam, and that today was Pam's 16th birthday and he had got her a radio-cassette player.

Dezzie's only response was the loud growling of her empty stomach.

"When's the last time you ate?" he asked.

She shrugged.

He jerked a thumb over his shoulder. "There's Pepsis in that cooler behind you, and some candy bars."

"I like Coke better," she said.

"Tough."

She was startled into laughter, and saw the easy humor in his eyes when he looked at her. "Thanks," said Dezzie.

On that ride to Portland, he explained that his wife's church group ran a shelter for homeless people, and Dezzie agreed to go. At a truck stop, Kevin bought a burger and fries – and a Coke – for Dezzie, and called his wife. Susie was waiting at the shelter for them when they arrived. Dezzie figured she'd stay one night, get cleaned up, and split.

But the next morning, freedom held no appeal; she looked at that open door and saw only the poverty, hunger and downward cycle of drugs and crime that waited for her. For the first time in months, she fought the need to start the day with a drink or a pill.

She turned to Susie, small and delicate, who stood beside her. "Can I stay? Please?"

* *

Over the next year, Dezzie and Susie argued and shouted, cried and laughed, and formed a strong bond. Susie, 23 years older than Dezzie, took no nonsense from Dezzie but she never belittled her or put her down. What Susie lacked in physical stature she made up for in strength of will. It was Susie who supported Dezzie during those first weeks of coming off the booze and the pills. It was due to Susie that Dezzie applied for, and got, a job as waitress in a diner, and then moved into an apartment with two girls not much older than she was, both steadily employed and leading respectable, sensible existences.

It was a life Dezzie would have scorned previously. Some nights, a part of her whispered in the dark of those heady early days with the band, the music and the highs, the crazy wild joy of simply being alive, being young and free – but she told it to shut up because she needed her sleep.

And sometimes she remembered a sky full of whirling stars, the rich cool scent of damp earth, and the thin cry of a newborn baby. Poor little thing, she would think, to come into such a world, and to have had such a mother. Where was she now? Had she even lived? It was harder to banish that memory than to banish the one of the band. Harder, too, to forgive herself.

Desdemona changed the short form of her name to Mona and insisted everyone call her that, another break with the past.

In addition to her shifts at the diner, Mona worked one day a week at the shelter.

"It's only right," Susie said. "In this life, we must give back part of what we are given."

When she was 19, Mona enrolled in adult education classes, determined to get the high school diploma she had previously written off as pointless. Among her fellow students was a young mechanic named Clive.

One day, about five months after she'd started going out with Clive, she and Susie were at the shelter, making an inventory of the bedding. Mona reached far back into the closet to retrieve a stack of sheets.

"Oh!" exclaimed Susie.

"What?" asked Mona, twisting to look at her. She saw where the other woman's eyes were directed. "Yeah. Four months." She patted the small bulge, then hesitated. "I've been trying to figure out how to tell you. I know you never trusted Clive – and like everything else, Susie, you were right! I told him about the baby two weeks ago, and I haven't seen him since."

"Oh!" exclaimed Susie again, eyes wide and voice angry. "Oh, I knew it! My poor girl!" And she threw her arms around Mona.

Mona laughed, and hugged her back. "Don't worry, Susie. I'll be fine. The doctor says I'm healthy as a horse and there's no reason why the baby won't be, too. He or she won't be the first baby born without a father."

Susie tilted her head back to look Mona in the eye. "You're sure about this? You truly want to raise a child on your own?" she asked. "This will change your life utterly. The baby will consume you."

Mona smiled down at her, this small woman who, by the sheer strength of her belief that things could indeed be better, had changed Mona's own life beyond all imagining. "Oh yes," she said quietly. "I've got you and Kevin, and my roommates, who are thrilled at the idea of a baby." Her hands cupped protectively around her growing baby. "And I've got this little guy. I'm not alone."

* *

A week after this talk with Susie, when Mona was on the afternoon shift at the diner, one of the other waitresses grabbed her arm and pulled her into the kitchen.

"I think he likes you," Lee-Anne said, pointing to the door.

The door had no windows, and Mona had no idea who Lee-Anne meant.

"At the counter," said Lee-Anne with a sigh, and exaggerated patience. "The thin guy."

Mona pushed the door open a fraction of an inch. "There are three thin guys."

"Really thin. With glasses. Black hair," added Lee-Anne helpfully.

There was only one man at the counter who fit that description. Mona recognized him, for he'd been coming in every day for almost two weeks. He hadn't said a word, though, beyond giving her his order.

"He doesn't like me," corrected Mona. "He never speaks to me."

"He watches you. As soon as he thinks you're not looking, he watches you."

Mona shuddered. "He sounds like a creep! Watching me, for God's sake!"

"He is not a creep!" declared Lee-Anne. "He's very nice. He's shy, that's all. He's not interested in me, so he does talk to me. He's smart, Mona! He has all sorts of university degrees, and a good job."

Mona scoffed. "Someone like that wouldn't be interested in someone like me! And this'll put him off, anyway." She patted the bulge, still too small to be really noticeable.

"If it does put him off, well, he wasn't worth it anyway. Dump him," said Lee-Anne stoutly. "But I don't think it will."

The idea that Mona herself might have a say in the worthiness of any man who wanted her, and that she herself might be the one to break things off, was so novel that Mona was speechless. A slow grin spread across her face.

"Yeah."

Lee-Anne took her shoulders and turned her towards the door. "He's nice. But he's shy. Now go out there and be nice to him." She gave Mona a push. "Oh yeah, his name's Edward."

Chapter 8

AN APPALLED SILENCE hung over the kitchen, broken only by the faint sound of a distant foghorn and by Mona's soft sobs. She was enveloped in Edward's arms, pulled hard against his chest. His face was pale, his eyes fierce and shimmering with unshed tears.

Janine was the first to speak. Revulsion and disbelief tinged her expression, and she sounded puzzled. "Mom, why are you telling us this? And why now?"

Mona's head came up in jerky movements, an inch at a time. "Don't you see?" she whispered. "That baby…in that park in San Francisco…." Her gaze fell on Nicola, and stayed there.

Greg put out a hand towards his mother, let it drop to the table. His eyes sought Nicola's, but she stared out the window, her eyes as blank as her face. "No!" he said vehemently. "We're not…she's not…no!"

Nicola's eyes swiveled to his, true as a compass to north. He saw the bleakness there.

"No," Greg whispered.

Then her chair crashed to the floor and she was gone, the cold damp wind seeping into the kitchen through the door she had wrenched open.

"Nicola!" he shouted, and ran after her.

She was still on the deck, huddled against a corner post with her hands pressed against her stomach. "I think I'm going to be sick," she said.

The rain had stopped but water dripped steadily from the bare tree branches, and beyond the railway tracks at the end of the garden was the Sound, still and calm, reflecting the heavy gray sky. From a neighboring yard drifted a child's laughter.

Greg reached out to touch her. She flinched, and was stiff when he put his arms around her. She tried to push him away but he was far stronger.

"Stop," he said gently. "Don't. It's me. Still me. Still us. That can't be true." There was a gaping pit inside him where an hour ago there had been joy and happiness.

"I think it can," Nicola said. "It all fits."

He shook his head. Gradually, her body softened against him, and she slid her arms around him.

"There are too many holes in her story," Greg argued. Christ, and what a story it was! His mother had been a runaway teenage groupie trading sex for drugs? If she hadn't told them herself, he would never have believed it. No wonder she had always refused to talk about her life before Edward came into it!

"But what if it is true?" whispered Nicola. The emptiness in her voice tore at him. "What if she is my mother? What if you're my half-brother?"

"Stop!" he said again, more forcefully, and gave her a little shake. "There's absolutely no point in standing out here and wondering 'what if.' I said her story is full of holes. We're going to go back inside and sit down and discuss this, sensibly and calmly!"

The look she gave him held the merest glimmer of amusement. "You don't sound either sensible or calm," she pointed out.

"I don't feel it," Greg admitted. He drew a shaky breath. "I cannot believe that my mother is right about you, but apart from that, can you imagine how I feel after hearing about her life? What would you think if Gwen suddenly revealed such things about herself? Poor Dad looked so shattered. And, oh yes, my real father was a shit called Clive, who got a girl pregnant and ran out."

"Oh my poor love," Nicola said. "I never thought of that. And Janine! She must be devastated. We should go in." She tried to pull away from him but he didn't loosen his arms.

Greg lifted one hand to Nicola's face, tracing the familiar curve of her cheek with gentle fingers, and searching her eyes. "It's not true."

"Oh Greg, I want to run away, far away, someplace all this can never find us!" Her voice quaked and her lips began to quiver, and then she was kissing him, with such unexpected violence that he was pressed against the post. "I love you!" she whispered.

"And I love you," Greg whispered back.

* *

The large kitchen felt stuffy and hot after the thin cold of outside, and with reluctance Nicola closed the door behind them. Only Janine was there, making another large pot of coffee. "I think we're going to need it," she said. "Probably the bottle of bourbon, too."

Greg nodded. "Probably. Where's Mom?"

"Upstairs. She went to shower and dress. Dad went with her. I don't think he had any idea, Greg. He looked so…dazed." Janine fumbled the lid of the coffee canister, and ground coffee spilled over the marble countertop. "Damn!" She flung the lid into the corner and turned away, her shoulders hunched and her back rigid. "Oh damn," she choked.

Nicola took a step towards Janine and then stopped, uncertain how much comfort she could offer, or if it would be accepted. One of the tumult of emotions rioting inside her was guilt, as if this terrible situation was somehow her fault. She began to sweep the grounds off the counter into her hand.

"It's okay," Greg said to Janine. "This is only coffee, and the other thing can't be true."

"But everything else? Everything she told us?" asked Janine, shaking her head. "At first, I refused to even consider that it was true. Mom! Our mother! But she couldn't invent a story like that! It explains a lot."

"Like what?" asked Nicola, not sure Janine would answer her.

But Janine said easily enough, "I was thinking of her volunteer work, mostly. I could never figure out why the issue of homeless people was so important to her, especially young ones. And she's always been dead set against any kind of drugs. The lectures she gave me!" She lowered her voice. "When I was 17, and had my first real boyfriend, she actually sat me down and discussed contraception. In excruciating detail. I was so embarrassed! I told her nothing like that was going on and she said, when it does, I had to be sure I used something."

Nicola couldn't imagine ever having such a conversation with her own mother. With Gwen, she thought uncomfortably. Oh God, it can't be true, this can't be happening.

The kitchen door swung open again as Edward and Mona returned. Mona looked more collected, calmer, but still drawn. Her damp hair was combed back from her pale face, revealing lines that Nicola didn't think had been there yesterday. Is it really possible to age overnight? she wondered. Her eyes met Mona's, jumped away and then came back. Mona was still looking at her, sadness and something like eagerness hovering in the blue eyes that were so very like her own.

"You all must despise me," Mona said, her voice so quiet that the words were hard to hear. "I spent all night wondering how I could ever bring myself to tell you such shameful things. It took me so many years to manage to almost forget them. But with what's at stake, how could I not tell you?"

"No!" denied Janine hotly, as if the strength of her support now would erase her first skeptical, sickened response. She flung her arms around her mother. "Oh Mom, we could never despise you."

Greg joined them, wrapping both sister and mother in his embrace. "But you've given us one hell of a shock," he admitted, his voice unsteady.

Mona's breath caught somewhere between a sob and a laugh.

Nicola stared down at the chair beside her, an outsider in this display of family closeness. Or, dear God, was this her family, too? Nausea, cold and clammy, swept through her again, and her nails dug into her palms.

It was Edward who broke the silence. "Let's sit down, shall we? I think we all have some things we would like to go over."

Wooden chairs scraped on terracotta tiles as they arranged themselves, and spoons clinked against mugs as they stirred their coffee.

Greg, who had insisted outside that his mother's story was full of holes, was silent. Nicola saw him look from her to his mother, slowly, as if comparing the one with the other; his lips tightened and he shook his head, as if in denial.

"Now, my dear," began Edward, taking Mona's hand. "Why do you believe Nicola is your daughter? Yes, she looks like you, remarkably like you, but how can you be certain of the date?

You describe being on drugs, or drunk, or both; how could you possibly remember with any precision when this happened?"

Mona tightened her hands around his, like a drowning woman clinging to a branch, and took a deep breath. "I know that my arrival in Portland ruined Pam's 16th birthday, and I know her birthday is on July 19th. It's in my little book, you know the one, where I keep dates and addresses. I remember the red, white and blue in Reno, so that was the 4th of July. I'm not sure how many days we took to get from San Francisco to Reno. Three? Maybe four?"

Here Mona paused and darted a look at Nicola, still and silent. "And Nicola said the doctors at the hospital put her birthday on June 30th. It fits."

"But how did she get to the hospital? Which hospital? When?" asked Greg in frustration.

Mona shook her head helplessly. "I don't know! That woman who helped me must have taken the baby."

"Is there any way to find out how many baby girls were abandoned in San Francisco in late June 1975?" wondered Edward out loud.

"I can't believe there was more than one," said Mona.

Greg turned to Nicola. "Do you know which hospital it was? That would narrow it down. If it was near the Tenderloin, or not, that would tell us something either way."

Mute, she shook her head.

"And another thing!" exclaimed Greg. "Mom was practically starving, it sounds like, living on alcohol and drugs. Was the baby full term? Premature?"

Mona lifted one slim shoulder. "I don't know!" she repeated.

"I rather doubt that any baby born to a mother in the condition you describe, my dear, exposed to high levels of alcohol and drugs from conception, could ever have grown into such a healthy, intelligent woman as Nicola," put in Edward. "Surely there would be problems. Nicola, were you sickly as a child? Unwell? How were you at school?"

She shook her head. "The usual things, chicken pox and measles, but nothing you'd call a problem. I've never heard that I had any developmental issues. At school, I was never at the head of the class, but I was nowhere near the bottom, either."

"So we're back where we started," said Edward. "Perhaps. Or perhaps not. All the evidence is so circumstantial."

They fell silent, all looking at each other as if the answer would appear in the air between them. All but Janine, who had been tapping on her tablet computing device for some time.

"Janine, for God's sake," said Greg sharply, "if you've got something more interesting to look at online, at least do it somewhere else."

She flashed him an angry look but didn't say anything, and turned the tablet so they could all see the screen.

"DNA testing?" said Nicola in surprise.

Janine nodded. "According to their website, the kit will take two days to arrive. You and Mom take a sample, which is no more than a swab from inside your cheek, and send it back. Once they get it, results take five to seven days. Then we'll know for sure. So yeah," she said, looking meaningfully at Greg, "I did have something more interesting to do than sit here and speculate wildly."

"Sorry," Greg muttered. He ran a hand through his hair, then stretched to touch Janine's hand. "Hey. I am sorry."

"How do we know this is reliable?" Edward frowned.

"It says that if the results are positive, if the DNA matches, the result is 99% sure. If the results are negative, it's 100% sure," Janine said, tapping again to bring up another screen. "Other sites say the same thing. It sounds straightforward. And it costs $400."

"Do it," commanded Mona. "Order the kit. I don't care how much it costs. It's the only way we'll know." A pause. "Nicola, do you agree?"

No! she wanted to shout. No! I know who my mother is, and she's in Sausalito right now pouring over wedding magazines. But…if she disagreed, if she refused to admit that there was any possibility that this stranger had given birth to her in a park in San Francisco, what would she be doing to her future with Greg? Greg, who just happened to be this stranger's son?

She met his eyes, and they held only misery.

Nicola nodded.

There was more silence as Janine brought up the order page. Greg flipped his credit card to her. "Get the kit sent here," he told her, "but the results to Nicola."

Nicola pulled her smartphone from her sweater pocket and looked up the website for herself. "It says two working days to arrive," she pointed out. "This is Saturday. They won't mail it until Monday. It won't be here until Wednesday. Then we have to mail it back, so let's say they get it Friday. Then it's five to seven more working days for results. It's at least two weeks before we'll know."

Greg took her hand. "And the wedding is three weeks from Monday," he said dully.

Mona drew a swift breath. "You must call it off!" she urged. "At least postpone it, until we know one way or the other."

Nicola pulled her hand from Greg's and wrapped both arms around her midriff, suddenly as cold as ice, and as lifeless. How am I going to tell my family about this? She wished, strongly, that she was at home right now, in the kitchen she'd known all her life, with her own family around her. Not these strangers, this woman.

"I can't stay here until Wednesday," she announced.

Mona looked at her sharply. "Here in Seattle, or here in this house?"

"Seattle, I meant. I have work."

"We can come back on Wednesday," suggested Greg. "Here and back in the same day is no problem."

Nicola nodded. "But," she said slowly, "since you mention it, would you prefer me to leave? I can stay in a hotel tonight."

Edward's expression was one of amazement. "Why?"

She squirmed on her chair and flashed a glance at Greg, who looked equally mystified. "I mean, if you're uncomfortable with the idea of us together. Um, in the same bed."

"Oh!" exclaimed Mona. "I hadn't even considered that." She looked from one to the other uneasily, and frowned. She opened her mouth, but was interrupted by her daughter.

Janine's laugh was the first any of them had heard for hours. "Oh, come on! You two are rarely out of touching distance from each other! I doubt you've been saving yourselves for the wedding night. Nicola going to a hotel tonight would definitely fall under the category of closing the barn door after the horse has bolted!"

Edward gave them a small smile, and although Mona still frowned, she was silent.

"And besides," added Greg, reaching for Nicola's hand again, "I would only follow you, so what's the point?"

* *

The Sound was almost flat, the wind almost non-existent. All around, islands receded into the mist. Gray water wavered into gray sky, and even the light seemed gray, with no hint of the sun. Only the cry of a gull or the forlorn bell of a buoy punctuated the still silence. It was no day for serious sailing.

"Quiet out here, isn't it?"

Greg nodded.

"I'm glad the rain stopped."

Greg nodded again.

"You going to speak any time soon?"

Startled by the question, Greg turned his attention from the water to the man whom he would always think of as his father. "I don't know what to say, Dad. About anything."

"Keeping it bottled up inside isn't going to help," advised Edward. He shifted on the wooden seat. "I think I've got a splinter in my butt."

Greg was surprised into a smile. "Ouch."

"She's too old, I know," said Edward. "I should have got rid of her years ago. But this boat holds too many memories."

"For me, too. You taught me how to sail in *Waste*."

Edward laughed. "I always did regret that her full name of *Waste of Time and Money* wouldn't fit. Your mother was very much against me buying a boat. That's what she christened it."

Greg knew that; he had heard the story a dozen, a hundred times. But it was comforting and familiar, part of his childhood. "Did you know?"

Edward might have assumed this was a reference to Mona's disapproval of the boat. He did not.

A spasm of pain and regret crossed his tanned, lined face, and he gave a long sigh. "No. I'd never heard any of what she told us, until you did." His hand on the tiller tightened convulsively, and the boat's head turned too close into the wind, what little there was. Edward loosened his grip.

Greg leaned over and grasped his father's shoulder, bony even through the layers of clothes and waterproofs. "Poor Mom."

"Yes." Edward stared out over the water. "I suspected, naturally, that whatever her life had been before I met her was... atypical, shall we say. She refused to talk about it. Completely refused, as if it had never happened. I had my own ideas, but they were nothing like what she told us this morning. I could never have imagined such horrific things, such a lifestyle.

"To me, Mona was a lovely girl with the bluest eyes I had ever seen, and a laugh that I couldn't resist. I knew she was catching up on her schooling, and working full time, and also volunteering in that homeless shelter. At 19! I admired her for that. I went into that diner day after day just to see her. I was jittery from all the coffee and sick from all the pie! To this day, I can't stand blueberry pie.

"I was over the moon when she finally agreed to go out with me. Before she said yes, she told me that she was carrying another man's child. I didn't care." He glanced at Greg, and smiled. "Although when you broke that store window playing baseball when you were 10, and I had to pay for a new one, I did have second thoughts."

Greg chuckled. "Funny, but I don't think you ended up out of pocket on that. I remember raking leaves and washing the car and taking out the garbage for a year to pay you back."

"Taught you the value of money, and of work, didn't it? Not to mention being more careful with your pitching," remarked Edward. He made a sound of impatience, and looked around. "I wish we had more wind."

The boat creaked on, happy in its old age to amble along on this whisper of air.

"Would it have made a difference? If you had known?"

Edward smiled. "Mona would have had to have killed some-one, I think, or done something equally as terrible, to have made a difference to how I felt about her. She wasn't the woman she is now, the one you have come to know as an adult yourself. She was defensive, suspicious, wary...but I could see, from the way she behaved with people she knew and trusted, like the other waitresses, that she was also warm, and kind." He smiled softly, his eyes unfocused as his mind flew back in years.

Greg looked around them, scanning automatically for ship-ping or navigation buoys. Nothing, so he relaxed, and drifted along with *Waste* and the wind and his father's memories. "Did Mom never want to go to college? Do more?"

Edward blinked, and came back to the present. "Yes. She wanted to become a social worker. I couldn't understand why, at the time. I...I wasn't supportive, or understanding," he said slowly. "My own family was very traditional. Mother never worked. I have no idea if she even wanted to. I expected my own wife to stay at home, too. We didn't need another income, and I'm sorry to say I talked Mona out of her plans – not kindly."

To Greg's surprise, his father laughed.

"Mona now would never for a moment put up with such caveman behavior, but Mona then was not as sure of herself," Edward said. He gave a small grunt of amusement. "And you know, Greg, I like this version of your mother even better."

"I wonder how she and Nicola are getting on at home?" asked Greg.

* *

"Where do you want these ones?" asked Nicola, holding up a handful of dried, wrinkled tubers.

Mona sat on her heels and brushed the back of her wrist across her forehead, leaving a smudge of dirt. "I don't know. I don't have any idea what they are. We may well be planting solid blocks of the same tulips, for all I can tell!"

"They do all look the same," said Nicola, eyeing the wizened blobs with doubt. She scooped up two handfuls and let them fall to the damp grass. "There. Mixed up. Oh! Maybe they were mixed up already, and I've put them back into solid blocks!"

"We won't know until spring," said Mona. "That's one of the joys of gardening."

Nicola dug the trowel into the turf, levered it up and dropped in a tulip. They had been out here for an hour, kneeling on mats on the grass – and by tacit agreement, neither had mentioned this morning. Talk had been of tulips, and gardens, of the incomprehensible foolishness of men who wanted to sail in this weather. Not a word about the things uppermost in their minds.

She looked sideways at Mona's hands, at her long, slender fingers. Her own hands were squat by comparison, the fingers short and blunt. But did that mean anything? For any one feature that was not like Mona's, Nicola could find another that was. The widow's peak of their hair. The hair itself, thick and almost straight, and so dark that it appeared black in all but the brightest light. Did Mona have a birthmark on her thigh? And would it mean anything if she did?

This woman cannot be my mother!

Nicola stabbed the trowel into the ground. It hit a rock and skittered to the side, the sharp tip scraping her other hand. She yelped, more in surprise than in pain.

"Are you all right?" asked Mona. She held out her own hand, an anxious look on her face. "Let me see."

Nicola extended her hand reluctantly, a confusion of emotions inside her. Her mother would say that, would sound just like that whenever Nicola had hurt herself as a child; what right had this woman to act like her mother! Oh God, it isn't true!

She snatched her hand back.

"It's nothing," she muttered.

Mona recoiled as if slapped.

Shame flooded through Nicola. "I–"

"Ahoy the garden!" called Edward in a loud and cheerful voice, as he and Greg clattered down the wooden stairs from the deck. "Come inside, you two, the heavens are about to open!"

She jumped to her feet and began gathering tools and mat and tubers, as full of a sense of reprieve as a woman whose cart trundling to the guillotine had turned to safety at the last minute. "I didn't expect you back so soon!"

Greg held open the sack for the tulips. "Have you looked up at all in the past 15 minutes? We're in for unpleasant weather."

Her laugh was only slightly too brittle to be genuine. "No, we were caught up in the planting!"

She looked at Mona, who was busy rolling up her own mat, back to them. Perhaps too busy. Nicola leaned over and brushed her hand against the other woman's shoulder. "Thank you for letting me help."

His mother's smile was only slightly too strained to be real. "Thank you for helping me."

* *

Dinner that evening had none of yesterday's spontaneity, none of the growing pleasure in one another's company. Tensions eddied, and thoughts went unspoken. The weather was a major topic of conversation.

The only one who seemed unaffected by the day's events was Janine. Her eyes sparkled with poorly repressed amusement, as if the whole thing was one big joke. Nicola sat with her after dinner on a sofa in the living room. She kept one eye on the clock, wondering when she could escape to their bedroom without leaving so early that it would seem ill-mannered.

The whole of this interminable day, Nicola had smiled, and been civil, and struggled to act as normal as everyone else seemed to be acting. Struggled to not give in to the impulse to shriek and to throw things, to blame Mona for the unthinkable disaster her life had become in one short hour. Or maybe everyone was pretending; maybe they were like characters in a play, going through motions and saying empty words. Well, probably not Janine. Nicola had to get away from them, somewhere she wasn't required to put on a good front.

"I always wanted a sister," Janine remarked.

"Did you?" said Nicola, with politeness more than anything else. And then the meaning behind the words hit her, and she reared back instinctively.

"If you're Greg's half-sister, you're mine, too," elaborated Janine. "Great!"

Nicola eyed her with disbelief. Was she kidding? Or merely incredibly self-centered? "Great?"

"Not so great for you and Greg, obviously!" laughed Janine.

"Obviously."

She wouldn't have said anything more, but curiosity got the better of her. "You don't seem disturbed by the idea that he and I might be half-siblings."

Janine swirled the dregs of her drink. "I guess I'm not. It's not as if you grew up with him, like I did. You're crazy about each other, anyone can see that. I think that's wonderful. So, no, it doesn't bother me that you have that sort of relationship."

A ribald laugh, and then Janine jabbed her thumb towards her own chest and said, "Though Greg better not get any ideas about this particular half-sister!"

Torn between reluctant laughter and repulsion, Nicola kept silent.

Mona put aside the book she had been reading – or had pretended to be reading. She hadn't turned a page in some time, and sat with her pale face propped in one hand. "If you will excuse me, I think I'll turn in," said Mona in a thin voice.

Choruses of goodnights and sleep wells followed her to the door.

Nicola gave it 10 minutes, 10 long minutes creeping past on the clock, and then announced with feigned heartiness, "I think Mona had the right idea. I'm off to bed."

She couldn't shake the feeling that anyone who had heard this morning's revelations would think she was doing something very wrong by sharing Greg's bed, and she thought that if they went separately perhaps Edward and Janine might somehow forget that point.

Greg foiled her plan by rising when she did, claiming to be tired, too.

"Sleep well!" called Janine after them, with a wink.

In their room, through half-closed eyes, Nicola watched Greg undress. How many times had she seen him naked, caressed every part of him? Yet, now it was as if he was new to her and this was the first time. How many more times would there be? What, she wondered bleakly, would they do if the test results were positive? How could she possibly give him up? How could she not?

They lay on their backs, not touching. Moonlight stole through the window to cast soft-edged silver shadows, and she thought she could hear the water washing against the shore. Was it too far away for that? The tension built to something almost palpable.

When his hand brushed against hers, she gripped it as if she would never let go.

"Greg?" she whispered.

"Unless there's someone else in here I don't know about it, it pretty much has to be, doesn't it?" he whispered back.

For a moment, her laugh ghosted on the air.

"Oh, Greg." The ghost was gone.

"Shhh, darling. Forget about everything. Go to sleep."

"I want you to make love to me, Greg. So badly. To make me lose myself in you, and forget myself so that I cry out so loud everyone hears. But we can't," she said, her voice breaking.

He turned on his side towards her, to slide his other hand over her waist and rest his cheek against her shoulder. "We did last night," he reminded her, then added, "Though you didn't cry out. I think you stuffed a corner of the pillow in your mouth."

"That was before we knew!" she said. "We can't do that now."

Greg gave her a sharp shake. "Don't! Don't say that," he commanded harshly. "We don't actually know anything. All we have right now is a crazy idea of my mother. I refuse to believe it's true until those results come back and tell me it's true, and even then I will demand another test from another laboratory. And I refuse to allow you to believe it, either!"

"Really?" Nicola was doubtful, but she turned to face him. From habit, his knee slipped between her legs and her arm went around his shoulders. "You think it's all right for us to have sex now? Oh!" His lips had drifted to her breast.

He raised his head. "Nothing has changed, Nicola. I'm still me, and you're still you, and I still love you."

"Oh, and I still love you, too!" she said with quiet intensity. "But Greg, I can't stop thinking that if your mother is right," she broke off as he rose above her, and she wrapped her legs around him, "if she's right, what we're doing now is inces—"

Greg's rough kiss stopped the word. "No! Don't say it."

Oh my love, Nicola thought, gazing up at him, his body heavy on hers. Not saying it doesn't make it go away.

Chapter 9

"CHURCH?" Nicola repeated dumbly. She lowered her arms, still caught in the sweater she was pulling over her head.

Greg nodded, and finished buttoning his shirt. "Why don't you come? It might help."

"You can't be serious," she stated, flinging the sweater onto the bed. "You think prayer is going to solve this?" Her voice rose with incredulity.

"I don't think it will solve anything!" he replied, his voice rising to match hers. "I do know prayer will make me feel better, and I thought it might help you!"

Something had changed between them during the night. All morning she had been prickly and irritable, he impatient and unsympathetic.

"I don't need help," she said sharply.

He took a deep breath and a step back, and she could almost hear him count to 10. "You were crying last night, Nicola," he said, his voice soft but his face still set in anger. "In the bathroom. I heard you."

"Oh." She looked away.

"I was halfway to the bathroom before I even knew I'd got up. Halfway to you. I couldn't bear to think you felt so bad, that you were alone in there and so unhappy," he said. The anger seemed to have passed. "But then I thought you wanted privacy, so I went back to bed."

"And you think talking to God will make me feel better? Should I try bargaining? Hey God, if I give up chocolate croissants forever, will you fix this?" She heard the taunt in her voice, and knew she should stop, but couldn't. All the doubt and fear that had churned inside her for the past 24 hours would not be repressed. "What sort of a God would do something like this? Have us meet, and fall in love, and then to liven things up a bit, oh, hey, let's see what they do if it turns out they've got the same mother! How can you believe in a God like that?"

"I believe in God. I never claimed to understand him," said Greg slowly.

His voice was level, but his eyes sparked with renewed anger.

Her laugh held no sound of humor. "Right now, I don't understand you. You're not going to give me that line about God working in mysterious ways and this all being for the best? Yeah, Greg, you go to church, for all the good it's going to do anyone!"

The sarcasm in her voice was sharp and heavy, and she saw him flinch. He stared at her with cold, level eyes, not saying anything, then turned away.

At the open door he paused, and without looking back, Greg said in a flat voice, "I don't understand you, either. At this moment, I'm not so sure I even like you."

The cushion she flung at him hit the wall with a soft thump. Nicola threw herself onto the brocade bedspread, last night's tears threatening to spill over again. She couldn't believe that of all the things they could have had their first fight about, it had turned out to be religion. No, that wasn't true, she knew that; religion had been only the excuse. Damn Mona!

She twisted up at the sound of a soft knock, ready to tell Greg to go to hell, or to church if that's what he preferred, but the angry words died when she saw it was Edward. He stood in the doorway, holding the blue cushion. The small, not-quite smile on his face said clearly that he knew what had happened.

"Are you a walker, Nicola?" he asked.

This was not at all what she had thought he might say, and she paused to consider her answer. "More of a runner, I think. But my mom likes to walk, and she drags me out sometimes."

The not-quite smile turned into a real one. "Then in that case, I shall have no compunction in dragging you out myself right now. They will be gone for at least an hour, and you and I can get in a good walk during that time."

She heaved herself off the bed and rummaged around for her shoes. "You don't go to church with Mona?" she asked, curious about how that worked out.

He shook his head. "I am, at best, an agnostic. Show me incontrovertible proof that God exists, and, more, that such a God demands weekly worship, and I may change my mind. Until then, my wife and I have, as they say, agreed to disagree.

Greg has adopted her religious beliefs. Janine's beliefs, such as they are, do not interfere with sleeping in."

That was so much like Nicola's own approach that she had to laugh. Outside, they strode along the sidewalk, under tall trees and beside solid fences. The day was sunny and the air was crisp, and her spirits rose with the exercise. She said, "I guess I didn't handle that very well, did I?"

"Marriage is compromise, my dear. It takes practice and commitment to get it right. You and Greg have barely got started. Give it time. You'd be amazed how far a simple 'I'm sorry' can go, regardless of whether you really are," Edward said with a small wink. "I think you and Greg will be fine."

Nicola looked at him sharply. "You talk like everything's going to work out." She took a few quick steps to keep up. Edward and her mother were roughly the same age, but they didn't walk at the same speed.

"I believe it will work out. Mona, despite the hardened exterior she likes to present to the world, is fairly emotional. I am fairly logical," he explained.

"Is that why you didn't want me to go to a hotel?" It was the only way she could think to phrase her question with any delicacy.

"Indeed. If you truly did have the same mother, that would be a different matter. I'm not certain how I would react to such a situation. Surely not with Janine's flippancy! Would I condemn you? Support you? I don't know," Edward admitted. "But, as I said yesterday, all the evidence for you being Mona's daughter is nothing but circumstantial."

Her spirits rose higher.

"Although, being circumstantial does not preclude it from ultimately being true," he added slowly.

* *

"You're going to dent the handle if you keep that up," commented Mona.

Greg looked at his mother in confused surprise.

"You've got a death grip on that thing." She took her eyes off the road to nod towards his right hand, clenched around the curved plastic attached to the car's door. "You told Nicola that prayer would make you feel better, but I don't think it has."

"How do you know what I told her?"

Mona smiled. "The two of you weren't exactly whispering. I don't think the neighbors heard, but we did."

"Oh." Greg uncurled his fingers. "That was our first fight."

"Fairly minor, as fights go," his mother observed.

"Minor? How would you know? I have never heard you and Dad raise your voices to each other!"

Her glance was brief, and she said pointedly, "Exactly. You never heard."

"You and Dad fight?" asked Greg, staring at her with as much astonishment as if she had suddenly grown purple spots.

"Oh for God's sake, of course we do! Every couple does. You and Jackie had some doozies, or have you forgotten that barbecue? All the neighbors heard that one!" They had stopped at a red light and she turned to him.

"Jackie and I had a fight every month since the day we met," Greg stated. "Nicola and I hadn't had one at all. I took it as a good sign."

Mona eased the car around a corner. "It is a good sign. That you've grown up, if nothing else."

"What!"

"You were sometimes self-centered and intolerant, Greg, when you lived here. Even when you were growing up, I often thought that you couldn't be bothered to understand someone else's point of view. But since you left," she said, and reached over to pat his hand comfortingly, "that's changed. I think that year on your boat did you a world of good."

He was speechless. Self-centered and intolerant?

"And I think," Mona added, "you'll need all that to get you through the next two weeks. We all will."

Greg watched her for a moment, noting the pinched look around her mouth, the dark smudges under her eyes. "I am a selfish bastard, aren't I? Thinking only about myself. How are you, Mom?"

The flicker of a smile. "You're not a bastard, Greg. Edward and I were married by the time you were born."

"Mom!" He didn't know whether to be amused or shocked.

The flicker faded. "I'm not sure how I am. How I feel. Relieved, in a way, to finally have it all out. I should have told Edward years ago, I know that. But how?" She sighed heavily. "I thought I had made peace with myself over that baby. But she's all I've thought of since yesterday. Your older sister. Who might be Nicola." She glanced at him. "Prayer didn't help me, either."

He wanted to put his arms around her, hug her, try to soothe that pain in her eyes, but traffic was heavy and it would be madness. Greg rested his hand on her shoulder, and squeezed.

"Mom…if Janine hadn't interrupted yesterday, what would you have said in response to Nicola's question about us being in the same bed?" He had seen the way she had looked at them in the kitchen, and had wondered.

She was silent, and he thought she might not answer. But then she pulled the car to the side of the road, and turned to him. "My gut reaction was shock at even considering it. But later, I was glad Janine did stop me. I think there's a good chance Nicola could be…that baby. Your sister. A good chance, but no certainty. Is it right to deprive you both of the comfort and love you can offer each other, while we wait?"

"Mom," he said gently, "you wouldn't have deprived us. I meant what I said. If Nicola had left, I would have gone with her. I may be mad as hell at her right now, but I'd still go with her."

Mona took his hand. "Even knowing it may be a sin?"

A deep breath. "I'll worry about sin when those results come back."

* *

Lunch had been awkward and uncomfortable. She and Greg had hardly spoken to each other, had certainly not apologized, and there was still coolness between them. Now, finally, it was time to leave, and they gathered beside the taxi in front of the house. Nicola tapped her foot, filled with impatience to be gone, at last, to no longer have to dissemble. If just one more time she had to pretend that calamity and tragedy were not hanging over them like an ugly shadow, she would scream.

"Come on," urged Janine, already in the back seat. "We'll miss our flights."

Mona stepped closer to Nicola, and took her hand. Her smile was hesitant. "You're a marvelous young woman, Nicola," she said. "I'll admit that a small part of me hopes that test is positive. I would love to discover that my daughter had turned out like you."

Nicola's tenuous self-control shattered, and she wrenched her hand free. "What? You would trade my future, and Greg's, just to appease your damned conscience?" she spat. "You think me being your daughter will make up for you being a drunk and an addict and a slut who can't even say who my father is?"

"Nicola!" Greg's face was white, and he pulled her roughly away. "How dare you speak to her like that!"

She jerked away from him. "You're taking her side?" she shrieked. "I can't believe it!"

Edward stepped between them and put an arm around Nicola's shoulder. With a strength she wouldn't have suspected his thin frame possessed, he overcame her rigid resistance and pulled her to him, holding her still. "Shh. Think what you're doing, what you're saying."

Nicola took a deep, shuddering breath, sanity snapping back into place with the abruptness of a shutter flung open. Had she really screamed such awful things at Greg's mother? How would any of them ever forgive her?

She smiled up wanly at Edward. "Thank you," she whispered, and stepped away from him.

Nicola did not dare look at Greg. She walked slowly in front of Mona, who was staring at the trees and blinking rapidly, like someone who refused to cry. "I'm sorry," Nicola got out. "I should never have said such things."

Mona's eyes brimmed with unhappiness when she finally faced Nicola. "No," she said softly. "You should not have. Even if they were true."

"Get in the taxi, Nicola," said Greg tersely, his face forbidding. "We'll be late." He went to his mother and hugged her tightly. "I love you, Mom." An equally tight hug for Edward and then he got into the car beside the driver.

Nicola huddled in the back seat, and closed her eyes, shaking with the empty adrenaline rush that comes with anger. Anger at Mona, who was the cause of everything going so wrong, and anger at herself, for having surrendered to the urge to punish Mona for that. She wanted only to get away from here.

The silence in the car was relieved by the taxi driver, prattling about football and oblivious to the undercurrents of friction among his passengers. When they reached the airport, Nicola roused herself to say the right things to Janine; she, at least, was blameless in this fiasco.

Greg walked beside her to their check-in counter, stiff and silent. Nicola matched him. Damned if she would be the first to speak.

Edward's voice was clear in her mind. "You'd be amazed how far a simple 'I'm sorry' can go, regardless of whether you really are."

I'm not sorry, she thought with a flash of renewed, petty anger.

"I'm sorry," Nicola said.

Greg tilted his head, his eyes cool. "For what, in particular?"

"In particular?" she repeated. Calm. Deep breaths. It wasn't working.

"For shouting sarcastic comments about my faith? For insulting my mother? For sulking in the taxi the whole way? I'm wondering what part of today you're actually sorry for," he said, in a voice like ice cubes rattling in a glass.

"What part are you sorry for?" she demanded.

The blue eyes, always before so warm and so full of love, had all the warmth now of a glacier. "I'm not sure I am sorry. For anything."

"Me either."

"You said you were."

"I lied."

More silence, from check-in through security and to the gate.

The flight back to San Francisco was an eternity longer than the one to Seattle on Friday. Never in all the time that they had known each other had they gone so long without talking, without touching. The urge to hold him, to apologize fully and unreservedly for anything he wanted her to apologize for, was almost impossible to deny, but it fought against a stubborn determination not to be the first to give in. Arms crossed, Nicola stared out the window.

They had driven in his car to the airport, so Greg took her back into the city, to her apartment in Polk Gulch. On California Street, they were slowed by a trolley.

"When will you tell Gwen and Arthur?" Greg asked. His fingers tapped in impatience against the wheel. "Or have you called them already?"

Relief that he had spoken, at last, warred with suspicion. It was "Gwen and Arthur" not "your parents"; was that intentional? "That's not the sort of news you can give over the phone! Tonight. I'll drive over when you drop me off."

"Shall I come with you?" Greg asked slowly.

Nicola shook her head. "You don't need to. It's a long drive from Sausalito to Richmond for you. And I may stay over."

"Right." The one word was clipped and cold.

In front of her building, she hesitated, and turned to him. His eyes looked straight ahead and his hands were tight on the wheel. With a sharp exclamation, she climbed out and opened the back door to retrieve her bag, resisting the impulse to slam the door shut. She turned on the stairs, but he had already pulled away from the curb.

Fine! thought Nicola. Drive off!

In the lobby, she jabbed at the elevator button. "Come on, come on," she muttered. In her apartment, she flung her bag onto the bed and then sank down beside it, unimaginably weary. The thought of that drive to Sausalito filled her with dismay. But she had to tell her parents. More than that, she craved the unquestioning love and comfort that only they could give.

The car's headlights swept across the front of their house as Nicola drew up, and a moment later, the porch light flashed on.

The door opened, but only as far as the security chain would allow. Gwen's face peered through the gap, her expression shifting from apprehension to surprise when she saw that it was Nicola. She opened the door wide. "Hello! What are you doing here?"

"Oh, Mom!" Nicola threw herself into her mother's arms.

Gwen staggered under the onslaught of this unexpected embrace. "What happened? Nicola, what's wrong?" she asked rapidly.

"What isn't wrong?" Nicola replied, stepping back. How could she ever find the words to tell them?

"Did you and Greg have a fight?"

"Yes."

Gwen smiled, and ushered Nicola into the house. "Oh, is that all?"

"No, Mom, that's not all," said Nicola, fighting back those damned tears. She hadn't cried in years, not even when Andrew left, and today it seemed she couldn't stop.

"Then what is it? Was his family awful?"

"They were very nice." She took a breath and looked down the hallway. Its apricot-colored walls glowed in the light of lamps, and at the far end a high arched window looked out onto the black night. From the living room came the sound of the television. "Mom, we'd better join Dad. He needs to hear this, too."

At first, Nicola's parents refused to believe that her story was not a tasteless joke. Eventually, though, disbelief gave way to stunned acceptance.

"That poor, poor woman," breathed Gwen. "To have gone through such a ghastly time."

Arthur shifted in his recliner. "And then to have to tell everyone about it so many years later."

"You would never in a million years suspect Mona of having a background like that," asserted Nicola. "In a way, she reminds me of Hélène. Mona has that same aura of calm control, and effortless elegance. You can tell she spends more on one visit to a hair stylist than I do in a year. All of her clothes look like she bought them last week, from an exclusive boutique."

Gwen leaned over to tweak Nicola's shapeless old sweater, and said, "She definitely can't be your mother, in that case!" She smiled, but it was strained.

Nicola captured the soft, wrinkled hand. "She will never be my mother!" she said fiercely. "Even if the DNA tests say she is, I know who my real mother is." With her other hand, she stretched out to touch Arthur. "And my real father! I love you both so much. Don't you ever forget that."

Gwen sniffed, and smiled again, without the strain. Arthur raised his daughter's hand to his lips and lightly kissed it.

"However," said Nicola, uncomfortable but determined to tell everything, "no matter who Mona turns out to be, I was inexcusably rude to her this afternoon. I completely lost control and said some nasty things. Greg was horrified. I have to call her first thing tomorrow and apologize properly. She didn't deserve that."

"Nicola!" said Arthur, in mild rebuke. "That's not like you."

She gave him a lopsided smile. "I haven't felt very 'me' since Saturday morning, Dad."

"The wedding!" exclaimed Gwen, looking horror-struck. "What will you do? What will you tell people?"

"We'll postpone it, of course," said Nicola. "How could we let everyone go on thinking nothing had changed?"

Arthur raised his eyebrows and his beer simultaneously. "You're going to tell everyone?"

Nicola shuddered. "God, no! Not the truth. Whatever that ends up being. No, we've decided to say that Greg's father is unwell and has an operation scheduled two days before the wedding date. We can't possibly go ahead until he's better, so we'll put it on hold. That gives us an indefinite breathing space."

"Good plan," commented Arthur in approval. "Very believable. Very logical."

"It was his father's own idea," replied Nicola with a smile. "Edward is very logical himself." Then she yawned, exhausted and drained by everything that had happened since Friday. "Can I stay here tonight? I can't face that drive home."

Gwen said crisply, "No, you cannot."

"I cannot?" replied Nicola, not sure she had heard correctly.

Her father's surprise matched her own.

"Where is Greg right now?" demanded Gwen.

"On his boat." She hated that note of defensiveness that had crept into her voice.

"Why? Why isn't he here with you, or you there with him?" her mother continued.

Nicola sighed. "I told you, Mom. We had a fight this morning. Then I shrieked like a madwoman at his mother. We've hardly said a word to each other since then. We both need some space."

"Is this about your fight? Or about what his mother told you?"

She opened her mouth to reply, then shook her head.

Gwen took her hand. "Sweetie, this is the first test of your relationship. Granted, it's beyond anything most couples could ever imagine having to face, but if your instinct is to run away then your marriage is doomed to failure from the start."

Nicola regarded her mother with wonder. "You sound like Edward. He said we would end up married."

"I look forward to meeting him," Gwen said.

"You'll like him, he's great. But don't go walking with him, Mom, you couldn't keep up," Nicola advised her.

Gwen rose, and pulled Nicola to her feet. "Now get out of here. I refuse to allow my daughter to become the sort of woman who runs home to mother."

Nicola held her hands and searched the other woman's familiar, beloved face. "You don't think it's wrong for us to…be together? Now?"

"I will think it extremely wrong for you to be together if Greg actually turns out to be your half-brother. 'Wrong' would not begin to describe it!" she replied with vehemence. "But there seems precious little real evidence for such a thing. I wonder if his mother is exaggerating? Maybe she's not as nice as you thought. People like that can be funny."

Nicola stepped back. "People like what?" She asked the question, but she had a good idea what the answer would be. She didn't often see the narrow-minded, intolerant side of her mother, and she didn't like it when she did. Earlier, Mona had been "that poor, poor woman"; now, she was "people like that."

"No decent person would ever behave like that. Drugs, and such promiscuous sex! There must be something wrong with her family for her to have turned out like that," said Gwen with cold contempt. "Thank heavens, Greg seems like a sensible young man. I can't imagine him ever behaving in such a way."

Nicola had the oddest urge to defend Greg's mother in the face of this attack, despite being uncomfortably aware that she herself had not exactly been forgiving or understanding during the course of these two extraordinary days. "She was only a kid when that happened, Mom! Fifteen when she ran away."

"And why did she run away, I ask you?" said Gwen sharply. Then she shook her head. "No, until that woman's story is proved true, I think you should carry on as before. Although I do admit, I would not be happy if it was happening under my own roof."

Nicola sighed, and looked down. Her fingers were knotted together, something she knew she did whenever she was upset. She didn't even know she was doing it.

Gently, Gwen asked, "Do you think it's wrong to be with Greg, sweetie?"

All of a sudden, her mother was back, shouldering away that harsh, judgmental stranger. Nicola hesitated. "Part of me does. Yes. I thought I would be physically sick when Mona told us she thought I could be her daughter. It's such a taboo! Imagine what people would say, what they would think, if they knew. Even now, when there's no proof." Nicola shrugged, aware of nothing but confusion, and wretchedness. "I don't know what to think. All I know is that I love him. I'll always love him. Even after spending a day being mad at him, I love him. Dad, what do you say?"

Arthur heaved himself out of the recliner and folded her in his arms, rocking her against his portly body as he had done when she was a child. "Gwen is right...in this, at least," he added. There was an edge to his voice that distanced him from some of his wife's views. "You and Greg won't be doing anything you haven't already done, I'm guessing, so staying away will only make you both unhappy. Yes, sweetheart, it is a great taboo, possibly the greatest taboo of them all, and if the worst comes to pass, you've already broken it. There's nothing you can do about that, and you're not to blame."

Arthur stepped back, and his face was grave. "You are my daughter, Nicola, always; I don't need a test to tell me that. I love you and trust you. I like Greg, and respect him. If this terrible thing is true, and he is your brother, well, I would have to think about how I felt about that. But for now, do as your mother says, and get out of here."

* *

Nicola waited at the red light. If she turned left, the road would take her over the Golden Gate Bridge and into the city; right, the Richmond-San Rafael Bridge would take her to Greg. She chewed her lip, trying to decide, and then yawned. So, so tired; couldn't making up wait until tomorrow? Loud honking from the car behind startled her into action, and she turned right without being aware of it, pulled to Greg by invisible strings.

The marina's parking lot was still and quiet when she arrived shortly after 11pm. A faint mist hung over the dark, calm waters, and she shivered in the cold. It crossed her mind that he might not be here. He could have gone to see Sam and Debbie, needing reassurance and comfort as strongly as she had. He'd certainly had none of that from her today. Would he even want to see her?

Please be here! Nicola thought, as she ran towards the pontoon. Please be happy I'm here. I'm sorry I was such an idiot!

The security gate across the pontoon brought her to an abrupt halt. Locked, of course, and at this hour there was no one conveniently coming or going. She fumbled out her phone.

"Oh, my darling!" he said. Her eyes filled again as she heard the joy and relief in his voice. "I should never have let you go off like that. Where are you? At your parents' house, or your place?"

"Actually, I'm in front of your security gate." There was no reply. "Greg?"

Then she heard the sound of feet slapping against the wooden walkway and saw his dark form running towards her along the pontoon, from bright to shadow to bright as he ran under the overhead lights. He wrenched open the gate and they were in each other's arms, laughing and apologizing and not quite crying, and kissing as if it was their only hope of salvation.

Chapter 10

"OH, NO! Nicky, how awful!" exclaimed Kylie, eyes wide and false eyelashes fluttering. Then her face took on a calculating expression, and she asked, "What is it that's wrong with Greg's father? I mean, can't he postpone his op for whatever it is?"

Somehow, not one of them sitting around the living room in Seattle, hatching this story, had considered that anyone would ask such a question. "I didn't like to probe. Man problems, you know," said Nicola delicately.

"But Nicky, your wedding! To have to postpone for some old man! I don't know…." Kylie's voice died away. "Wait, I do know! Why don't you two go to Las Vegas and get married there, and then have a big party back here when the father-in-law is up for it?"

Nicola stared up at Kylie, perched, as usual, on the edge of her desk. Was she serious? "Interesting idea. But we both want our families at the actual wedding, so I think we'll have to wait."

"Too bad," said Kylie. "I read about this amazing hotel in Vegas, where all the rooms have a different theme. Little Bo Beep, or a bordello, or the Wild West. I'd love to stay there!"

Looking at the expressions on people's faces, Nicola decided that she wasn't the only one unable to understand how Kylie wanting to stay in this peculiar hotel had any bearing on Nicola's wedding. They had all been curious to know how Nicola's meeting with her future in-laws had gone, and sympathetic at the news of the postponement. All but Kylie.

Max said thoughtfully, "It does seem strange that this operation wasn't mentioned before. I mean, you'd think that if a man planned to go into the hospital in three weeks, he'd tell his children."

"They didn't want to worry Greg and Janine," replied Nicola smoothly. That line had been Mona's idea when Janine made the same objection. "Apparently it's not serious."

He frowned at her. "Not serious, but it can't be rescheduled?"

"Ah, the surgeon is booked up for months," Nicola said, clutching at any plausible reason.

"I have it!" cried Kylie. "There's no op at all! His parents don't want you to get married because you haven't known each other very long – which, admit it, Nicky, is what all of us said – so they came up with this operation scam to make you wait!" She looked around in triumph.

Nicola wondered if Greg had this same problem with his accounting colleagues, or if only journalists doubted everything.

Max regarded Kylie with approval. "Hey, that's good."

From behind Max, someone asked, "Hold on, what about the operation day? What happens if there really is no operation but Greg or his sister turns up at the hospital, worried about dad? His parents would be caught then."

Silence, as they all worked out answers to that.

Nicola seized the chance to get out while she could. "Tell you what, I'll leave all you investigative reporter types to figure this out on your own. I'm meeting a friend for lunch and I'm late already."

"Say hi to Greg, I mean 'your friend,' for us!" a voice called.

Good-natured laughter followed Nicola as she swiped her security card and pushed open the glass door leading to the elevators. She walked past them, to the fire stairs door. It was only three floors to the street, and the stairs were invariably faster than the elevators. And the stairwell was private. Nicola sagged against the scuffed wall and let out an uneven breath. That had gone better than she had feared, and, at the same time, worse. She hadn't expected anyone, especially not Kylie, to doubt that there actually was an operation.

For late October it was a glorious day, sunny and warm, so she and Hélène had agreed to meet in the same small park where Greg had taken Nicola for their first lunch months ago. It was one of Nicola's favorite secret spots in San Francisco, and the frog fountain always made her smile. Someone had told her it wasn't even a proper park, that it was intended for the people who worked in the Transamerica Pyramid next door, but anyone could use it when the gates were open. As Nicola hurried into the park, she inhaled deeply, savoring the clean scent of the redwood trees, so unexpected among the shiny office towers.

Hélène was waiting, sitting alone on one flat, wide bench, surrounded by multiple plump bags from designer boutiques. As Nicola approached, she saw another woman gesture at the bags, obviously asking Hélène to move them so she could sit. Even from 20 feet away, Nicola heard the stream of outraged French; the other woman backed away, looking embarrassed. Hélène spotted her then, and waved, and began plucking the tissue paper from the bags and folding them down. She slid the small pile into the largest bag.

"Hélène, were they all empty?" asked Nicola, starting to smile as she sat down.

Hélène looked surprised. "But of course. They are my secret weapons in the battle for outdoor seating in San Francisco. That, and my ability to unleash a torrent of incomprehensible French if needed," she replied.

"Oh, Hélène!" Nicola exclaimed, and laughed as she had not laughed since Friday.

"So, how were the in-laws?" From the large bag, Hélène pulled out a lunch that consisted primarily of lettuce and rice cakes, and began to nibble.

"Oh, Hélène," Nicola repeated, the laugh replaced by misery.

"*Mon Dieu*, what is the matter?"

Hélène was the perfect person to whom to tell this incredible story. She did not once interrupt, never exclaimed or clutched at Nicola, and having no personal stake in the outcome of the DNA tests, she remained her analytical, cool-thinking self. It was an immense relief to Nicola to have only non-judgmental silence as she related the events of the weekend.

"Is the resemblance truly so great?" Hélène finally asked.

Nicola nodded. Her sandwich lay in her lap, untouched. "Mona is 53 but looks five years younger. Too young for anyone to think she could be Greg's mother, let alone mine, but no one would have any difficulty believing she's my older sister. It's uncanny."

"And so you believe that she could be your mother?"

"It doesn't matter what I believe. The test will prove it, one way or the other," she replied.

Hélène gripped Nicola's hand. "Yes, it does matter! It affects you. You believe it, I think, and so you are depressed and unhappy."

"If you think I'm depressed and unhappy now, imagine how I'd feel if I spent the next two weeks being cheerful and optimistic, and the results came back with 'positive' stamped in gigantic letters!" protested Nicola.

"That is a point," conceded Hélène. She toyed with her lettuce. "And Greg? How is he taking it?"

Nicola said, "About as well as you'd expect. He insists he won't believe it's true unless the results say it is, and since there's nothing we can do about it, we should carry on as normal. Apart, that is, from the small matter of not getting married right this moment."

"So you are still...?"

The blush on Nicola's face was answer enough. Their reunion last night had been emotional and passionate, their lovemaking more intense than ever before. Nicola was sure she had actually screamed, which was something she had thought happened only in films. Few of Greg's neighbors lived on their boats, so likely no one had heard, which was a relief. But still...she'd had no idea she could respond like that.

"I called her this morning," said Nicola abruptly, tearing her thoughts away from last night.

Sculpted eyebrows rose in delicate crescents of inquiry.

"Mona. I was awful to her yesterday. I made her cry, Hélène," confessed Nicola quietly. "I felt so bad. I had to apologize for that. Regardless of what she did in her teens, she didn't deliberately set out to hurt me. I mean, if she is my mother." She shrugged helplessly.

"Oh, *chérie*," whispered Hélène.

Nicola picked at her sandwich. "And Greg can't go with me on Wednesday. There's a meeting he has to attend. Mona offered to come out to the airport with the kit; she said we could take the swabs there. That would save me going all the way to their house and back. But I couldn't agree to that, Hélène, not after being so horrible to her. And," she added, hesitantly, as if revealing a secret, "I would like to talk to her. Just the two of us. I did like her, you know. I remember thinking, that first night, before I knew, that I'd got lucky with a mother-in-law. And now she may be responsible for ruining everything."

Hélène gazed at her with sympathy, and patted Nicola's hand. Then she asked, with the brisk air of one moving on to practical matters, "So, what about the postponement? Do you require help with anything?"

Nicola shook her head. "It's all in hand. As you knew, the ceremony itself was small, only immediate family and closest friends. It was going to be at Greg's church in Richmond, he arranged that part, so he's dealing with, uh, what's happened. Mom cancelled the reception venue this morning and they gave us back our deposit. That only leaves telling the 100 or so people who assumed they would be invited to said reception that it's on hold. Approximately 80 of those 100 are from my side, so guess what I'm doing this evening?" she finished with a grimace.

"If you like, I will come over and top up your wine glass while you call them," offered Hélène.

"Imagine those final calls if you did!" laughed Nicola. "No, most can be done with email. Greg will be there, and that's what he will be doing – copy-and-paste postponement emails. I hope he doesn't get carried away and copy 'Dear Barb,' say, into the email for Sue."

Hélène smiled, but it turned into a frown. "Why so few from Greg's side for the reception? Truly only 20?"

"Strange, isn't it?" agreed Nicola. She tossed the remains of her sandwich into a nearby garbage can. "Debbie, Sam and Peter, of course, plus some friends from Seattle, but not many relatives. His mother was an only child, her parents died in a car accident before he was born, and Greg says he has never met any relatives on her side. That's the most bizarre thing! There are relatives on his father's side, but they– oh, did I tell you that part of Mona's story about Greg's real father being a moron called Clive?"

"No, you did not!" Hélène listened with every evidence of fascination. "*Mon Dieu*, Mona has had a very interesting life," she observed, in quiet understatement. "So, go on, Edward's relatives...?"

"Greg says his grandparents, that is, Edward's parents, died when Greg was in his teens. Edward is also an only child, so Greg has no aunts or uncles or cousins at all. Imagine that!" Nicola's voice was full of wonder at such a concept, for her whole life had included large numbers of aunts, uncles and cousins from both of her adoptive parents.

Hélène murmured, "How convenient for Mona."

"What do you mean?"

"If one wished to erase one's past life, it would be difficult to do so with relatives telling stories," explained Hélène. "Remove the relatives, and you remove the stories."

Nicola was amazed. "You think she lied?"

"She has lied regarding so many other aspects of her life, why not that?" Hélène's lips pursed and she shrugged, that simple French gesture of dismissal. "What time do you return on Wednesday?"

"Whenever I want. It's a flexible return. Janine has arranged it; she's a travel agent. She got me a discount, too," laughed Nicola. "A useful sort of sister-in-law!"

Hélène smiled. "Indeed. Why don't you and Greg come to dinner that night? Neither of you will be in the mood to cook, I am sure, and you don't want a noisy, public restaurant."

But Nicola said no, with thanks. "I think we'd rather be alone after a day in which I take the first step in finding out if his mother is also my mother."

* *

Greg invited himself over to Sam and Debbie's house on Tuesday evening. Sam, of course, was his best man for the wedding – if there was a wedding – and this wasn't something that he wanted to tell them over the phone, or, worse, in an email. Going through that list of emails last night, copying and pasting the same words over and over into messages to people he didn't even know, had somehow dulled the import of the words themselves. It had been harder on Nicola, on the phone with people, telling that same lie about his ill father and then having to make cheerful conversation.

"Come to supper," Sam had said this morning, when Greg phoned, but he had declined. With Peter there, he would be unable to talk freely.

So, it was after 8pm when Greg parked outside their house. Peter would still be up, but not for long; Debbie was a rock when it came to bedtime, unmoved by tears or pleas. Greg was walking up the path when the door opened and Peter burst out, running to meet him.

"Hey, sport," Greg said, and swept the boy up to swing him in a circle. He grunted when he set Peter down again. "That was easier when you were two. You're getting too big now."

Peter nodded. "I'm almost 10."

"So I heard," said Greg. It was all he had heard for weeks.

"Where's Nicola?" asked Peter, sounding disappointed.

Greg hid a smile. Peter's regard for him had only increased when Nicola was introduced, which had taken everyone by surprise, particularly Nicola, who was not used to being the object of a boy's affections. She had been touched, but embarrassed, by the effort Peter had put into finishing his rope floor mat so that it could be a wedding present from him. "She's busy tonight."

Debbie had appeared in the doorway by now, and she hugged him hello. The look she gave him was part worry and part speculation. As she had said that weekend on *Drifter*, he couldn't fool her. It was clear that Debbie suspected this was more than a social call.

Once Peter had gone to bed, they sat in the living room. It was small and on the shabby side, cluttered with the books and DVDs and toys that no one seemed to get around to tidying. The drapes in front of the window were noticeable for being the only new-looking things in the room. Greg refused a beer, but accepted a coffee, and now he held the mug in his hands and wondered how to start.

"Is there any significance to Nicola being 'busy' tonight?" asked Debbie bluntly.

"No. It's Tuesday, and that means Pilates," he replied. "Nothing gets in the way of that. After the class, they all go to a health food café, drink herbal tea and compare favorite detoxes and purges. I've rarely seen Nicola on a Tuesday."

Debbie glanced down at her own rounded body, which hadn't exercised in years and had never been purged or detoxed.

Both men laughed at the amused, rueful look on her face when she glanced back up. Sam patted his wife's hand. "Don't even consider it," he advised.

"If the wedding isn't off, then what's the matter?" Debbie asked. She drew a sharp breath, and leaned forward. "Or is it off?"

"I don't know. It's certainly on hold." He told them what had happened in Seattle.

"My God," she breathed. She got up off the couch and walked to Greg's chair, and hugged him. "You poor, poor man. And poor Nicola. And poor Mona!"

"You see why I didn't want to talk in front of Peter," Greg said.

Sam nodded. "And the test? How long does that take?"

"We won't know for around 10 days."

"Hell," was all Sam said, conveying his sympathy and horror in one syllable.

Greg grimaced. "Yes. It is."

He left soon after that. There wasn't really anything more to say, although he felt better for having been with them. Their house was only a short drive from the marina, which was one of the reasons he had chosen that one. The night was cool and misty, heavy with damp, and he hurried from his car towards the pontoon. He was almost at the gate when he heard the soft thud of a car door closing, and then Nicola's voice.

Greg whirled around, and a thrill of happiness shot through him at the unexpected sight of her coming towards him. He had walked right past her car, which was parked as close to the water as she could get. How long had she been waiting for him?

"What are you doing here?" he asked. "I told Sam and Debbie I never see you on a Tuesday. I would have come back sooner if you'd told me you were coming! Why aren't you purging and detoxing and God knows what elsing?"

"I didn't go."

He put his hands on her shoulders. "You didn't go to Pilates? And the world didn't end?"

She gave him the smile of one who is forced to explain the obvious. "Of course I went to the class! Not the café after. It seemed...I don't know. Trivial."

His arms slid around her. "I've noticed that. At work today, I wondered what the point of it was. Why I was bothering."

She nodded against his shoulder, so soft and pliant in his arms.

"Are you staying tonight?" Greg asked. He couldn't stop himself from nuzzling along her neck, working his way down to that sweet little spot where her neck met her chest. Lower, alas, was blocked by her jacket.

"If you don't mind. I didn't want to be alone. But maybe I'm ruining your Tuesday! I don't know what you normally do," she said, her voice light with teasing. "Maybe you've got a poker game with the boys. An all-night porn movie session. Or–"

"Poker and porn!" Greg exploded with laughter, nuzzling forgotten. "Oh yeah, that's me all right. Every Tuesday night, I indulge my baser instincts." He shook his head, still chuckling. "Did you bring a bag?"

She pointed to her car.

As he watched her walk back and collect the bag, her yellow jacket glowing under the streetlights, he marveled at her imagination. Poker and porn! Of all the things.

"Do you want to know what I normally do on a Tuesday, while you're off twisting yourself into knots and swallowing peculiar herbal concoctions?" he asked, as they walked along the pontoon.

Nicola admitted, "I have wondered."

"I fire up my laptop and go online. Then I log on to a particular website that only people with the right passwords can access."

"Porn," she said, sounding smug. "I knew it."

He slung an arm around her shoulders. "CPE."

They were at the corner where the main pontoon branched off towards his berth, and there was enough light to see the frown on her face.

"CPE. Complicated Pornography...uh, Environment. No, that's stupid. Complete Porn Experience!"

"I find it interesting that you're convinced it's porn, rather than poker. Also a P word," he pointed out.

"Computerized Poker Extravaganza?"

"You are going to be so disappointed in me," Greg warned. He held her hand to steady her. "Watch the railing as you climb over."

They stood in *Drifter*'s cockpit, arms around each other lightly.

"Well?" she demanded.

"Continuing Professional Education. I have to do a certain amount of learning each year, to get the required CPE points and keep my license."

She looked disgusted. "Accounting? That's what you do when I'm not here?"

Greg kissed her in consolation. "Told you you'd be disappointed. Now go below and get into my bed, and you can explain to me why are you obsessed with porn tonight."

Chapter 11

NICOLA LEANED her forehead against the small window and looked down at the ground, still so far below even though the plane had begun its descent into Seattle. A red car crept along the thread of a road, no larger than a pinhead from this height.

She always asked for a window seat. Even after all the flights she had made, both for work and for pleasure, she never tired of this god-like view of the world. When she lifted her eyes to the right, there was Mount Rainier, its peak bulking large against the flawless blue sky and dominating everything. Up here, it was possible to forget all of life's problems. It was a limbo, a place that didn't count, where nothing you did would affect anything back in the real world.

But she couldn't put it off forever, and the real world was waiting at Seattle airport in the form of Greg's mother.

The flow of passengers and the crowd at the gate hid Mona from her view, and Nicola came to a halt. People behind her muttered, and someone deliberately bumped her in passing. Then she saw her, as impeccably groomed as Nicola remembered, searching the passing faces with anxiety. Nicola threaded through the people between them and stopped a few feet from Mona, feeling awkward. Were they expected to hug? Air kiss? Why was there no rulebook for this?

"Hello," said Mona, looking relieved, and solved the hugging question by tucking her arm lightly through Nicola's and turning her in the direction of the exit. "How was your flight?"

"Fine. Short, which is always a bonus," replied Nicola.

Mona gave her a glance of amusement. "I suppose, with your work, you've had some very long ones."

Nicola grimaced. "Oh yeah. Worth it, though." She stopped walking and pulled Mona to one side. "Mona, I want to say again how extremely sorry I am for my behavior on Sunday. Nothing could excuse what I said to you, and the way I said it." She looked earnestly at the other woman, trying to convince her by sheer good will that she meant everything she said. "I never act like that. Ask anyone."

"Oh, my dear," said Mona softly, and touched Nicola's shoulder in what might have been an aborted hug. "Of course you don't. I know that."

"How could you possibly know that?" asked Nicola, an edge of tartness in her voice. After all, Mona had seen little evidence of her alleged good nature.

Mona said simply, "Greg would never have fallen so much in love with you if you did act like that."

And then they did hug, briefly, but heartfelt on both sides.

"The car is outside," said Mona, and pointed.

Conversation was fairly easy between them on the drive north. General, and safe, but they needed that if they were ever going to feel comfortable enough with each other to be able to speak of things that were more personal. In the middle of the city, traffic slowed, and Nicola could see the top of the Space Needle off to the left, above buildings.

"Why did you and Edward leave Portland for Seattle?" she asked. "Didn't you like Portland?"

"I did like it, very much. It was the first place I remember ever being happy," said Mona. "But Edward was offered a job with a drugs company here, where he has been ever since. Neither of us imagined what that move to Seattle would lead to. In Portland, we had a little apartment over a shoe store, whereas here things seemed to go from better to better. I didn't want to leave Portland, to be honest. Greg was only three months old, I think it was, and I had friends to help with the baby. Edward had a job waiting for him in Seattle, but we knew no one. But Edward had a dream!"

Nicola smiled, to think of Edward as a dreamer, and to think that anyone could possibly ever dream about pills and potions.

"What sort of work did Edward do then?" she asked, curious. They were halfway across the Aurora Bridge now, over the ship canal, and she knew it wasn't far to the house in Blue Ridge.

Mona shrugged. "I have no idea. Honestly!" she insisted, when Nicola looked doubtful. "I was 20 years old, and overwhelmed at dealing with a baby on my own in a strange city. I told you what my life had been before Portland; that hardly prepared me for a screaming infant and dirty diapers, and absolutely never enough sleep! I was far too self-absorbed in the early days to sit down with Edward when he came home and discuss chemicals and compounds and blind trials. I often think it's a miracle we survived those first couple of years of marriage," she finished.

Nicola turned to her. "How did you?"

"Edward," said Mona, as if that one word explained everything. "I've never understood what he saw in me in the first place, but it got us through all that."

"I like him," stated Nicola.

The car came to a stop in front of the house. "Me, too," said Mona with a sideways grin, and they both laughed.

Their lingering laughter died in the kitchen. The swab kit, still in its packaging, sat in the middle of the table. It was only a small box, wrapped discreetly in nothing that would betray its nature to curious eyes, but it seemed out of place in this warm, lived-in family space.

"It didn't seem right to open it," explained Mona.

"No."

Silence.

Nicola said, absently, "All of you were right, it is a glorious view." The sun was shining, and through the windows she could see bare branches silhouetted against the sparkling water. Large ships and small yachts moved along safe channels between the green islands.

"It's nicer in the summer," said Mona, coming to stand beside her. "You must be sure to come back and see it then." A pause. "Whatever happens."

"Thank you, but if 'whatever' happens, I doubt I'll be back," Nicola replied emptily.

Mona's hand brushed Nicola's so lightly that she wasn't sure she had felt it.

"If it is positive, I would hate to never see you again," Mona said quietly.

"Oh Mona, how could I? I want Greg as a husband, not you as a mother!" cried Nicola. The anguish on the older woman's face matched that in her own heart. "I'm sorry," she whispered.

Mona turned away with a jerk, and Nicola saw her knuckles whiten as she gripped the edge of the counter. Then Mona's shoulders straightened and her head came up, and, striving for normality in this situation that was so inconceivably far beyond normal, she asked, "Would you like something? A coffee?"

Nicola admired her self-control. The question triggered the memory of Janine making coffee on Saturday morning, saying they might need the bourbon, too. "A bourbon?" suggested Nicola with a smile.

Mona smiled back. "What the hell?" she said with a shrug. "It's a DNA test, not a breath test."

She opened one of the wooden cupboards and took down the bottle of Southern Comfort. "I can't stand bourbon," she announced. "Are you okay with this?"

Nicola nodded.

Mona poured a small amount into two squat glasses, and the women – who might be mother and daughter, or might not be related at all – clinked glasses and downed the amber liquid.

"Right," said Mona briskly, handing Nicola a small knife. "Open the damned box and let's get this over with."

It was an anti-climax, in a way. The box held clear instructions, a pre-addressed return envelope, and what looked remarkably like the cotton-topped sticks each of them used for removing eye make-up. "We swipe these against the inside of our cheeks," said Nicola, reading the instructions, "put them in this," she held up a container, "put that in the envelope with the bottom half of this sheet, and mail it back to the lab."

"And then wait," said Mona dryly.

"And then wait," agreed Nicola.

Mona splashed more Southern Comfort into their glasses. "Courage, my dear," she said, and drank, and picked up her swab.

And that was it. The envelope, sealed, sat on the table, as innocuous as the box had been. It needed only a stamp. They sat on opposite sides of the table, the envelope between them, and regarded it.

"It seems a lot of trouble for you for such a small thing," commented Mona. "Having to take a day off work, I mean."

Nicola shrugged. "It had to be done. You could have done yours, and then mailed it to me, and I could have done mine and sent it to them, but how many more days would that have added?" She lifted the bottle with a look of inquiry, and, at Mona's nod, she poured another measure into their glasses.

"Is it far to the post office?" she asked.

Mona shook her head. "A five-minute drive."

Nicola gestured to the bottle with a smile. "I think we'd better walk, don't you? Imagine telling this story to a police officer in an attempt to explain why you're over the limit at 1pm on a Wednesday!"

The post office was in a small mall that held an upscale grocery store, a dry cleaner, a pet store and an Italian restaurant. Nicola held open the slot on the mailbox while Mona pushed the envelope inside. They both heard the soft thump as it landed.

"Are you hungry?" asked Mona.

Nicola nodded. She'd had only toast for breakfast, hours ago, and the Southern Comfort sat uneasily on her empty stomach.

"The restaurant is very good. Shall we?"

The owner greeted Mona with cries of welcome, and ushered them to a table beside the panoramic windows overlooking Puget Sound. They ordered salads to start, then mushroom risotto for Mona and linguine with pesto sauce for Nicola.

"And wine?" prompted the owner, as she filled their water glasses. "We have a new Pinot Grigio, from a little winery in Tuscany."

"Is it good?" asked Mona, giving Nicola a smile that said this was a familiar routine.

"Good?" exclaimed the woman, her ample bosom quivering with her outrage. "*Mamma Mia*, 'Is it good?' she asks!"

Mona looked penitent. "I'm sorry, Maria, of course it's good. May we please have a bottle? And would you join us for a glass?"

Her face wreathed in smiles, Maria walked briskly off, giving orders left and right to scurrying wait staff.

"We must go through this every time," confided Mona. "We've been coming here for years, and it's always the same. I hope you like grappa," she added in a rapid undertone as Maria reappeared, the wine bottle in one meaty hand and a terracotta cooler in the other.

Grappa? wondered Nicola.

Maria had only half a glass of wine with them, for the restaurant was popular, even at lunch on a weekday, and she was too busy to linger.

"This is nice," remarked Nicola, looking around at the framed posters of Italy and the warm glow of the brick walls as the sunlight fell on them. "Does Greg like this restaurant?"

"Very much," Mona said. "We came here for his 18th birthday, and sat out there." She pointed through the window to the terrace, desolate now, its flower urns sadly empty, but Nicola could see that it would be delightful in warmer weather.

Nicola toyed with a bread stick, one of those dryly unpalatable creations in slim paper sleeves that she saw only in Italian restaurants. "I'd like to ask you something," she blurted out.

Mona's smile was tinged with sadness. "I'd think you would. Probably more than one 'something.'"

"Do you mind?" asked Nicola anxiously. "I feel caught between wanting to know more about you and thinking it's none of my business."

"Tell you what," said Mona. "You ask what you want, and I'll retain the right to refuse to answer if I think that it is none of your business."

Nicola smiled. "That seems fair."

But she was silent for so long that Mona finally prompted, "Well?"

"Did you ever see Susie again? After you left Portland?" asked Nicola.

Mona looked taken aback, as if of all the things she might have expected Nicola to want to know, this had not been one. "Yes. Twice. I took Greg to see her when he was three years old. I was settled by then, you see," she explained, a distant look in her eyes.

"I had, much to my own surprise, fallen in love with Edward at some point after we arrived here. Oh, I had liked him," she added hastily, "liked him very much, and no one in my life had ever made me feel more safe, or cherished. That's why I married him. I had no idea why he felt that way about me, and it wasn't until I began to have a sense of confidence in myself, and my own worth, that I could see him in that way in return. And I wanted Susie, who was so instrumental in all of that, to know what she had done for me."

They were interrupted by the waiter, who whisked away the empty salad dishes and put down their meals with a flourish. He topped up their wine glasses, gave them a dazzling smile of perfect white teeth that stretched his moustache wide, and left them.

"Mario," said Mona, with a nod of her head. "Maria's youngest."

But Nicola wasn't interested in the restaurant staff. "Go on. Didn't Edward go with you?"

"No. Susie and her family had been at our wedding, of course, so Edward knew who she was. But he didn't know how I knew her. I had never told him," she faltered, "never told him what I told all of you Saturday morning. I should have. But I didn't want to disappoint him. Oh Nicola, I had such a low opinion of myself for so long! Can you imagine how important it was to me that this one man who truly loved me should never think of me what I thought of myself?"

A tear slid down Nicola's cheek and she scrubbed it away, then reached over and gripped the other woman's hand. "No, I can't," she said.

"I'm glad you can't," said Mona. They gazed at each other, closer at this moment than ever before.

"When was the second time?"

Mona blinked. "What?"

"You said you saw Susie twice. When was the second time?" asked Nicola. She picked up her fork, put it down again.

"Oh." Mona stared out the window. "When she was dying."

"No!" Nicola somehow had assumed the redoubtable little woman was still ministering to the homeless of Portland.

"We didn't visit, or speak on the phone often, but we wrote to each other. Almost once a week. Nothing happened in my life that Susie didn't know about – or comment on," added Mona wryly. "And then, no letters. After two weeks, I got a call from Kevin. She was in the hospital. Leukemia. I got there in time to say goodbye, at least, and tell her I loved her." Mona drained her wine glass in one long swallow.

Nicola could barely see Mona through the haze of tears in her eyes. "Oh, Mona. When?"

"Twenty years ago. She was only two years older than I am now. Greg will probably remember," she said thoughtfully. "He was 13, and I was upset for some time after she died. He didn't know why, of course."

Nicola was filled with an overwhelming gratitude that her life had been full of love and support, that she had grown up in an environment that had given her unthinking strength and confidence in herself. That her life had been nothing like Mona's. "You must have had a terrible childhood," she observed, thinking out loud.

Mona's expression shifted to amused surprise. "No, not really."

"But then why…?" Nicola didn't know how to finish the question.

"Why did I run away when I was 15 and a half? And become a groupie for a band that made up in volume what it lacked in talent?" Mona asked, still looking amused. She seemed far less emotional talking about her childhood than about what had come after it.

Nicola nodded blankly.

Mario returned, uttered sounds of disapproval over their cold, barely touched lunches, topped up the wine glasses again and left.

"I grew up in Omaha. My father owned a hardware store. My mother…." Here she hesitated. "My mother and I never got along. She always found fault with me, and I responded by being worse at anything she didn't like. My sister, two years younger, could do absolutely no wrong in my mother's eyes. Charlene was perfect. She even had blonde ringlets! I know nothing about genetics, and maybe it is possible that two dark-haired people could have a blonde daughter. I always wondered, though. I do know that nothing I did was right, and nothing Charlene did was wrong. But to say it was a terrible childhood…no. I merely got tired of always being wrong.

"There was one particular night my mother wouldn't let me go out. We had an awful fight, screaming at each other. She told me to go to my room. I didn't. Instead, I went to her room, took all the money from her purse, stuffed a few things in a bag and climbed out the window. The band was in town. I hung around when the show was over."

Nicola gaped at her. "That's it? It's as simple as that?"

"Yes."

Mona reached for the wine bottle, but they had emptied it. Mario, though, ever the attentive waiter, sidled up with another.

Nicola drank off half a glass in one go, then looked across at Mona but didn't say anything.

"What you're thinking is exactly right. I was a silly, naïve child, with far more attitude than sense," said Mona, dismissing her long-ago self with contempt. "Look what happened to me. Some people would think I got what I deserved."

"No!" exclaimed Nicola. "How can you say that?"

Mona shrugged. "Why did I stay with the band? Why couldn't I see what was happening?"

"Because you were a silly, naïve child?" asked Nicola gently.

The laugh caught in Mona's throat.

"Are they…can I ask, did your parents really die in a car crash?" ventured Nicola. And this sister, the aunt that Greg seemed not to know about?

Mona shook her head once, sharply. "This is the part when I tell you it's none of your business. I told you about my childhood only so you didn't go away thinking it was horrific, or I was abused. I wasn't. But I refuse to talk about it. My life before Portland does not matter."

Nicola sat back in her chair, rebuffed. Mona did warn me, she reminded herself. She took a healthy swallow of wine in preparation for the next question. "Can I ask you something else?"

Reaching over to touch Nicola's hand, Mona answered with a smile, "Yes, with the same condition that I may not answer."

"It's about…the baby," she began hesitantly. She glanced at Mona, who looked troubled but didn't stop her. "Did you ever try to find her?"

It was Mona's turn for a bracing drink of wine. "No. Shall I tell you why?" When Nicola nodded, she continued, "I wondered about her, of course. Where was she? Was she all right? Had she even lived? But my life changed so much during my time in Portland, and I tried so hard to forget everything before then, that most of the time I managed to forget her, too. Then there was Edward, and so soon after Greg was born we moved to Seattle. I was all alone with a crying baby and a husband whose understanding of a father's role did not include hands-on baby care but who did expect his supper to be ready when he got home – this was before Edward discovered the delights of cooking – and, Nicola, I was on the verge of collapse for quite a while." She raised a hand as if to forestall objections. "I know, other women have done the same thing, and coped better than me. Eventually, I got the hang of it, but for a few years that baby was nothing more than an occasional regret.

"And then, when I did consider telling Edward, and perhaps trying to find her, I had no idea how to start. Where would I begin looking? Walk into a police station and spill out my story? I think it's illegal to abandon a baby. What if they prosecuted me? Sent me to prison? I would have been no good to either Greg or that other baby. And even if I wasn't arrested, and somehow we found the baby, she would have been a girl by then. Fostered, or adopted. Was it fair that I, a stranger, took her from what settled life she had?

"Then Janine came, and we moved from an apartment into our first house. We had friends here by then, and my relationship with Edward had grown. That baby retreated back into being no more than an occasional regret."

Here Mona paused, at last, and looked levelly at Nicola. "So once more, perhaps, I did not do the right thing. That's not to say I don't hate myself for what I did." A deep breath. "If indeed you are her…." Mona's voice tailed off.

I'm not, I'm not! thought Nicola. But if, somehow, being

Mona's daughter did not mean sacrificing Greg, Nicola would have agreed, if for no other reason than to ease the distress on Mona's face.

"What is this Mario tells me?" demanded Maria, descending on them in a flurry of tight, ruffled organza. Her bustling arrival broke the feeling of despair that threatened to grip both of them, and they looked up with relief. Maria pulled out a chair and filled her glass. "My cooking is so bad you don't eat? The pesto is my own grandmother's recipe!"

Even Nicola, emotional and slightly drunk by now, could see that behind the bluster was real concern. "It was wonderful," she declared, forcing herself to respond appropriately. "I guess I wasn't hungry after all, and the salad filled me up."

Maria eyed her with suspicion, but allowed herself to be soothed and convinced.

It was after 3pm by now and the restaurant was almost empty, with only their table and a large family group on the other side of the room. Their talk turned to Seattle, and San Francisco, and then to Italy when Maria learned that Nicola had once spent a week not five miles from her family's farm in Piedmont.

The wine bottle slowly emptied. Maria would have called for another but Nicola, rather blearily, claimed she had a flight to catch.

"You must have grappa!" insisted Maria. "From my family's farm!"

Nicola frowned. "In…Piedmont?"

"No," scoffed Maria. "In California! My brother Alberto makes it."

"I warned you," whispered Mona, looking rather bleary herself.

* *

Nicola managed to text Greg with her arrival time moments before the flight attendant appeared in the aisle, frowning down and insisting that all electronic devices must be turned off at this time. With exaggerated care, Nicola punched the "off" button, turned the phone to show him and then stuffed it into her bag. She missed, though, and the phone fell to the floor. She leaned over to retrieve it, but the seatbelt caught her, so she unbuckled it and slid down. Still couldn't reach. She groped around with one foot, and knocked it into the aisle. With a look of extreme irritation, the attendant bent down, picked up the phone and handed it to her, and watched closely as she carefully put it into her bag.

"Hmm," he said, looking at her with suspicion.

When he turned his back, Nicola stuck her tongue out at him.

She was asleep before the aircraft's wheels left the ground.

Chapter 12

GREG PACED back and forth, back and forth. The flight had landed on time, the stream of passengers had thinned to a trickle, so where was she? And why had she stayed so long in Seattle? It couldn't have taken more than five minutes to deal with the DNA kit, yet here it was, after 8pm and still no sign of her.

There! He spotted Nicola and moved towards her, relief turning to concern. She looked awful. So pale that the sprinkle of freckles across her nose stood out starkly, and her hair straggled down. She stumbled, and Greg leaped forward to sweep her into his arms.

"Nicola!" he exclaimed. "What's wrong? Are you sick?"

She seemed surprised to see him. "Greg! Come here, my gorgeous hunk of manhood!" She flung her arms around his neck and kissed him, passionately if sloppily.

He disentangled himself and stared at her with astonished disbelief, and rising amusement. "You're drunk!"

"Am not!" she declared. And hiccuped.

Greg looked at her sternly, trying not to laugh. "Are too."

"Might be." Her blue eyes blinked at him, once, solemn as an owl. "But so's your mother. And Maria. I should never have had that second glass of grappa," she said, shaking her head sadly. "And definitely not the third."

"You had three glasses of Maria's brother's grappa?" he asked, torn between admiration that she was still walking and worry over what she'd feel like in the morning.

Nicola followed without protest as he took her hand and led her towards the door. "Yes. Oh, and two bottles of wine," she added with deliberation. "Really, Mona had one and I had one. But Maria had some, too. So I guess I didn't have a whole one."

Greg stopped walking. Nicola, whom he had never seen drink more than three glasses of wine in the course of an evening, had drunk most of a bottle of wine plus three glasses of Alberto's grappa? Large glasses of grappa, he knew, because that was the only size Maria poured.

He put an arm around her, afraid she would keel over. "Well," he said comfortingly, kissing her forehead, "at least that was all you had. You know the saying, never mix the grain and the grape."

Outside, the night air hit Nicola, and she stopped as abruptly as if she had walked into a wall. "Greg?" Her voice sounded weak.

"Yes, my darling?"

"Does Southern Comfort count as a grain?"

"Oh Christ!" he exclaimed, and towed her rapidly towards the nearest bush.

Once he eventually got her into the car, she fell asleep. A less kind man might have used the words "passed out." Greg looked across at her when they stopped at a red light, her head back and her mouth open, making little snuffling noises as she breathed. The poor girl is going to feel like hell, he thought with sympathy. He couldn't begin to imagine how Nicola and his mother had ended up drinking so much.

At her apartment building, he helped her up the stone stairs and through the ornate wooden doors. Waiting in the lobby for the elevator, she whispered, "Did I really throw up into that bush?"

"I'm afraid so," he said, grinning.

Nicola swatted his chest feebly. "Wipe that smirk off your face," she instructed, but the hiccup undermined her. She leaned against him. "Ohhh, Greg, I'm so embarrassed."

She hiccuped all the way to the fifth floor, her slender frame shaking with each one, and Greg struggled manfully not to laugh. He steered her to her door, then bent over to retrieve her keys when she dropped the whole set onto the carpet. Inside, he unzipped her jacket and pulled it off. Her arms flopped back to her sides, and she wobbled.

"Do you want anything to eat?" Greg asked.

She looked as if she might be sick again. "I just want to go to bed," she said, sounding woeful. Nicola wandered off to the bathroom, bumping against the doorsill as she went.

Greg shook his head in wonder as he watched her unsteady progress.

She might not want food, but he was starving. He had assumed they would eat when she got back from Seattle, and had assumed that would be hours ago. The sound of splashing water assured him that she hadn't curled up on the bathroom rug, so he walked into the kitchen to see what Nicola's cupboards could provide. Soup, that was good, and there must be sandwich makings in the fridge. He was rummaging for a pan to heat the soup in when he heard her slippers scuffling along the hall's linoleum flooring.

She was swathed in a voluminous white cotton nightdress with blue ribbons around neckline and wrists. Her hair was brushed back and her skin scrubbed clean, and when she came closer, he caught the scents of toothpaste and soap. He opened his arms and Nicola snuggled against him.

"You look like a little girl," he observed. "All clean and ready for bed. Did you wash behind your ears, young lady?"

A faint giggle, and she nodded against his shoulder.

"Let me see." Greg gently folded one of her ears forward to look, then on impulse he kissed the skin where ear met scalp. "I don't think I've ever kissed you there," he commented. "I wonder if there's anywhere else I've missed?"

"You're not going to find it tonight," she said, the words disappearing into a yawn.

He turned her around and walked her to the bedroom.

"I didn't know you even had things like this," he commented, stroking the soft cotton.

There was amusement in her voice when she replied, "I don't bother putting anything on when you're here because I know it will only come right off."

"You are safe tonight, my darling drunk," he assured her. "You'll be comatose the moment you lie down, and quite immune to my advances."

"I am not a drunk," said Nicola with immense dignity, slurring her words only a little.

He pulled back the embroidered white bed cover and fluffed up the pillows, keeping one eye on Nicola as she swayed gently, like a frond of delicate seaweed in the current. Her nightdress was luminous in the faint light from the hallway. He got her into bed and tucked the blankets around her; her eyelids fluttered closed and she gave one enormous sigh, as if she was deflating. Against the white sheets and pillowcases, her hair was a spill of darkness. Greg leaned down to smooth it from her face.

"Goodnight."

Her hand battled free of the covers to clutch his sleeve. "You're not going to leave me, are you?" she whispered, fighting the pull of sleep long enough to ask.

"Never. I'm going down to my car for my suit and stuff, but I'll be right back. Now go to sleep and I'll join you in a while." He kissed her lightly.

How had she got into such a state?

Five minutes later, Greg eased open the apartment's door and gently closed it behind him, but when he entered the bedroom again he realized he could have slammed it going out and coming back and she would never have noticed. Nicola was, as he had foretold, comatose. And snoring, loudly, which he had never heard her do. He pushed aside clothes in the crowded closet and hung up his suit and shirt.

Back in the kitchen again, stirring the soup, he pulled out his phone.

"Hello, Greg," his father answered in an amused voice. "I thought you'd call. How is Nicola?"

"How is Mom?"

Edward laughed. "Asleep."

"Same here," said Greg. "What the hell did those two get up to today? And do you know if they actually did what they were supposed to be doing?"

"According to Mona, that was what caused it all. They had a few shots of Southern Comfort to steel themselves, it sounded like, then walked to the post office," explained Edward.

Greg reached for a bowl. "Ah. And the post office, of course, is right beside Maria's."

"One thing led to another, it seems."

"More like one drink led to another!" retorted Greg. He stared into the fridge, wondering if she had any cheese. "I have never known Nicola to drink so much."

There was silence for a moment, and Edward replied, "They were both nervous. Understandably. I hope you haven't been hard on her."

"No, Dad, of course not. I might have laughed," Greg admitted.

"So did I," confessed Edward, and chuckled. "The sight of your mother sprawled on a sofa at 6.30pm, dead to the world and snoring merrily, is not one I ever expected to see."

No cheese. Damn. Greg dug out sliced ham. And lettuce. Why are women's fridges always full of lettuce? he wondered. No cheese, no tomatoes even, and only this bottle of fat-free imitation mayonnaise stuff plus bread sliced so thin you could almost see through it, but lots of lettuce. Tomatoes…something stirred in his mind, but he was distracted by his father's voice.

"And now we wait," Edward was saying.

"It won't be long," said Greg confidently. "And then we'll all be back to normal."

"Greg, have you thought about what will happen if things are *not* back to normal? You don't seem willing to accept that there is even a small chance the results will be positive."

Greg laughed. "Oh, Dad! That story of Mom's is preposterous. No, I'm sorry," he added quickly. "The story is heartbreaking. But the idea that Nicola is that baby is preposterous. What would the odds be that I would ever meet, let alone want to marry, Mom's long-lost baby? I refuse to take it seriously. It's the sort of thing that happens in movies, not in real life."

He heard his father's heavy sigh.

"I hope you're right. I fear that your mother has almost convinced herself that Nicola is her abandoned daughter, and she is imagining a rosy future in which we're all one happy family. With you and Nicola, needless to say, married to other people," added Edward dryly.

"Oh God, poor Mom." Greg stopped trying to open the package of ham one-handed. "I had no idea. Does she really believe that, Dad? It doesn't sound like her."

"Mona is not as tough as she likes to have people think. I suspect that baby has preyed on her mind since she was born. Who can blame Mona for thinking that, miraculously, her daughter has been restored in the form of this lovely, intelligent young woman?" Edward said sadly.

Greg's heart sank. No, Mom, he thought. No.

A sudden hiss and a pungent burning odor as the soup boiled over brought Greg back to the present. He yanked the pan off the burner. "I've got to go, my soup's made a hell of a mess on Nicola's stove."

Edward laughed softly. "All right. Goodnight, son."

"Dad, wait!"

"What is it?"

"Tell Mom I love her."

"She knows that, Greg. But I'll tell her."

Greg surveyed the mess on the stove, and figured it could wait until after he'd eaten. He carried his soup and his ham-and-lettuce sandwiches to Nicola's small dining table. It was under a window, but he had no hope of seeing anything through that jungle she had growing in front of it. Not that there was much to see apart from the windows of apartments opposite and the blinking traffic lights below. He took a bite of one sandwich and rummaged through the newspapers and magazines on the table. Last Sunday's travel section was on top; it would be, he thought in amusement. His attention was caught by the cover's striking photograph of an ugly tree, gnarled branches ending in spiked leaves, silhouetted against a colorful desert sunset. He shoveled up some soup and pulled the travel section closer to read.

Kitchen tidy and stove fairly clean, Greg wandered into the small living room. He wasn't tired enough to go to bed yet, but it felt strange roaming around Nicola's apartment while she was asleep. Almost as if he was a trespasser. He stood in the middle of the room, hands on hips, and surveyed it.

Sofa covered in a pattern of big abstract flowers, matching armchair, a surprisingly delicate desk with a laptop, a television, lamps and overflowing bookshelves, with a stereo system perched on top; nothing unusual, apart from the wall of plants where any normal person would have curtains. There was no spare space, no empty bookshelves or vacant corner. The closets and drawers in her bedroom were equally full, he knew. So where would he put his own stuff, his clothes and his few belongings, when he moved in while they house-hunted?

Tomatoes. It came to him all of a sudden why there were none in Nicola's fridge. She was allergic to them. Just like his mother. Like…her mother?

"Greg, have you thought about what will happen if things are *not* back to normal?" His father's words echoed in his head.

"No!" he said intensely, fists clenched. "I have not! I will not!"

He flicked off the light switch with one decisive swipe and strode down the hallway. It wasn't a long hallway, though, and didn't lend itself to striding, and after only a few steps he was in the bedroom.

Nicola didn't seem to have moved at all, although, thankfully, she had stopped snoring. Greg undressed and walked around the bed, to what had become his side. She stirred, and mumbled something, when he slipped under the covers. He turned on his side and slid over so that their bodies touched, not enough to wake her but enough so he could feel her against him.

Dear God, to never feel her like this again? Never make love to her, never see her eyes glow with warmth when she saw him in the morning? Never hold their children in his arms?

"It isn't true," he whispered.

* *

The alarm clock shocked Nicola into unwelcome wakefulness at 7am and she fumbled a hand onto the bedside table, succeeding only in knocking the clock to the floor. "Shit." She heaved herself closer to the edge of the mattress, finally grabbing the clock and stabbing at the off button. She flopped back against the pillow, willing the room to stop spinning.

Greg loomed up on one elbow beside her. "And how are we today?" he asked, with uncalled-for cheerfulness.

She squinted at him. "What are you doing here?" she muttered with a frown.

"I met you at the airport?" he prompted. "Brought you home? Tucked you into bed?"

It all flooded back into her mind. "Oh God, the bush," she moaned, and covered her eyes with one arm.

"Never mind," he soothed. "Your gorgeous hunk of manhood was on hand to take care of you."

Nicola shifted her arm. "My what?"

"You described me as 'my gorgeous hunk of manhood,' quite loudly in fact, before kissing me in a manner that in certain societies would have got us arrested," Greg elaborated. Looking thoughtful, he added, "No one's ever called me that before. I kind of like it."

"Oh God," she moaned again, and closed both eyes.

The sudden flinging-back of the covers was followed by Greg tugging her into a sitting position.

"Get up," he urged with a smile. "You need a long hot shower, a lot of water, a couple of painkillers and some food."

Her head flopped against his shoulder and she groaned. "No food. I couldn't face it."

"Yes, food," he insisted. He clambered over her to stand beside the bed, then grabbed her hands and pulled. "My old university roommate, Debbie's brother, always had a big greasy fried breakfast when he was hungover."

Nicola's stomach churned in an unpleasant way at the idea of a big greasy fried breakfast, and she put both hands over it.

"Maybe not," Greg said hastily. "Janine swears by chocolate milk and potato chips."

"You're kidding?" she asked faintly.

He kissed her cheek and guided her towards the bathroom. "I'm only repeating it, I'm not recommending it. From what I saw in your kitchen last night, we're both going to have to settle for microwaved oatmeal and skimmed milk. And one overripe banana, which I will generously share with you."

She nodded slowly. "Okay, I could manage that. And maybe tea? Weak tea?"

"Very weak, in your case."

Nicola watched him as he walked down the hallway to the kitchen, and smiled when he hitched up the blue boxer shorts with the absent-minded gesture that had become so familiar.

A white t-shirt hung loosely from his wide shoulders. The far end of the hallway was a brilliant dazzle from the sun that poured into the kitchen, and as he neared it, he became a silhouette, his hair surrounded by light and his bare feet dancing on the cold linoleum.

"Hey, Greg?"

He half-turned towards her, the sunlight falling on one side of his face and showing her the heavy stubble.

"I've always thought you were gorgeous. I just never said it."

She saw the flash of surprise, followed swiftly by the smile, then he disappeared into the kitchen.

* *

Being hungover was not a state with which Nicola had any familiarity. She vaguely recalled youthful binges and student parties in her college days, but nothing like these waves of feeling not too bad followed by waves of feeling like death. But, she told herself sternly, staring into the mirror of the ladies' room at 2.30pm, that was 15 years ago. She grimaced at her reflection, pale and puffy. You'd make a poor alcoholic, she said to her mirror self, which, all in all, was just as well. She splashed cold water onto her face.

In the hallway, her cell phone gave a blast of trumpets. Greg's ringtone.

"Hey," she said, and leaned against the wall between the ladies' room and the glass door that led into the office.

"Hey, yourself. How are you?" His voice was warm and comforting, and definitely amused, and she wished that somehow she could wrap it around her like a blanket.

"I've been better," Nicola admitted. "Only three hours to go."

He chuckled softly. "You'll sleep like a baby tonight."

"Should I come over?"

A pause. "Do you want to? Wouldn't you be better on your own?"

"I'm always better with you," she said softly. "And you were at my place last night, so this is fair. Did I ever tell you what my mom said on Sunday, before I turned up at the marina so late?"

"No."

"She said she wouldn't let me be the kind of woman who runs home to mother. This would be the same. When we're married, I can't say, 'Sleep somewhere else tonight,' now can I? For better or worse, Greg," Nicola said. "There are worse things than hangovers, but right now I can't think of one."

"Seasickness?" he suggested brightly.

"Oh, ha ha."

He hesitated, then asked, sounding like a man feeling his way across a minefield, "Do you really think we'll still be married, Nicola?"

"Oh my love," she replied, her voice breaking. "I don't dare think anything else."

She heard his breath catch. "No. Me either," he said. "Love you."

"Love you, too."

Nicola somehow got through the next three hours, which dragged almost to four because Greg had a meeting that ran late. She sat at her desk in the nearly empty office as night fell outside, observing like a voyeur the happenings in the insurance company next door. Two men were arguing in an office, arms waving and faces red with anger. She wished she could hear them, but had to content herself with supplying the words for them. In this building, on other floors, where the news journalists were, for example, it would still be busy, but here in travel, lifestyle and fashion there was rarely a need to work late.

She was aware of Greg behind her a moment before his hands rested on her shoulders and he pulled her back against him. It wasn't something he would ever do if anyone was near, but no one was in the immediate vicinity to see. He bent over to kiss the top of her head.

"Sorry I'm so late," he said. "You ready to go?"

Nicola nodded. "I was ready at 9.30 this morning," she confessed.

Traffic came almost to a standstill once they were off the Bay Bridge, and they crawled towards Richmond. Nicola leaned her head back and closed her eyes.

"Hey, don't go to sleep yet!" Greg warned.

She smiled. "I'm awake. Just resting my eyes. Talk to me, that'll keep me awake."

"Let's go away this weekend," Greg suggested.

Nicola snorted. "We went away last weekend. Not a great deal of fun, as I recall," she said pointedly.

He laughed softly, and she felt his hand close briefly around her own. "No, I mean really away. No family, no friends, only us. Somewhere we've never been. The two of us, alone. We'll leave all this mess behind us."

That had definite appeal. "I like that idea. Where did you have in mind?"

"India? I've never seen the Taj Mahal."

Nicola laughed, and sat up. "India! For the weekend! That would be a neat trick. Anyway, I've been to the Taj Mahal, and you said someplace we've never been, so that's out."

"I said someplace we, you and me together, have never been," he corrected. "But I take your point about the impracticality of it. London?"

"I suppose we might be able to get there in a day, and back in a day, but that would give us two hours in London, at the most. Not much time for sightseeing," she said, amused.

The traffic holdup had eased, and the car was quickly approaching his marina now.

"All right," said Greg, with the sigh of a man who has given up. "India's out, so's London. That just leaves Death Valley."

"Death Valley! Your idea of a romantic weekend away to take our minds off 'this mess' is Death Valley?" Nicola twisted around to stare at him in amazement. "Wait a minute," she said slowly. "India, London, Death Valley...."

He brought the car to a stop and turned off the engine. "Your travel section from Sunday. I read it last night, while you were snoring loud enough to wake people in London, if not in India."

She slapped his arm. "I was not! I don't snore."

Greg laughed and put an arm around her as they left the parking lot and walked across the damp grass. "Before last night, I would have agreed."

"Oh, God," she moaned. "I accosted you in the airport, I threw up in a bush, and I snored. Please tell me there's nothing you're hiding from me, to spare my feelings. I'd rather know it all now."

He considered for a moment as he pulled out the swipe card for the gate. "No, I think that's it. So, what about Death Valley? Ever been? That article didn't have your name, so I'm guessing no."

"No, you're right. And I'm not that eager to go now," she said.

"Why? It sounds fantastic. I'd love to see a tree like in the picture on the cover."

"It was a good photo, wasn't it?" Nicola asked with satisfaction. "I was really torn between that and one of the Taj Mahal at sunrise, but went with the Joshua tree."

He turned to her in surprise as they walked along the pontoon, their footsteps echoing in the quiet night. "Did you choose that?"

"I am the editor," she replied with dry amusement. "Who else do you suppose agonizes over cover photos?"

He reached out a hand to help her over *Drifter*'s railing. She'd been on the boat countless times by now, but Nicola was the first to admit that she would never be much of a sailor. If a rope was lying on the deck, she would catch her foot in it; in the calmest sea, she would lurch unsteadily. Remarkably, though, she was never seasick.

Downstairs, the wood and pale walls glowed softly in the light of the lamps, giving the cabin a snug, cozy feel. It was chilly, however, and Greg flicked the switch on the heater.

"I haven't got much food," he said, surveying the contents of the tiny fridge. "Scrambled eggs and toast? Or we can order something, or go to the yacht club."

"Eggs are fine," Nicola said, and yawned. She curled up on a bench and watched as he disappeared into the dim bedroom. "You'd better keep talking or I'll nod off right here. Do you really want to go to Death Valley?"

"Yes." His voice was muffled, and a moment later he reappeared in jeans and a sweatshirt. He tossed another sweatshirt to Nicola, who nodded thanks and pulled it over her head. "I thought we could fly to Vegas after work tomorrow, and stay there. I'm not the camping in the desert sort, and somehow I don't think you are, either. Correct me if I'm wrong on that front," he invited.

She pulled a face, and yawned again.

"We could rent a car on Saturday and drive to the valley," Greg continued. He held a hand over the frying pan, gauging how hot it was. "Your article said it's only two and half hours."

"Oh, yes," Nicola said, more interested in the plan now that it involved more than deserts and salt flats and weird trees, not to mention a variety of snakes and scorpions that would kill you as soon as look at you. "So we're really going to Las Vegas, with a side trip to Death Valley?"

"You could look at it that way, yes," he admitted.

"Why do you suppose toast always smells so good?" Nicola asked, feeling more alert than she had in the past hour. She didn't really expect an answer, and didn't get one.

"But Greg," she said, disappointed, "neither of us has time tomorrow to arrange all this."

He put the plates of eggs and buttered toast on the table and slipped onto the bench beside her. "Janine will do it. She does this sort of thing all the time, it's her job. I'll call her after supper. What do you say?"

Nicola leaned over and kissed him. "Yes."

* *

He woke sometime in the night. His arm was outside of the covers, and it was cold. Even the rest of him, under the covers, was cold. The whole cabin was cold, with winter approaching, and although to admit it would be like a betrayal of *Drifter*, he was glad to know that he wouldn't be living on the boat this winter. Nicola's apartment had big old iron radiators in every room, and would be wonderfully warm.

Dread settled on his chest. If….

Greg shook his head. No ifs!

He became aware that another reason he was cold was that Nicola wasn't pressed against him. He reached out and patted the bed, but it was empty. She could be in the bathroom, but he'd been awake for a few minutes now and all was silence. He got up.

In the cabin, he realized why it was so cold. The main hatch was open and icy air funneled down. He reached back for a t-shirt and went on deck.

Nicola was at the front of the boat, sitting on the deck and wrapped in a blanket. She was no more than a dark shape silhouetted against the city's lights across the water.

"Hey," he said quietly, sinking down cross-legged beside her. "What are you doing out here? It's freezing."

He saw her swipe one hand across her cheek. "Nothing. I couldn't sleep," she said, but the tear-choked roughness of her voice gave her away.

"No, no." Greg gathered her to him, rocking her. "Don't cry, my darling. It will all be fine. You'll see."

She sniffed. "I tell myself that, and I try to be strong like you, but sometimes I think that it must be true. Just look at us! I look like Mona, and like you!"

"Coincidence! It's only a coincidence!" he insisted. "Like you both being allergic to tomatoes. It doesn't mean anything!" Then he added quietly, "And I'm not all that strong, either."

They sat silently, drawing warmth from each other. She tweaked a corner of the blanket to cover his legs. A gust of wind ruffled the water, sending the reflections of lights into crazy wavering patterns. The night was clear and moonless, the stars overhead a glittering blaze.

"How was it yesterday?" Greg asked after a while. "You haven't told me."

"Surreal," she said against his chest. "I couldn't believe we were really taking DNA samples. It seemed…so mundane. A swipe with a swab, and you're done."

Greg smiled in the dark. "Lots of time for hitting the booze afterwards, I guess?"

She punched him lightly. "Not funny!"

He heard the smile in her voice, though. "I'm sorry."

"Anyway, the Southern Comfort was before we did the swabs.

We were nervous. Scared," she said. "And no one told me how strong grappa is!"

"Especially the way Alberto makes it," Greg observed. "So what did you do when you weren't drinking?"

She punched him again, harder this time, and he captured her hand and kissed it.

"We just talked. Do you remember," she asked, "when you were 13, your mother being upset for a few months but she wouldn't say why?"

"Yes, I do!" he exclaimed. "I remember being so worried, and confused, too."

"Susie had died," Nicola explained.

He whistled softly. "Poor Mom. After that story she told us, I imagined Susie still going strong, intimidating homeless people onto the path to righteousness."

"Greg! That's no way to put it!"

"Sounds like that's what she did for Mom," he replied, unrepentant. Then he shivered, for this was no place to be wearing just a t-shirt.

"You're freezing! I'm sorry, let's go back inside."

Greg got hastily to his feet, rubbing his hands against his frozen backside to get some life back into it. She struggled up, hampered by the blanket, and he grabbed her arm to steady her. Then hugged her against him, hard.

"It isn't true," he whispered.

Chapter 13

FROM THE corner of her eye, Nicola saw her phone flash silently. She glanced at it, one eye still on her computer screen. Greg.

"Hi."

"I had an email from Janine. We're all set. The flight is at 8 tonight and she's booked us into a hotel. She even arranged the car rental for tomorrow!" Greg added. "I know how much you're looking forward to Death Valley, so I thought you'd want to know."

She smiled, and traced one fingernail in idle patterns on her desk. "Of course I am. It will be the highlight of the weekend, I have no doubt." She paused, then said, "I got an email, too."

"From my sister?"

"No, from the…the company. To let me know they received the package," Nicola said quietly.

"Oh." Silence. "Well, that's good."

Nicola gave a small, humorless laugh. "They emailed me on Monday, too, to confirm it was on its way. Great customer service. I'll recommend them to anyone I know who needs…this."

"Don't think about it, Nicola," Greg urged. "There is absolutely nothing you can do, so don't let it spoil our weekend."

"You're right, of course. I promise I won't!" she vowed, but quietly, aware that Max at his desk could hear everything she said. "I'll see you in the lobby at 5.00."

* *

Nicola had the window seat but Greg pressed against her as the plane came in to land, trying to glimpse the astonishing light show she had described below them.

"No good," he said, easing back. "All I can see is night-time in the desert."

Obligingly, the plane banked, and he leaned closer again to see Las Vegas unfold in garish, brilliant neon. "I'd hate to have to pay that electricity bill!" And then, since he was squashed against Nicola anyway, he kissed her. "This will be great."

She grinned back.

They were like kids in the taxi, or small-town tourists, pointing out hotels along the Strip they'd heard of but never seen, and gawking at the glittering, flashing lights on both sides.

"Look, there's the Eiffel Tower!" exclaimed Nicola. And then she squealed. "Guy Magyck!"

Greg looked at her in disbelief, not sure what astonished him more – that sound she had just made, or this hitherto-unrevealed passion for Guy Magyck. He followed her pointing finger and there, in glowing neon on a giant billboard, was the name of the singer-comedian-magician.

"No," he said faintly.

Nicola didn't appear to have heard him. "Do you suppose we can get tickets?" she asked, her words tumbling out in a rush of enthusiasm. "Oh, I wish Mom was here, she absolutely loves Guy Magyck! I never thought I'd see him in person!"

"No," Greg said again, more firmly. "Nicola, I refuse."

"Give it up, buddy," advised the driver. "They're all like that. The minute they see the sign, that's it. She'll be singing in a minute."

Sure enough, Nicola broke out with, "Oooh baby baby, hey maybe maybe?"

Greg covered his ears. He loved her, no question. She told bad jokes that made him laugh, she offered up pithy observations that made him groan, she could write about somewhere he'd never heard of but make him want to hop on the next plane and see it, made him laugh, made him want to shake her in exasperation, made him mad for her body – but, dear God, the woman could not sing.

She broke off to exclaim in dismay, "What if it's sold out? I'll die!"

This is getting more improbable by the second, thought Greg. He clung to the hope that, yes, the show was sold out. No luck.

"Don't worry, lady," soothed the driver. "Mr Magyck's been here over a year now. Lots of shows."

"Wow!" breathed Nicola, and she looked at him, her face alight. "Can you believe it?"

"No," Greg muttered.

Her face fell as his lack of enthusiasm finally penetrated, and then she brightened. "A wise man – that's your dad, by the way – told me that marriage is compromise. You want to go to Death Valley, and I don't, very much, but I'm willing to go along because it's important to you. And I want to see Guy Magyck, and you don't, very much, but you'll come with me because you love me. Won't you?" She slipped her fingers through his, and she smiled.

How could he possibly say no when she looked at him like that? "Yes. But I'm not singing along," he warned.

A laugh came from the front seat. "They all say that, buddy! But when I take 'em back to the airport, it's a different story."

The hotel Janine had chosen wasn't on the Strip itself, but it was only a block away. The outside looked disappointingly plain after the glitz and spectacle of the big hotel-casinos. "It was probably too last-minute for Caesar's Palace or Bellagio," reasoned Nicola, walking past him as he held the door open.

"Oh," she said, sounding disappointed.

"What?"

"I had hoped I could write this up as part of the series we do on weekend getaways, but," she waved a hand around the lobby, "I can't see me recommending this sea of beige and glass to anyone. I guess I can't claim it, after all."

He had spent too many years as an auditor with a Big Four firm in Seattle to let that pass. Greg stopped walking, and because they were holding holds, so did she. "You really, really do not want to be telling me things like that. Faking expenses, and so on. I have a CPA license. I belong to professional bodies. I signed up to a code of ethics. I can't just turn a blind eye. Not even for you."

Nicola flushed, and then moved against him. She wasn't batting her eyelashes, was she?

"Our secret, okay, big boy?" she whispered. "I'll make it worthwhile." And the hand he wasn't holding ran up his thigh.

"Nicola!"

But now he saw that she was laughing at him.

"Greg! That's how it works. What, you think I rock up to a hotel I want to review, hand over my pre-authorized account from a well known newspaper, and then get standard treatment?" She shook her head at his innocence. "If you want to get upgraded to the presidential suite, sure. If you want an honest review, you pay up front, then claim it back."

He licked his lips, glanced away, glanced back. "I knew that. I was testing."

Her eyes narrowed and her head titled, and she smiled. "Right."

While he checked in, she browsed through the pamphlets on a nearby rack. The clerk turned away to answer the phone, and Greg turned to watch Nicola. How could any woman be so desirable doing nothing but looking at advertising?

"Bordello?" He caught only the tail end of what the check-in clerk had said. He must have misheard.

"Oh yes!" she said. "Your travel agent asked for it particularly. We already had another couple penciled in there, but since you wanted the room so badly we gave them the Wild West instead."

Nicola was frowning, he saw.

"Oh. Thank you," said Greg weakly.

He exchanged a look of uncertainty with Nicola, and they walked towards the elevator.

As the doors closed, she snapped her fingers. "This is the hotel Kylie told us about!" she exclaimed. "Where all the rooms have different themes."

"And my sister ensured we got the bordello one," replied Greg. The doors whooshed open, revealing a foyer as beige as the lobby had been, and he said, "Maybe it won't be as bad as I'm expecting."

They found their room and he swiped the key card, with Nicola hanging over his shoulder for that first glimpse inside.

"It's worse."

"Look!" Nicola giggled, and pointed to the mirror above the heart-shaped bed, which itself sat in regal splendor on a raised dais against one black-and-white striped wall. Vaguely erotic paintings in heavy frames hung on the other walls.

As they ventured inside, Greg bumped against a little table, on which a half-bottle of champagne nestled in a silver ice bucket. Beads of moisture clung to the bucket and an envelope rested against it.

"Have a great weekend! PS, I hope you like the room. Love, Janine." He tossed the note down. "I'm going to kill her," he added, in a conversational tone. He slung his bag off his shoulder and onto the bed.

"No, don't!" cried Nicola, digging in her own bag. She pulled out her camera case. "Pick that up and stand behind me, so you're not in the pictures."

"You're going to photograph this?" he asked in disbelief, but obediently moved his bag and smoothed the satin.

"Of course! This will be one of my best 'weekend getaway' articles ever!"

When she gave him permission to move again, Greg wandered over to the window and pulled back the heavy red velvet curtains, swatting away a dangling fringe from the gold braid swag. There was the Strip, spreading before them in all its glory. "Good view, anyway," he commented after a minute. "Look at this."

There was no reply, and he turned around. No Nicola. But she emerged from a side door, which he assumed was the bathroom, her face alive with delight.

"What shall we do?" he asked. "It's only 10pm, and Las Vegas never sleeps. You want to gamble away all your savings? Eat? Try out that bed?"

She shook her head, and smiled, that look of delight growing stronger. "I want to have a bath."

"You do?"

Nicola grabbed his hand and towed him into the bathroom, another eye-watering exercise in red and black and gold.

"Only a shower," he said, pointing to the glass stall in one corner.

She led him to an arched opening in the wall, with a red velvet curtain behind it, and beyond that was another room. One whole wall was glass, with that same view of the Strip, but what was impossible to miss was the huge circular bathtub, almost as high as his thigh.

Nicola's fingers were busy on the top button of his shirt. "I want to have a bath," she repeated, and kissed the skin of his chest revealed by the first open button. "With you. And that champagne. And all these candles. You can make sure I wash behind my ears." Another button, another kiss, this one followed by a flick of her tongue. "And anywhere else that interests you."

Desire flashed like lightning along Greg's spine. "The window," he protested, but not very strongly.

Another button. "It's got a coating. We can see out, but no one can see in. There's a sign over there." She pulled his shirt-tails free of his jeans and ran her hands up his chest and over his shoulders, leaving trails like sparking electric wires where she touched him. His shirt fell to the floor.

Her lips were against his neck, soft and moist. "You get the champagne, and I'll light the candles and turn on the water," Nicola suggested. "Unless you'd rather feed the slot machines?"

He seized her bottom in both hands and pulled her against him, hard, so she could feel for herself exactly what he'd rather do. "What do you think?"

"Oh dear," she said, eyes wide. "I think we had better do something about that."

He ran to the bedroom for the champagne, and turned back to the bathroom. Glasses. Where were the glasses? He banged the ice bucket onto the table and strode over to a large, ornate cabinet. Yanking open the doors revealed a large flat-screen television – and a mini-bar, thank God. Greg dumped the glasses into the bucket and hurried out, through the bathroom and into the bathtub room.

He blinked in the sudden dimness. A dozen small candles flickered around the room, but after the glare of the glittering chandelier in the bedroom, and the lights in the bathroom, it seemed dark.

She was standing by the glass wall, her back to the door, and his heart clenched just to see her.

"I'm back," he announced.

Her smile was brighter than any crystal chandelier, and she came to him, arms wide.

It took a while to fill a bathtub that size. Enough time for all of his clothes to come off, and hers, for lingering kisses and wandering caresses. The water was almost too hot, the heat crawling up from his toes to his knees and to his waist when he lowered himself down. Foam from the bubble bath she'd insisted on adding rose in scented mounds, and he batted it away. Greg snaked an arm around her and pulled her down into the water with him, just their heads emerging from the fine white bubbles. The damned tub was so big they could almost stretch out in it. She was smooth and slippery in his arms, and her eyes sparkled with laughter and love.

"I'm awfully thirsty," she said, and her eyes swiveled to the ice bucket on the ledge behind him.

He pulled himself into a sitting position. "Is this going to end with you snoring loud enough to wake the neighbors? Shall I have reception send up a nice bush for you?"

The handful of bubbles she deposited on his head dripped onto his nose.

"Do you suppose they have nice bushes?" she asked.

With an explosive pop, the cork came free of the bottle "It's the bordello room. I'd guess they would have had stranger requests than that."

"Eww!"

Greg pulled the chilled glasses from the ice bucket and poured the champagne in a frothing stream.

"To this weekend." He held his glass up.

"It was a great idea," she agreed, and clinked her glass against his.

"I never expected to be wallowing in a bubble bath, drinking champagne and looking out at a view like that," he said, one arm going around her shoulders. "I may forgive Janine, after all."

"I already have," Nicola said. She stretched across him to deposit her glass on the ledge, then stretched more and kissed him. Her body, slick and soapy, was in danger of sliding down his own soapy body, and her arms twined around his neck. Greg fumbled his glass to one side and ran his hands down her back, clasping her sweet round bottom to keep her in place.

"Mmmm," he groaned, as she kissed her way from his mouth, along his jaw and to the soft spot behind his ear.

"Don't you find it odd," she whispered, "that you hate it when I lick your ears, but you love it when I do this?"

"No," he said faintly. This was no time to be discussing the logic of erogenous zones.

Her fingers teased and slid down to another little hollow, that one at the base of his spine.

"Nnnnn," he groaned, and relaxed his grip on her.

Mistake. Nicola slipped in a soapy rush straight down his front, landing with a splash and an explosion of bubbles.

Greg groped for the rim of the tub to stop himself slipping down with her, and his eyes flew open. There was the Strip, a kaleidoscope of colored lights through the light mist of steam on the window. He looked down to see her face against his belly, her chin resting just below his navel. Her eyes smiled up at him, mischief lurking in those enchanting sapphire depths. She blew a froth of bubbles off his abdomen, then winked at him, took a deep breath and lowered her head under the water.

Oh, Christ. It was extraordinary, the feel of her mouth on him and the water around him, her fingers splayed over his thighs. The bobbing of her head made little waves that splashed against his belly. He wanted to lower his hands, to run his fingers through the wet strands of her dark hair as it floated around them, but he knew that if he let go of the sides of the tub, he would slide down. How long could she hold her breath? Oh Christ if she doesn't stop I'm going to—

Nicola burst out of the water, gasping and grinning, to fling her arms around his neck and her legs around his waist, her heels digging into the small of his back. Greg grabbed her hips and he thrust, hard and deep. The water sloshed madly in response to their feverish rhythm. She bent back, tight against him and her hands clutching his shoulders, and she cried out.

One final thrust and…and…the clenched muscles of his backside lost their precarious hold on the smooth bathtub and he and Nicola crashed down into the water, sending a wave slopping against the side of the tub and cascading onto the carpet.

Nicola hauled herself to her knees to peer over the edge of the tub, her wet bottom inches from his face. Over one foam-clad shoulder, she grinned at him.

"Oops."

* *

The shrilling of the telephone woke them at 7am, the wake-up call that Greg had insisted on placing so they were up in time for their Death Valley trip. Nicola opened her eyes to a dimly glowing sea of red, the sun through the curtains casting everything in crimson shadows.

"This is like those documentaries on television, where they put cameras inside you. Everything's red," she said, plucking at the sheets to illustrate.

"They're red anyway." Greg's voice faded into a yawn. "So are the cover and the pillows. If you want a bird's eye view, look up."

"Oh my God," she giggled. She had forgotten about the mirror. There they lay, two mounds on a heart-shaped bed, their faces no more than pale blobs against the shimmering satin. She reached behind her head, shaking one of the slender metal uprights that followed the indented curves of the top of the heart. "This is more like a fence than a headboard."

"The bed is such an odd shape, I'd think it would be easy to roll off if you weren't paying attention. If you were, shall we say, occupied with something else. Or someone," Greg added. Then, as she turned towards him, he said, "Oh no you don't! Take that look off your face and your hands off my person. I will gladly be seduced at another time, but today we have plans."

Nicola sighed, and rolled over. So much for her last-minute ploy to stave off a day in a car looking at desert and rocks. It seemed that Death Valley's charms were greater than hers – this morning, at least. Bright sunlight flooded in as Greg dragged back the curtains, and she stretched in its warmth.

"I can't get over this view," he said.

She twisted around to see him. He had dragged back not only

the heavy velvet curtains but also the light privacy ones beneath them, and stood now before the window, looking out, his hands scratching his backside. "Did you notice a sign by that window, like the one in the bathtub room, that said no one could see in?" she asked.

Greg's look of puzzlement changed to alarm. He leaped back, then sidled along the wall to where his bag lay on the floor, and fished out a pair of boxer shorts. "Stop laughing and get out of bed, before I come over there and drag you out," he threatened.

She stuck her tongue out. "Bully. And if you think I'm getting out of this bed before you close those privacy curtains, think again."

"Bully, huh? That's rich, from the woman who's inflicting an evening of Guy Magyck on me," he retorted with a smile.

Nicola brightened. "Maybe I can download some songs to my phone, so we can listen to them in the car."

He paused, curtains half closed, and stared at her. "Great idea."

Greg hustled her into her clothes, hustled her through breakfast, and hustled her out the door. The morning was sunny but chilly, and she thrust her hands into the pockets of her jacket. "It can't be much more than 50 degrees," she commented. "It's hard to believe it could reach 80 this afternoon."

"Typical desert. Not that I've ever been to one before!"

They followed the cracked sidewalk, and beside them weeds grew at the base of a sagging wooden fence encircling a garbage-strewn empty lot. It was nothing like the lights and glitter of the Strip. "You sure this is the right way?" Nicola asked, doubtful.

He pulled a printout from his pocket. "It's around this corner, apparently."

At the corner, they detoured around two women sitting on stained cardboard, their backs against the fence. Their clothes were dirty and torn. Faces that could have been 18 or could have been 30 peered up from under disheveled hair, and one woman held out a grimy hand, palm up.

Greg put his arm through Nicola's and steered her around their feet, but she shrugged free and turned back. "Here," she said, holding out a five-dollar bill.

The outstretched hand snatched the money, and dull brown eyes met Nicola's for a fraction of a second. "Thanks."

"They'll only buy booze with it, or drugs. You know that," Greg said, disapproval in his voice.

She shrugged. "If I was living like that, I'd probably want something to make me forget it, too."

The look he gave her held considerable surprise, and a degree of thoughtfulness. "I've never seen you give money to someone on the street before."

"I haven't. But they reminded me of your mother's story," she said.

"Oh." He was silent for a few steps. "I thought we had agreed not to talk about that this weekend."

Nicola exhaled sharply. "And that's going to wipe all memory of it from our minds? Make our little problem conveniently vanish for two days?"

"No, of course not," he retorted. "But I would like to think of happier things for two days. I'd like us to be like any other couple that's come to Vegas for a holiday, not a headline in a tabloid newspaper. I can see it now: 'Man marries his own mother's abandoned daughter!'"

She grabbed his sleeve and swung him around, then flung her arms around him. "Don't you ever say that! This will never end up as news."

His arms tightened around her. "Have you forgotten where we work? If even one of those reporters finds out…." His voice trailed away. "All in all, I'd really rather enjoy this weekend."

"Me too, oh Greg, me too! It's been great so far," she assured him.

He pulled his head back to gaze at her. "Last night was certainly great. I'll never look at a bathtub in the same way again. Though that one is more like a small swimming pool. I had no idea you could hold your breath for so long."

Nicola blushed. "I, uh, was kind of thinking of other things. And now we've got Death Valley to look forward to!" She put as much enthusiasm as possible into her voice at that prospect, and was rewarded with his smile.

"And Guy Magyck," he added.

"Can we stop for tickets on the way out of town? I'd hate to miss out," she said, as they walked into the car rental office.

Car rented, show tickets bought and tucked securely into Nicola's backpack, they headed out of Las Vegas on Highway 160 to Pahrump.

"Our first road trip," announced Greg, in the voice of a man who is satisfied with life.

She glanced sideways at him. "Yup, it's a great view of rocks and scrub and dirt. With, I believe, what look suspiciously like hills ahead of us. You don't see many of those around."

"You wait until we get there, and you see the Devil's Golf Course, and Badwater Basin, and the view from Zabriskie Point. It will all be worth it then," he promised.

"Tell me, had you ever heard of the Devil's Golf Course, or Badwater Basin, or Zabriskie Point before you read my travel section on Wednesday night?" she asked.

Greg shook his head.

That freelance writer must be better than I realized, she thought.

"Do you want to know why it's called Death Valley?" Greg asked.

"Let me guess. Someone died there?"

He shot her a look that said he really had expected better of her than that. "A group of pioneers got lost there on their way to California to join the 1849 gold rush. When they finally got out, someone looked back and said, 'Goodbye, Death Valley.'"

"So how many died?"

"Ah, I'm not sure. The website didn't say."

She smiled at him. "That's all right. I'm impressed you read up on it."

"I've got a whole raft of printouts and maps in my bag."

"You sound prepared. Were you a boy scout? Can you tie knots? If we get lost and have to camp out in this car, can you forage for food? Kill supper with your bare hands?" Nicola laughed at the mental image of Greg zigzagging over the desert in pursuit of an animal, a lizard maybe.

"Yes, I can tie knots, but that's because I've been sailing for 25 years," he replied. "I can forage for food if we happen to find a supermarket, but I'm not killing anything with my bare hands. Not even for you, my darling." He took one hand off the wheel and patted her thigh.

She gazed out at the harsh landscape, dry and barren, still nothing but dirt and rocks. A lot of dirt and rocks, in assorted browns and beiges. Hills rose steeply on the right, and to their left were occasional tantalizing glimpses of the valley and mountains beyond. Not a tree anywhere, not even one of those Joshua trees. "Imagine crossing this back then, on foot, or at best on horseback. It's a miracle any of those people survived. What did they feed the horses?" she wondered.

"Hell, what did they feed themselves?" he asked. "They must have badly wanted that new life in California to have risked so much. To leave behind everything and everyone they knew, and start over. I can't imagine ever doing that."

Nicola turned in her seat to face him. "You left Seattle," she pointed out.

"On a whim. With no threat at all to life or limb," he said. "And I knew Sam and Debbie. It's not the same as those 49ers."

"No, you're not likely to find gold anywhere," she laughed. Then she pointed ahead and to the left. "There's your Zabriskie Point lookout, I think."

They got out of the car and stretched, happy at the prospect of moving around again. Nicola peeled off her jacket and threw it onto her seat. "It's a lot warmer than this morning," she observed.

Hand-in-hand, they followed a sand-colored path up the slight incline to the viewing platform. Small jagged peaks thrust up haphazardly around them, rising above the fingers of bedrock worn away over millennia. Across the valley rose the wall of mountains, a seemingly impenetrable barrier.

"Wow."

Greg grinned, and pulled her against him. "I told you it would be great. Apparently, it's even better at sunrise and sunset, when the rocks glow with color."

She pointed. "You can see parts of the valley floor. Look how white it is! I suppose that's dried salt." She shook her head. "Imagine seeing that, and knowing you had to get across it, and then over those mountains."

"I'm just as glad we've got air conditioning," he said.

"Some pioneer you'd make!"

"I like my modern comforts, I admit it," he replied. Then with a wink, "Like bathtubs."

Nicola swatted his arm, and he laughed. After one last admiring look, they turned back towards the parking lot.

Next stop was the Furnace Creek visitor center, where they both headed straight to the restrooms. Outside again, she spotted Greg reading a pamphlet and walked towards him. His phone trilled. "I guess we're back in the modern world, if there's a cell signal." He glanced at the display, and said, "It's Dad."

Nicola wandered around, reading display boards and looking at maps and photos, all the while keeping one eye on Greg. He had sat on a bench and was staring into the distance, frowning, listening to Edward.

"Is everything all right?" she asked, as they walked back to the car.

He shrugged. "It's Mom. Dad's worried about her." He negotiated the crowded parking lot, and after a few minutes turned onto Badwater Road which would take them along the valley.

"Why is Edward worried?" asked Nicola, when it didn't look as if he would elaborate.

Greg glanced at her. "Dad said that since she met you, and particularly since Wednesday, Mom has become more and more convinced that you are her daughter. Dad's afraid she actually wants you to be her daughter."

"That would be a disaster!"

He hesitated. "For us, yes. But she would have found her long-lost daughter at last."

Nicola snorted. "Yeah, right. She hasn't made much of an effort in the past 36 years to find her long-lost daughter. I don't think she was all that concerned."

"Try to be more understanding," he suggested, in a tight voice. "This isn't easy for her, either."

"I am trying!" Somehow, understanding had been easier on Wednesday, when it was just her and Mona. Now, with Greg's presence reminding her of everything that was at stake, Nicola's concerns were more selfish.

"You're not trying very hard, it seems to me!"

She twisted towards him, the seatbelt catching at the suddenness of her movement. "You actually want me to be her daughter? Your half-sister? Just so she can feel good about her past?"

"No, of course not!"

"That's what it sounds like," Nicola said, and flipped back into her seat, staring stonily ahead. She heard him draw breath to speak, but she cut in with, "I swear to you, Greg, if those results come back positive, there is no way in hell I am playing some perverted form of happy families! I will never speak to that woman again!"

"'That woman' is my mother!"

She gave a bitter laugh. "Oh yeah, jeez, thanks for reminding me."

The silence in the car grew, cold and hard. Spectacular views flashed by on the right, stunning colors of banded rock on the left, but neither commented on what was outside.

Finally, Greg said, in a remarkably conversational tone, "Did you never wonder who your parents were? Your real parents?"

She took a deep breath, forcing herself to calm down, to meet him halfway in this attempt to lower the level of angry emotion. "No." But inherent honesty compelled Nicola to say, "Yes. In my teens, if I'd had a fight with Mom about something, or Dad ticked me off for something, then yes, I would think to myself, 'My real mother/father wouldn't say that!' I flung that at her once, I remember, when I was 13 and she wouldn't let me get my ears pierced, and she came right back with, 'Then she wouldn't love you as much as I do!'"

His soft chuckle was a welcome sound after their recent harsh exchange. "It's hard to argue that one."

Nicola was silent for a minute, then said in a small voice, "But I admit, I've wondered more about my real parents, whoever they are, in this past week than in my whole life." She sighed. "What about you? Your real father?"

A light shrug. "Same as you. Never, unless we disagreed about something." His hands tightened on the steering wheel. "And after learning about that bastard Clive, I thank my lucky stars that Dad walked into that diner in Portland."

It came out before she could stop it. "At least Mona could identify who your father was."

He slapped one palm hard against the wheel, and the car veered. "Christ, Nicola!" The anger in his voice was as sharp as the edge on a steel blade.

"It's true," she insisted. "You heard that story! God knows how many men she had sex with while she was with that band. She sure didn't know!"

Greg pulled off the road and jerked the car to a halt. He turned to face her. "I refuse to talk about this any longer," he stated. "This is exactly why I told you not to think about it."

"How can I not think about it?" she cried. "You may be able to put it away in a box and ignore it, but I can't! It's in my mind all the time. This thing is hanging over us, Greg! It's the rest of our lives, our life together, and it may all fall apart!"

"That's my point! It may. Or it may not! We don't know. We won't know before Friday, at the earliest. And there is not one damned thing we can do about it, either way!" Greg's fingers dug into her shoulders and he shook her, not gently. His eyes were narrow slits, the dark blue glinting with anger and frustration. "So why must you go on and on, like a doomsayer, raking it over and bringing it all up again?"

The idiotic tears were blurring her vision, and she turned away before he saw them.

"Are you coming?" he demanded.

"Where?" she asked blankly.

Greg waved a hand at the expanse of glittering white valley floor in front of them, shimmering in the heat. People were walking across, those in the distance no more than wavering shapes. A sign right in front of the car announced that they were at Badwater Basin.

"No." She crossed her arms. "I'll ruin my shoes. You didn't tell me there would be a hike involved."

"Your…shoes." He flicked one glance of dismissal at her feet, then opened his door. Heat gushed in, a dry blast.

She heard him open the door to the back seat and a moment later slam it shut. Then he appeared in front of the car, striding down the boardwalk and struggling into his backpack, and was gone.

Chapter 14

GREG REFUSED to look back. Let the damned woman sit in the car, sulking, and wallowing in her useless "what ifs." Some romantic weekend this was turning out to be!

He marched across the ground, eyes on the distant mountains. A small white dust devil whirled into existence feet away, and disappeared as quickly. Gradually, the brisk exercise calmed him, as did the need to watch more closely where he put his feet once he'd gone far enough for the trail to roughen. Irregular lumps of mineral deposits littered the ground, and he had no desire to twist an ankle because of a carelessly placed boot. Nor did he especially want to step on a rattlesnake.

Christ, it was hot! And this was November; what must it be like in summer? he wondered.

Heat radiated from the cracked ground, and the dry wind sucked the moisture from his body. Greg pulled his hat lower over his forehead, and stopped to swing the pack from his back and rummage for the water bottle. It was quiet, even quieter than sailing, for then there was always the sound of the water, and the rigging or the sails. Here, there was only the eerie keening of the wind.

"At least Mona could identify who your father was."

Against his will, Greg heard the words again, and the harsh, resentful tone in Nicola's voice. Until last Sunday in Seattle, he had never seen or heard that side of her. All of her words had been teasing or playful, or thoughtful, or straightforward and without artifice, or, after their relationship had deepened, rich with love or desire for him. This cutting, hurtful woman was a stranger.

He knew that she could no more be sweet and even-tempered all the time than he could. No one could. But it shook him to see them act like this to each other. In the car, she had brought him closer to the man he had been in those furious fights with Jackie than he had ever wanted to go again; unlike Jackie, Nicola had turned away and fallen silent.

Yet she was still Nicola. Still the woman he loved. The quickness to anger, the biting remarks, were Nicola struggling to cope with the change that his mother's story had wreaked on their relationship. She would not let it go, and he would not accept it; two different ways of trying to deal with the same situation.

Greg kicked moodily at a rock and watched it roll away in a small puff of dust.

And Mom. Christ, poor Mom, the unwitting cause of their conflict. Dad had said on the phone that every day she felt more guilt over the baby abandoned so long ago, coupled with this growing belief that the baby had now appeared in the adult form of beautiful, intelligent, maddening and infuriating Nicola.

Greg stuffed the water bottle back into the pack and resumed walking, shaking his head at the mess everything had become.

I should go back, he thought. I can't leave it like that.

People were coming towards him, a small group on their way back to the parking lot. One raised an arm and Greg waved in reply, but the other man lifted his arm higher and gestured at something behind Greg.

He looked, and far behind him was the shape of a person, running, it seemed, although in the heat shimmers and whirls of dust it was hard to tell. Who in their right mind would be running out here? Greg started to turn back, and a flash of deep pink caught his eye. The t-shirt Nicola had put on this morning was pink; "fuchsia," she had informed him loftily when he had commented on its color.

He took a step. It couldn't be Nicola? She wasn't running over this stony, uneven ground in those flimsy little shoes? Greg took another step. The woman – for it was clearly a woman, she was close enough to see that, at least – definitely was dressed in a pink t-shirt and jeans. Another uncertain step, and then he began to run towards her.

Nicola collapsed into his arms, her breath coming in great heaves and her face a worrying shade of red. "I'm sorry!" she gasped. "I was so stupid!"

Greg flung off the backpack and wrenched out the water, thrusting it into her hands. "Drink this!" He pulled out a map and started to fan her with it, not convinced that the hot air would be much help in cooling her.

She swallowed greedily, between deep gulps of air. "I had to come after you," she said, and one hand gripped his wrist. "We have nothing if we don't have each other. We're going through this whole horrible experience so we can be together. I think I forgot that."

Relief washed through him like a cool spring rain. "It's all right," he said. "We're both on edge. I was more worried you would fall, running like that."

"I did fall." She held out her hands, showing him her scraped palms and the smeared blood, then gestured to the torn knees of her jeans.

"Oh, you crazy woman!" he exclaimed, and clutched her tight against him, sheltering her with his body. "I would have come back. You could have told me then."

The vigorous shaking of her head flipped her ponytail against his neck. "It wouldn't have been the same."

"This was certainly more dramatic," he admitted, lips tugging into a wry smile.

That group of people had caught up to them by now, and as they passed one of the men said, "You know the lady, then? Everything all right?"

Greg laughed, and pulled Nicola even closer, if that was possible. "Everything is fine."

* *

Back at the hotel, he made her sit on the toilet seat while he cleaned her palms in the sink. She flinched as the hot water bit into her abraded skin, and tried to pull her hands free.

"I know it stings," Greg said, working soap gently but thoroughly into the cuts and scrapes. "But you don't want any infections, do you?"

She shook her head, looking so resigned that he bent over and kissed her forehead.

"When this is done, you're going to have a shower, and then you're going to lie down on the bed," he instructed.

Her eyes widened with interest. "Oh, yes? And what will you be doing while I'm lying on the bed?"

"I will be sitting beside you, rubbing antiseptic ointment into your palms and knees."

She pulled a face. "That sounds like fun."

"And then," he continued, "if you are very good, and you behave, I may think of other things to rub."

"With antiseptic ointment?"

"No."

* *

Greg would have held Nicola's hand as they walked towards the theater where Guy Magyck was performing, but, despite his ministrations, her palms were still tender, so he contented himself with tucking her arm through his. Her eyes were shining and her skin was glowing, and the dark blue dress she wore, with its long sleeves and V-neck, hinted at every curve of her delicious body. Dangling silver earrings caught the light and matched the necklace that drew his eyes to her breasts. Not that he needed anything to draw them there.

"You look fantastic," he said.

Her eyebrows lifted, and then she smiled. "Thank you."

"I don't say that often, do I?" Greg asked, when he'd figured out why she looked so surprised. "But I think it a lot. No matter what you wear, you look fantastic."

Her arm tightened on his and she moved closer, and the subtle scent of her perfume rose to hover around him.

"And coming from a gorgeous hunk of manhood like me, that means something, let me tell you," he teased.

The blue eyes narrowed and she glanced around. "If you ever tell anyone I called you that, you're in big trouble," she threatened.

He laughed. "Half of San Francisco airport heard you call me that, but I promise, my lips are sealed."

They had reached the door, and her reply turned into an exclamation of delight when the attendant handed them both a glowstick. Greg held his gingerly, as if it might go off at any moment. He wasn't actually expected to wave this thing around, was he?

Their seats were at a shared table in the first row of the second tier. The show wasn't sold out, but all the tickets for the private tables close to the stage were gone. Their table mates were already there, a couple in their 40s. The man stood up when it became clear that Greg and Nicola were joining them, tipped back his baseball cap and thrust out his hand.

"Hi," he drawled. "I'm Stan, and this here's my wife, Trish."

Greg shook the hand. "Greg and Nicola."

"You sit down here, honey," said Trish to Nicola, one hand patting the seat beside her and the other patting the precarious-looking blonde tower of her hair. "Us girls should have the best seats for Guy, don't you think?"

"Absolutely!" agreed Nicola.

"Where you from?" Trish asked. She took a long draw on the straw sticking out of her bright green drink, cheeks sucked in and eyes moving from one to the other. They lingered longer on Greg than he liked. "We're from New Orleans."

"San Francisco," Greg replied, and then to the hovering waiter he said, "A beer and a white wine, please."

Stan gave a hearty laugh, and waved at the waiter as he prepared to leave. "Hell, since you're here anyway, let's have another bourbon and one of them green drinks for the lady."

Trish giggled. Then she grasped Nicola's left hand, and leaned closer. "What a beautiful ring! When's the wedding?"

Greg exchanged a glance with Nicola, and then he brought out the by-now well rehearsed story about the postponement due to his father's ill health.

"Oh honey, you should just drag this man into any old chapel tomorrow morning and get it done, Vegas style," the woman advised Nicola. "I'd be quick if I was you."

There was no mistaking the message in the look Trish flashed at Greg, and he glanced uneasily at her husband. Stan was six inches taller than Greg himself, and big; a lot of the big was fat, but a lot was muscle. He hoped the man was as easygoing as he seemed, and not given to sudden flashes of jealousy. As proof of his own harmlessness, Greg lifted Nicola's hand to his lips and kissed it.

"Unfortunately, we promised our families we would wait," he said.

"Good man," said Stan in bluff approval. "Family is what counts."

Nicola smiled around at everyone, and picked up her small satin bag. "If you'll all excuse me, I must visit the ladies' room."

"Me too, honey!" said Trish, grabbing a large purse decorated in sequins and rhinestones. "Don't want to be answering nature's call while Guy's on stage, now do we?"

The men stood and pulled back their chairs to let them out. In passing, Trish's hand brushed Greg somewhere he wasn't used to anyone but Nicola brushing him, and he hoped to hell that Stan hadn't seen. Come to think of it, he hoped to hell that Nicola hadn't seen, either.

"Why do they do that?" asked Stan, frowning after the women. "I'd never go to the toilet with another man."

He shook his head in bafflement. "One of the many things we mere men will never understand about women."

Stan picked up a glowstick. "And this here's another thing. What do they possibly see in that joker?" He laughed. "The things we do for love, huh?"

Greg grunted in agreement. He was thinking not only of the prospect of two hours of soppy 1980s love songs and cheesy jokes, with a handful of basic magic tricks thrown in for variety, but of that pointless argument in the car this afternoon. "Can't live with them, can't live without them."

"Yeah, but they sure do make the livin' a whole lot more fun," said Stan, and with a laugh Greg raised his glass in agreement.

* *

"Let's go for a swim," Nicola suggested.

Greg yawned, then rolled over and propped his head on his hand. "In our own miniature pool, you mean?" He pulled down the red satin sheet far enough to drop a kiss on one breast. "I warn you, I can't hold my breath as long as you can. But I'll do my best!" He winked.

Nicola snatched at the sheet and pulled it up, preempting

what looked like a plan to kiss his way lower. "No, in the real pool. The swimming pool."

"That's a lot of effort for a Sunday morning," Greg protested. He hooked one finger around the sheet, and tugged. "We could just stay here."

She slapped his hand. "Swim. Now."

On the way back from the pool, white cotton courtesy robes wrapped around their wet bodies and flimsy white slippers on their wet feet, they had to walk through the lobby to get to the elevators.

"Oh, sir! Sir, excuse me!" cried the woman who had checked them in on Friday evening. She scurried out from behind the counter carrying a narrow white box, looking flustered. "Oh sir, I'm so sorry! This came for you yesterday morning but somehow it was misplaced, and I just found it now. I hope it's not important!"

Greg took the box she held out to him, and looked at the courier's labels. "It's from my sister, so I doubt it's important," he said to her.

"Oh, thank goodness!" she exclaimed, and returned to her domain.

"From Janine?" asked Nicola. She shoved wet hair out of her face and leaned against his arm to look at the box. It was roughly two feet long, and six inches on its other sides. "What do you suppose it is?"

He shrugged, and tucked it under his arm. "No idea. But I'm much more interested in a hot shower and breakfast." In their room, he tossed the box onto the bed and stripped off his robe.

"Aren't you going to open it?" Nicola asked, throwing her own robe onto the chair with his. She was wearing her favorite bikini, the one with ruffles and polka dots.

Greg turned back from the bathroom door, and hitched up his wet swim shorts. "You really want to know what's inside?"

She nodded, and he came back. They sat on the edge of the bed while he flipped open the ends with his thumbs.

The first thing to come out was a piece of paper. "To get you in the mood," they read.

"Mood for what?" wondered Nicola aloud, and leaned closer to see what came out next.

Like Guy Magyck on stage last night, Greg slowly pulled a long piece of shimmering, flame-colored silk from the box.

"What...?" She looked at him, wondering if he had any idea what this was, to see that he was grinning. "What?" she demanded.

"Hold your hands out," he commanded, and she did, palms up and a foot apart.

"Not like that!" He pressed her palms together and quickly looped the silk around her wrists.

She looked at her wrists, then at him.

Greg rattled the box. "Sex toys," he said. "You are now my sex slave."

Nicola burst into laughter. "Yeah, right."

"This is off to a good start," he commented.

"Is that really full of sex toys?" Nicola asked, intrigued, and bent over to look.

"I think 'full of' might be overdoing it, but there's definitely something in here," he replied.

She looked at her hands. "Ah, I see. And I am meant to lie here submissively while you have your wicked way with me, is that it?"

"I opened the box," he said, sounding reasonable. "I tied your hands together. I seem to be the one in charge."

"Shouldn't my hands be tied to the bedpost? So I can't run off?" she asked, and twisted around to look. "No real bedposts, but there is that metal fence-headboard thing."

Greg heaved a sigh. "You are being very difficult, considering you're my slave. All right, lie down and get closer to the headboard."

She wriggled up onto the pillows until she could reach back and grasp the metal with her hands. "How's this?" His fingers played over her wrists and then her hands were free. "Hey, you untied me!"

"Only to do this properly," Greg said with a grin. He leaned over to give her a quick kiss. "Never fear. You'll be quite helpless."

She felt his fingers again, brushing the insides of her wrists and tugging on the silk, and then each of her hands was tied to a different piece of metal. "Ooh, very nice. I can grab hold of one with each hand," she said with approval. Nicola gazed up at him, standing beside the bed and looking down at her with an indulgent smile. "You beast," she said, opening her eyes wide in mock terror. Then giggled.

Greg rolled his eyes. "I think you need to practice your sex slave routine." He folded his arms across the smoothly muscled bulk of his bare chest, and regarded her critically. "That wasn't smart. You're still wearing your bikini."

"And you're still wearing your swim shorts. You're not going to ravish me with them on," she pointed out.

He stripped the shorts off and tossed them aside.

She wriggled her hips. "You'll have to pull it off. With your teeth, maybe."

He snorted. "We'll be here all day if I do that, and the flight's at 2pm." He hooked his thumbs into the bikini bottom, but the fabric was damp and it clung to her skin. "Lift your hips."

Nicola lifted, and twisted, but her tendency to collapse into giggles every time she looked up and saw their contortions reflected in the mirror did not help matters. Greg's backside was startlingly pale compared with the tanned skin of his back, and stood out like a beacon against the red sheets as he fought for leverage on the slippery satin.

"Finally!" grunted Greg, and flung the bikini bottom into a corner. "This dominant alpha male thing is not what it's made out to be."

His expression changed from humorous disgruntlement to something else as he ran his eyes over her, sprawled on the rumpled satin wearing only her bikini top, with her arms pulled back and her hands tied to the fence. He now looked…chagrined.

"How will I get the top off, with your arms tied like that?" he grumbled. "I'll have to cut the straps."

She gave him a severe look. "You harm so much as one polka dot, and I'll tell Kylie you broke my heart."

That stopped him in his tracks. "You'll what?"

"She said that if you ever broke my heart, she'd cut your balls off," Nicola explained. She jerked her chin meaningfully towards his groin.

Greg's hands instinctively covered that vulnerable area, and he shuddered. "Knowing The Man Eater, she'd probably bite them off."

"So the polka dots are safe?" she demanded.

"And the ruffles." He reached down and undid the clasp at the front, and spread the halves of the top wide. "Best I can do."

"Oh, I think you can do better than that," she purred, and wriggled her shoulders so that her breasts wobbled.

Hands on hips, Greg looked down on her, eyebrows raised slightly. He moved his hands behind his back with slow deliberation, and bent to meet her challenge. The heat of his mouth on her damp skin, the feel of his lips and tongue, sent waves of sensation radiating from that single point, and Nicola could no more stop herself arching up to him than she could stop breathing.

Then the contact was broken. Nicola opened her eyes, and blinked, and focused on him.

His eyes were definitely amused. "I'm in charge, remember?"

Nicola sank back against the pillows with a nod. "Just you wait until we swap positions," she said. "I'll have you begging for mercy."

"Is that a threat, or a promise?" Greg asked with a grin. "When you're in charge, will you wear one of those black leather things?" His hands motioned, as if cupping the breasts he didn't have, then skimmed down to his waist. "With laces up the front."

She frowned. "You mean a bustier? Why? Would you like me to?"

He licked his lips and glanced away, then back. "No. Not really. Maybe. If you want to."

She squirmed over to the side of the bed, close enough to run her left foot up his leg. "Is there anything else you don't really care if I wear? Boots? Leather pants?" Her foot reached the top of his thigh and she rubbed her toes against him. Nowhere near as flexible as her fingers, of course, but Nicola was gratified to see that the effect was similar.

Greg grabbed her foot and kissed her big toe. "Stop that. No, not pants, but fishnet stockings would be good. With a seam at the back." His finger tracing up the back of her leg sent shivers through Nicola. He stopped mid-thigh. "But no higher than here."

"Why not?"

"I don't want to spoil the view."

With her knee bent and her foot against his chest, Nicola figured he had a pretty good view at the moment. "Okay. And boots?"

He shook his head. "No, you have great legs, I wouldn't want them covered up. Black stiletto heels. No, red ones."

She laughed. "Greg, I don't own any stilettos, regardless of color! I have never in my life dressed like that! But if you want me to, I will. Why didn't you say anything before?"

His face colored and he ran one hand over his stubbled chin. "I didn't know how you would react. It's only been a few months, after all."

"But you thought that me being tied to the bed would be an ideal time to share this with me?"

"It does seem to have broken the ice," he replied, with a crooked smile.

Nicola had a sudden insight into the benefits of Janine's box of toys. Would he have mentioned this little fantasy if they hadn't found themselves in this position? Although she had to admit that with her hands tied above her head, and her legs apart, she was the only one in a "position."

Greg kissed her grazed knee and released her leg, then sat beside her and picked up the box. "Now, what have we got in here?"

"Surprise me," she said.

Greg held up an ostrich feather, dyed red.

She raised her eyebrows. "Are you going to tickle me into a state of quivering ecstasy? Or merely dust me?"

He shook the tip of the feather behind her ear, and she screeched and pulled her shoulders up. Greg traced it along her neck and around each breast, and Nicola writhed. "Stop!" She pulled her knees up and twisted onto her side, protecting her stomach, only for the feather to brush against her bottom. "Stop, stop!" she laughed. "Ravish me if you will, you brute, but no more feathers!"

He shrugged and tossed it to one side, and Nicola straightened out again, still smiling. "What other instruments of sexual sadism have you got in there?"

It was a slender piece of finely worked leather, with a small flexible tab at one end. Greg flicked it against his palm as he stood. "Riding crop," he said with satisfaction. "Now you're in trouble, wench."

"Wench?" Nicola repeated. "Is that customary terminology in these situations?"

"How should I know?" He swished the crop in a swift downwards arc and it made a whistling sound, followed by a loud crack. "Ow! Holy Christ! Ow!" Greg flung the crop away and hopped in a circle on one leg.

"Greg! What's wrong? What happened?" She twisted and pulled against the ties that held her, but all she saw was his naked form disappearing into the bathroom. "Greg!"

"It's okay," came his voice. "I'm fine."

She heard the water running, and then silence, and then he hobbled out again, bent over and holding a wet facecloth against his calf.

"What?" Nicola cried. "Show me!"

He pulled the facecloth away to reveal an angry red welt four inches long, with a fine track of blood oozing from it.

"Oh!" she exclaimed.

"What sort of sick bastard would ever get turned on by hitting a woman with that thing?" he demanded, sitting on the edge of the bed. His face was red and his jaw clenched so tightly that the muscles bunched up by his ears. "Imagine if I had hit you with that, even in play, having no idea what it could do?"

"Maybe you should spank me instead," she suggested, looking as naughty as she could manage. Anything to lighten that dark fury on his face.

"What!" He turned to her as if not believing what he'd heard, then began to smile.

"I've been a very bad girl, and I must be punished." She managed to get the words out and not laugh at the absurdity of saying such a thing.

"Punished, huh?" Greg's eyes tracked slowly over her body, and he flexed the fingers of his right hand. "Alas," he said, "if I were actually tempted to spank you anywhere, you're lying on it."

Nicola got a good grip on the headboard, tucked her knees up again and swiveled her hips so her bottom flashed at him, then twisted over so she was on her back again, laughing.

"Oh no you don't!" he said, laughing too, and climbed onto his knees so he could wrestle her onto her side again. He slapped a hand against one buttock. "Take that!"

She looked back at him. "You call that a spank? All those muscles, and that's the best you can do?"

Greg's eyes glittered and his mouth narrowed, and for one uneasy moment Nicola reflected that goading him into spanking her the day after that argument might not be such a good idea if he was still mad at her. He didn't seem to be mad, but....

His palm whacked against her bottom with two sharp smacks.

"Ow!" she screeched, as pain flared red-hot. "Owwww!"

"Nicola!" he cried. "Oh my darling, did I hurt you? Stop howling, people will think I'm beating you!"

She was tied to the bed, her bottom on fire, and he was afraid people would think he was beating her? Nicola's howls veered into uneven laughs.

The bed heaved as he jumped off, then nothing.

"Greg?"

Something hard and cold pressed against her flaming skin, and she shrieked. "What the hell is that?"

The bottle of white wine from the mini-bar was dangled in front of her face, and Nicola exploded into laughter. "Put it back on my bottom, please!"

Greg rolled the bottle back and forth over the painful area, stopping every so often to kiss her tingling skin. "Better?"

She nodded. "I hope you wipe that off before you put it back," she said with a grin.

He tossed the bottle onto the thick carpet, along with the

discarded feather and the riding crop.

Nicola rolled onto her back again, and looked up into his worried eyes. "Hey, it's all right," she said softly. "Took your mind off your leg, didn't it?"

With a startled look he touched his calf and grimaced, and then smiled.

His body was a welcome, familiar weight as he stretched out beside her, entwining his legs with hers. He propped himself on a bent elbow, his other arm around her waist. She gazed at him, before his face went all fuzzy as he leaned closer to kiss her.

"You are the most amazing woman," he said, nuzzling below one ear.

She wriggled under him. "Why don't you untie me, and we'll do this properly?"

"May as well," he said. "You make a bad submissive sex slave, I've noticed."

"We'll see how good you are the next time!" Nicola retorted. "When I don my dominatrix outfit and tie you up."

His face lit with laughter. "If you tied me up, the knots would take hours to undo!"

"And yours won't?" She yanked her arms against the bonds, which held firm.

Greg reached one hand over her head, and in the mirror above them, she saw him pull on the loose end of the silk cord. The knot unraveled and her hands fell free. "I told you I knew knots," he said. "You could have done that yourself at any time. I would never restrain you, Nicola. I think I would do almost anything to keep you, but never against your will."

His lips traveled down her neck and along her collarbone, and she wormed her fingers into the thick warmth of his hair. "I want a willing partner, not a submissive doll. Someone who takes as much pleasure in what I do to her as she does in giving pleasure to me." His fingers were gentle, his mouth insistent, and she strained closer, wanting more of him. "I love that little sound you make when I do that," he whispered, "and I love the way you run your fingers through my hair and pull my head closer to tell me you want me to do it. You could never do that if you were tied up."

Chapter 15

"AND SO YOU did not gamble away your life savings in Sin City?" asked Hélène, from one end of an overstuffed sofa in her living room.

"We only went to one casino," replied Nicola, from the other end. "Neither of us is really interested in gambling. I found it fascinating to watch the other people. Some of them sit there for hours, feeding the slot machines. They get their food and drink brought to them. I think if they could get a toilet delivered, too, they'd never leave!"

Hélène reached for her glass of wine on the coffee table. She smiled as the cheers and groans came to them from the next room, where Antoine, Philippe and Greg were playing something on Philippe's video game console. "They never grow up, do they?"

Nicola smiled and shook her head. "Can you imagine us playing pretend hockey, or basketball, or whatever they're doing in there, with a computer, and taking it so seriously?"

"I cannot imagine us doing it at all, seriously or otherwise. But it is good to hear Greg laughing. He is quiet tonight. He did not seem to enjoy the *boeuf bourguignon*, and I know it is his favorite," Hélène said, concern in her eyes.

"More left over for you and Philippe for tomorrow night," suggested Nicola. "Since Antoine will be at that conference for the next few days, you'd have to cook otherwise."

Hélène made a delicate moue of horror at the very thought. "No, tomorrow night we will have pizza. Big, thick pizza dripping with mozzarella cheese and laden with spicy pepperoni, scented with the cardboard boxes in which they will be delivered." She winked conspiratorially at Nicola. "Antoine is convinced that pizza is an American abomination, so Philippe and I can have it only when he is away."

They laughed together at the idea of Antoine as the self-appointed food police.

"Maybe that's why Philippe didn't eat much tonight, either," suggested Nicola. "He's saving himself for that pizza."

"Perhaps. He said he has a sore stomach, also. I hope he has not caught a virus. But Greg," said Hélène, picking up the conversation, "I thought he refused to dwell on your situation. Being the strong man, and believing only in a happy ending."

"As the days drag on, it's all anybody dwells on. It's only Wednesday, and everyone knows we won't hear anything until Friday, at the earliest, but my whole family phoned me today. Edward and Janine called Greg," said Nicola. She hugged a cushion, resting her chin on it. "And the closer it gets, the less sure any of us is about that happy ending. Even Greg, although he refuses to discuss it. I tried to get him to talk about it on Saturday, and we ended up in a huge fight."

"Did you? Greg seems too easygoing for what you describe as a 'huge fight.'"

Nicola grimaced. "You wouldn't have thought that if you'd seen him go marching across that desert."

Hélène toyed with the stem of her glass. "How will you find out?"

"The results, you mean?"

She nodded.

"We asked for email, because it's quicker. They'll also mail a hard copy," explained Nicola.

Restlessness drove her to her feet and she wandered around the large room. Tonight, the pale green silk wallpaper and furniture in soothing shades did not have their customary relaxing effect on her. In front of the glass doors leading to the balcony, she paused and looked out. The city spread its sparkling nighttime finery before her, disappearing into the inky nothing of the bay and then reappearing on the other side. "You have such a great view."

Hélène did not reply to the meaningless pleasantry. "If it is a happy ending, what will you do?"

"Get Mom back to looking for venues! Book the church, and email everyone with the news of Greg's father's full recovery." Nicola smiled, but it was strained.

"Aaagggghhhhh!"

Hearing Greg's bellow of disappointment, Nicola smiled for real.

"And if it is not a happy ending?"

Dull emptiness washed through her, too devastating even for tears. She shook her head blindly. "Part. Never see each other again." Throw myself off the bridge, she wanted to add, but knew she would never have the courage for such a thing.

"Why?"

Nicola stared at Hélène in incomprehension. "What do you mean, 'why'? Do you really need to ask why I can no longer be with Greg if he's my half-brother?" She heard her voice rising in something that might have been hysteria, and took a long, shaky breath.

"Yes, *chérie*, I do." Hélène rose and came to stand beside Nicola. "Why, in and of itself, is it so terrible that you stay with the man you love, even if you have the same mother?"

"He…we…Hélène, it's wrong!" spluttered Nicola, unable in her shock to articulate all the reasons why it was so very wrong.

Hélène's cool gray eyes regarded Nicola. "Who says?"

"Everyone! Society. The church. It's just one of those things. A rule that can't be broken."

"Ah, so it is wrong only because other people say it is wrong?" Hélène tapped one manicured nail against her chin, as if considering the merits of her argument.

"You can't have children with your brother!" Nicola exclaimed.

Sympathy radiated from Hélène. "No. That is true. But you can adopt other children."

Nicola shook her head, trying to clear the chaos of thoughts. "What are you saying, Hélène?"

"I am saying that if no one knows you are brother and sister, and you do not have children, where is the harm? Whom do you hurt?" she persisted. "Will society, or the church, crumble and fall because two people who love each other stay together?"

Nicola groped behind her, found the back of the armchair and collapsed into it. She gaped up at her friend. This was not something Nicola would ever have considered, and the cold rationality of what Hélène suggested stopped her breath.

Hélène kneeled on the carpet and took Nicola's hands in her own. "It would demand extraordinary strength from you. From both of you. The test of your love might prove too great. But, *chérie*, surely to be with Greg in this way would be better than not being with him at all?"

Somewhere deep inside, hope flickered. "But...." Her voice died away, while she considered. "Some people know already. My God, my mother would die!" She stumbled to a halt in the confusion of mothers. "Gwen."

"I know you mean Gwen. She is your mother, always. Yes." Hélène nodded. "Some people do know, and some of them may not accept. Like a parent who struggles to accept a homosexual child. They will see it as very, very wrong. They may refuse to have anything more to do with you."

Who? Nicola wondered, her family springing into her mind as clearly as if they stood here in Hélène's living room. Who among the people whose love she took for granted might turn their backs? Her mother, she was certain, would disapprove very strongly of Nicola having any sort of romantic relationship with her half-brother – but did that mean Gwen would reject her? She had no idea how Arthur, solid and gently humorous, would react. Stuffy Bill, Alison who seemed focused only on her family, and their spouses and children. Her extended family, her colleagues, her friends? Hélène, obviously, would stand by her, but what about her own husband and son?

Nicola's head fell into her hands, her hair brushing against her cheeks. "Hélène, I don't think I could do that."

"Not even to keep Greg?"

"Keep Greg, and lose everyone else?" she whispered in anguish. "What kind of a deal is that?"

Hélène's fingers were gentle as she tucked back Nicola's hair. "A deal with the devil, I fear. Sometimes, that is what it takes."

A loud shout of triumph from next door and Greg strutted into the room, hands clasped over his head in victory. "Yes! Champion of the world!" he exclaimed. Then he frowned. "Nicola?"

She forced a weak smile. "It's okay. A headache."

"We should probably go, anyway," said Greg. "Philippe here has soccer practice before school and needs his sleep. Though if he plays it for real as well as he plays it on the game console, he'll be fine." He clapped a hand against the boy's thin shoulder, and Philippe beamed.

Outside, it was crisp and cool, a hint of damp in the air. They strolled the two blocks to Nicola's apartment hand-in-hand, in what passed for the still quiet of the night on California Street. Her spirits picked up. What a crazy idea of Hélène! She chuckled softly in wonder that she had even considered it.

"Your head better?" Greg asked.

She nodded.

But in bed, her arm around Greg's waist and her body pressed against his just enough to feel the rise and fall of his chest as he slept, the crazy idea wouldn't go away.

* *

Nicola stared unseeing at the monitor, her hands motionless on the keyboard. Around her the background sounds of people talking and phones ringing, the pit-a-pit of fingers on keyboards, were so familiar they barely registered. She was writing up that bordello hotel in Vegas, or, rather, that's what she should have been doing. Her mind kept flitting off to last night's conversation. It had been doing that all day.

She had gone for a walk during her lunch break, needing to think about it without the distraction of work, or of Greg. Hands thrust deep in her pockets, head bowed against the wind, Nicola had walked block after block. And come to no conclusion. One moment she would decide yes, to stay with Greg she would give it all up; the next moment it would be no, how could she possibly abandon everyone and everything, how could she live a lie for the rest of her life?

And what would Greg think? She hadn't mentioned this to him. She wouldn't, until she knew in her own mind that it was something she could do.

She had returned from her walk windblown and cold. She was no closer to a decision, but something quite awful had occurred to her on the way back to the office.

Nicola glanced around, guiltily, as if people could read her thoughts, or there was a camera behind her, or the newspaper had installed keystroke-logging software that recorded everything she typed. She clicked on the internet browser, and glanced around again.

In the search bar, she began to type. "Incest California law"

"Nicky, have you seen this?"

Nicola fumbled for the alt-tab command to switch applications. She had done it thousands of times, without thought or even looking, but now she stared at the keyboard as if she had never seen one before.

A competitor's weekend fashion magazine was thrust under her nose. "Look!" insisted Kylie. "This is a fashion show in Madrid. Their writer got the front row, and I was way at the back! I'm going to phone that place and give them a piece of my mind!" Off she flounced.

Nicola sighed, and brought back the browser. A minute later, she sat back, her heart thumping and her breath coming fast.

Illegal. It was illegal to marry your half-sibling. The point, apparently, was to prevent having children with birth defects – but there was no opt-out clause if you agreed not to have children. No get out of jail free card.

Prison!

The quiet meow of a cat startled her, and it took her a moment to recognize Hélène's ringtone.

"Nicola, can you come?" Hélène's voice was strained, and closer to tears than Nicola had ever heard.

"Where? What's the matter?"

"It is Philippe. He collapsed at school; the doctor is doing tests now. She thinks it is his appendix." Scratchy silence for a moment, and in the background a faint announcement. "I do not like to take you from work like this, but Antoine is away and I am a coward where my baby is concerned."

Nicola gripped the phone more tightly. "Hélène, of course I'll come! But he'll be fine, you'll see. That's fairly routine," she soothed. "What hospital are you at?"

She hung up soon after, and started gathering her things. It was 4.15pm, so not too outrageously early to call it a day. "Max,

I have to head off." Her voice was muffled, for she was doubled over to swap her heels for her street shoes. "If anyone needs me, give them my cell number, will you?"

Max swung his chair around. "Is anything wrong? Is Greg okay?"

"He's fine. It's my friend's son." She stuffed page proofs into her bag and swung it over her shoulder. "See you tomorrow."

Outside, scanning the street for a taxi, she called Greg and told him what had happened.

"Poor kid!" he sympathized. "I thought he didn't look too good last night. I had mine out when I was about his age, so you can tell him from me that he'll be fine."

"You never told me that."

The warm sound of his laugh brought a smile to her face. "It didn't seem important. Let me see.... I broke my right forearm when I was 16, playing football. I don't think I told you that, either. But I don't want you to think I'm keeping things from you!"

"Idiot," she chided, her voice soft. "Look, about tonight. I don't know how late I'll be."

"Don't worry. The other woman in my life needs some attention too, so I'll stay there tonight."

She shook the phone, not sure that she had heard what she thought she had heard. "The other woman?"

"*Drifter*, of course! Good God, Nicola, you can't have thought I meant a real woman!" His voice held amused disbelief, and he added, "Now who's being the idiot?"

"Funny. See you tomorrow. I love you."

"I love you, too. But you know that, I hope."

Nicola smiled as she climbed into the empty taxi that had finally appeared. Yes, she knew it. The taxi paused to let a speeding police car go past, sirens wailing and lights flashing, and that word slammed into her mind again. Illegal.

She found Hélène in a waiting room, picking apart an empty coffee cup with nervous fingers and staring at the wall. Her face was pale and drawn, but other than that, she was her usual immaculate self. She swung anxious eyes towards Nicola as she neared, then jumped up when she recognized her.

Nicola hugged her. "Well?"

"It is the appendix, the tests confirmed it. Philippe is in surgery right now," said Hélène.

"Sit down," urged Nicola. "He'll be okay. Greg said to tell you that he had his appendix out at that age, and look at him now." She figured Hélène needed the reassurance more than Philippe. The boy was tougher than his wiry frame indicated and, at any rate, he was anesthetized at the moment.

Hélène smiled. "That is kind of Greg."

"Did you get hold of Antoine yet?"

"Yes, and he tells me not to be such a worrywart." She pronounced the word with care, but it still sounded odd in her accent.

Nicola's lips curved with delight. "A worrywart? You're not going to tell me Antoine used that word?"

The apprehension in Hélène's gray eyes lightened. "We were speaking French, but he said that word in English. He is picking up an alarming amount of American slang for someone who so admires the Académie française. Ah, that is like the watchdog of the French language," she explained.

They fell silent. Other people in the little waiting room spoke in quiet tones, and a woman cried in a man's arms. A wall-mounted television played with no sound, people and places sliding across the screen without meaning. A floral arrangement on a table, perhaps intended for a patient's room, released the faint scent of roses, all but drowned out by the smells of the hospital itself.

Nicola tried to imagine what Hélène was going through, or, worse, what the mother of a much more ill child would be going through. Helplessness, fear, anxiety. But she had no child, so could only guess at the pervasive, consuming depths of those emotions. The cold realization came that she may never have a child, not one of her own flesh and blood, depending on those test results. She was swept by a rush of love for her parents, who had never in any way indicated that she was less precious to them than their own flesh-and-blood children.

She gripped Hélène's hand. "He'll be fine," she insisted, as if picking up an earlier conversation.

"I know," Hélène said. "Deep down, I know. And I know he is not a baby any more, and he would be mortified to have me fuss over him when he wakes up. But even when he is 60 and I am 87, I will worry! It is what mothers do. You'll see."

Nicola sighed. "Will I? It seems unlikely. If the results are negative, then it's full steam ahead in the baby-making department," she said, and could not resist laughing at the idea of her and Greg having sex even more often than they had now. It was like a drug: the more they got of each other, the more they wanted. It was difficult to imagine that future time when this consuming passion would fade, as it did for all couples; when the sight of Greg would not make her want to rip his clothes off. "But if not, there's only adoption, and who knows how long that could take? If we do as you suggest."

"Have you talked to Greg yet?"

She shook her head. "I don't even know how I feel about your idea. And I think he's more…rigid, I guess is the word, in his outlook. But Hélène, it's against the law! Did you know that?"

"*Mon Dieu*, no! You are sure?"

"I looked an hour ago. California Penal Code 285. Up to three years in prison for marrying your sibling. Prison!" That same cold fear flooded through her.

Hélène frowned. "And then what?"

Nicola's mind was a blank. "Then what?"

"Once the government in its wisdom has punished you for your love, what happens? Is the marriage annulled? And living together, is that illegal?" pressed Hélène. "When the couple is released from prison, what is to stop them cohabiting? Or not marrying in the first place?"

"You are the most pragmatic person I have ever met!" exclaimed Nicola, torn between admiration and disbelief. "I would never have thought of all that. I don't know." She shook her head in bafflement. "Oh, but Hélène, I'm talking about my own troubles, when I came here to be supportive and helpful to you! I'm so sorry."

"You are being supportive, simply by being here. And talking about you helps to take my mind off Philippe," Hélène assured her. "I wonder if I could bring you croissants in prison?"

"Hélène!"

The sobs of the woman behind them stopped, mercifully. Nicola had opened her mouth to speak when the woman shrieked, once, a drawn-out note of denial and loss that raised sudden goose bumps on Nicola's skin. She turned to see the woman being led out of the room by the man, followed by a doctor.

She and Hélène exchanged a sober glance.

"He'll be fine," she said again, as if the sheer repetition would make it true.

* *

Greg was in *Drifter*'s sail locker, wrestling the spinnaker back into place, when his phone rang. He considered ignoring it, for the sail was awkward and the locker was small, but it was the trilling birdcall ringtone he had assigned to Nicola. With a muttered curse, he dropped the sail and scrambled into the cabin.

As he snatched up the phone, he saw the time: 11.30pm. Later than he had realized.

"Hi."

"Hi to you. You sound out of breath. Have you installed a running track on your boat?"

She was a fount of witty little quips like that. Greg rolled his eyes. "No. I've spent the evening checking over my spare sails for tears, or mildew. I was in the middle of stuffing the last one back into place when you interrupted me."

"Sorry." She didn't sound it, but he forgave her nonetheless. "How's Philippe?"

Her laugh was a tinkle of bells in his ear. "Lacking an appendix, but awake again. He was surprisingly happy to have his mother make a fuss. The hospital told Hélène there was no need for her to stay overnight, so we left. I got home a few minutes ago."

Greg considered going over, but by the time he sorted out that spinnaker and drove into the city, she would be asleep. "I'll miss you tonight," he said.

"I'll miss you, too. The bed looks empty without you in it. I'll have to dig out my hot water bottle to warm it up, I guess," she teased.

"Warming it wasn't what I had in mind," Greg said, smiling.

Her laugh this time was low and husky, the one that made him want to fling her onto the nearest bed, or sofa, or table even. Christ, that time on her dining table, when with one thrust of his arm he had swept everything to the floor and then hoisted her up. He could see her now, eyes unfocused and lips parted, her head flung back as he…his hand rubbed against the front of his jeans. Just thinking about her was enough to arouse him. Phone sex. They'd never done that. He had a startling vision of her lying on her bed, naked, her phone against her ear and her hand between her legs.

"Greg? You still there?"

He swallowed. "Yeah."

"You sound breathless again."

Would she go along with it? She was…certainly not prudish, but certainly not adventurous, in her approach to sex, he had found. She hadn't minded being tied to the bed in Vegas, but she hadn't taken it seriously, either. "Jogging on the spot," he said. "It's cold in here." Cold, think of cold things. Ice, snow, blizzards, gelato, beer, anything.

"Greg…."

"What?"

"Nothing. Goodnight. Sleep well."

Sleep was going to be a long time coming tonight. "Goodnight."

Chapter 16

IT WAS WORSE today than yesterday. All Nicola could think of was that DNA test, and Hélène's suggestion. Minutes crept by, or were frozen entirely. And now her sister was on the phone, again.

"For God's sake, Alison, will you stop calling me every five minutes?" exclaimed Nicola. "No, we don't know yet, and yes, I'll tell you when we do."

Alison's voice was aggrieved. "Back off, Nicola, we're all concerned. You've been snapping at everyone for days. You said it would be today, after all!"

"I said it would be today at the earliest," said Nicola, carefully enunciating each word. "I can't make them go any faster!"

"Do you suppose they lost your sample?" wondered Alison out loud. "Just think how awful that would be!"

Nicola, to whom this catastrophe had not even occurred, said, "I have to go. I have work to do. Goodbye."

She swiped at her smartphone's display, longing for the satisfaction that came with slamming down a receiver. Placing the phone back on her desk, she met the worried brown eyes of Max.

"You okay, Nicky?"

She resisted the urge to tell him to mind his own business. "My sister's driving me crazy. You know how they are!" she said with false lightness.

"No, I don't have a sister," he replied, forehead still furrowed. "You sure nothing's wrong? You've been on edge all week."

One. Two. She wasn't going to make it to 10. "She's driving me really crazy. Incredibly crazy. Round the bend, bonkers, howling at the moon crazy. Okay?"

She regretted the look of hurt surprise that appeared on his face. Max was nice, and he behaved as well towards her after she had turned down his date suggestions a year ago as he had before. He didn't deserve to be on the receiving end of her stretched nerves. "Sorry, Max," Nicola said. "It's nothing, really."

Nothing. Yes, if you could call it nothing that her whole future rode on this stupid test and it was impossible to forget it for a second. She had checked her email 50 times since 9am, refreshed the page and sent herself a message just to ensure it still worked. Alison had phoned five times, her mother twice, her father once. Even Bill's wife had called, something that rarely happened. Hélène, bless her, had sent one text message of support from the hospital and left her alone.

She had heard from everyone today except Greg. She hadn't seen him since yesterday morning at her apartment. Was he at his desk, working industriously at whatever it was he did all day (and she was ashamed to admit that she had little idea of what that was)? Having determined he could do nothing to influence the outcome, had he sensibly dismissed the problem from his mind? She envied him that ability.

"Nicky."

She looked back at Max, who pointed in the direction behind her.

As if her thoughts had conjured him from the air, Greg stood at the end of her row of cubicles. He was talking to someone, but the tap of his fingers against his leg gave away his impatience. His eyes flickered to her as she turned and his face softened into a brief smile. The other man saw it, and turned, then gave Nicola a wave and Greg a quick handshake, and was gone.

She watched as he covered the 20 or so feet between them, moving with a lightness that had at first surprised her in such a solid, muscular man. He wore that pinstriped suit that fit his body so well, a red-pink-yellow-striped tie and a white shirt, and Nicola's heart clenched in her chest at the thought that this man, who loved her and who made her breath catch just at the unexpected sight of him, could be lost to her forever.

Greg put one hand on the back of her chair and leaned down to say in her ear, "I can't take any more of this. I can't concentrate, I can't think of anything but what might be in your inbox. Can you leave now?"

Nicola had an article to finish writing and two more to edit, a breezy editorial for the website to write and photographs to commission, all of which should have been completed yesterday. "Yes."

She reached to turn off her computer, then brought up her private email and refreshed the page again. Nothing. Their eyes met, and he shrugged.

On the street, she asked, "Where are we going? What did you have in mind?"

"Timbuktu? The middle of the Australian Outback? Anywhere without a cell phone signal!" he said. "If it's not my family, it's Debbie, every five minutes."

She smiled in understanding. "Me, too. Alison accused me of snapping at her, and then I took it out on Max by snapping at him."

Greg put an arm around her and they began to walk towards where he had parked his car. "He'll get over it," he said, dismissing Max. "There is something I would like to do."

She gave him a questioning look.

"Let's go for a run."

Inquiry turned into astonishment. "A run!"

"I want to do something that requires no thought. Just pure, physical action. Will you take me on that run you do with Hélène?" Greg asked.

"In the Presidio?"

He nodded.

There was enough daylight left if they were quick, and not thinking for a while was an attractive prospect. "Do you have enough gear at my place?"

"Most of what I own seems to be at your place," he said, with a wry smile. "Why do you think I'm wearing this hideous tie today? All the others are in your closet."

Nicola laughed, and opened the passenger door. "I did wonder why I'd never seen it before!"

* *

She never took days off work for no reason, never called in sick if she wasn't actually sick, so for Nicola, being out of the office on a sunny early-winter Friday afternoon had a feeling of wickedness. You are so sad, she told herself, pounding along the packed dirt of the track, if this is the best you can do for wicked.

Behind her were the sounds of Greg's breaths, deep but ragged, and of his running shoes striking the ground. The tangy scent of pine trees and the bite of the ocean hung in the cold air as they ran though the deep shade along this stretch.

"Stop for a second!" he called.

Nicola came to an awkward halt, regretting the loss of the swift mindless rhythm of the run. Greg was down on one knee, fiddling with a shoelace, and she jogged back to join him.

"That's the second time your lace has come undone," she observed. "Shall I tie them for you? In double knots?"

He looked up, self-conscious mischief in his blue eyes, his chest heaving. "Then what will I use for an excuse to catch my breath?" Greg stood up, hands on hips and head back. "You're like a gazelle! It's no wonder you caught up to me in Death Valley so quickly."

She stepped closer and took one of his hands in hers. Turning it over, she kissed his palm. "If you fall, I promise to look after you just like you did for me."

Greg's arms slipped around her waist. "It's a shame you have only a shower. Otherwise, you could certainly look after me."

Nicola kissed him, but quickly, then slapped one hand against his backside. "Come on, we've got to be fast to finish this before it gets dark. And you've still got the stairs."

Scorn flitted across his face. "How tough can stairs be?"

"Wait two minutes, and you'll find out. Every French swear word I know, I learned from Hélène at the top of those stairs."

* *

It was true; her apartment had only a shower stall. But it was a large shower stall, and two people with no interest in the concept of personal space could fit into it easily.

On her knees, Nicola ran the soapy sponge up his calf, scrubbing and scouring, then switched hands and moved her attention to his other leg. His fingers were in her hair, kneading and massaging, working the shampoo into her scalp. With her eyes necessarily closed as suds and water ran onto her face, Nicola moved the sponge higher by feel alone.

"Careful with that thing," Greg warned. "It's rough, and you're near somewhere very delicate."

She patted one hand along his leg in exploration. "So I am!"

He got his hands under her arms and pulled her to her feet, rinsing off the shampoo in the spray of water, then pressed her against the tiles. She gasped at the coldness of them against her back after the heat of the water. It was cut off by his mouth against hers, urgent and demanding. With his knee, he pushed her legs apart, then cupped both hands around her bottom and lifted her against him.

"I can't wait," he whispered hoarsely. "I want you so much. Always."

"I am yours. Always."

* *

They were on the sofa, his arm around her shoulders. The television was on, showing something that called itself a comedy, but neither of them laughed.

"Do you think I should check again?"

Greg shook his head, and brushed his lips against her hair. "Too late now. It's long past business hours."

She sighed in frustration. "Two more days of this."

"Are you sure you don't mind about the weekend?"

"I'm sure. Peter will turn 10 only once, after all. You agreed ages ago to this men-only sailing trip. It would be so unfair to him to break it off now," Nicola said. She leaned forward for her mug of tea, turning her head so that her hair fell forward and hid her face. A large swallow, and the smile was in place as she turned back to Greg. "You have fun."

"I should go back to the boat tonight. She hasn't been out in a while, and I need to do a few things before they arrive. I thought I could make a start last night, but the sails took longer than I expected." His arm tightened around her. "I hate to leave you. But I'll be back here Sunday night. Promise."

She laughed, and if it was forced, he didn't seem to notice. "Don't be silly. I'll be fine."

"What will you do? Will you go to your parents?" His fingers drew lazy circles on the sleeve of her sweater.

"Sunday afternoon, probably. Tomorrow I'll go into the office for a few hours. I left a lot of work on my desk."

Greg kissed her forehead. "Sorry. I dragged you away this afternoon, didn't I?"

"I wanted to be with you," Nicola said, a simple statement of fact. She looked around, then frowned. "And I really have to do something about this apartment."

He looked around too, and frowned, but he sounded puzzled when he asked, "Why? What's wrong with it?"

"It's filthy, for one thing!" she exclaimed. "I haven't been here for the past two weekends, which is when I usually give it a good clean." Nicola swiped a finger over the top of the coffee table and showed him the smear of dust.

Greg laughed. "My little housewife."

The word "wife" hit the floor like a lead weight.

"Greg," she began hesitantly, but he put his finger on her mouth.

"Don't, Nicola. Please, let's not go over it again." His eyes were sad, but his face was stern.

She jerked her head away with an exclamation of impatience. "This isn't about that. Well it is, sort of, but not." Oh God. Now that she finally had steeled herself to bring it up, she was bungling it. She rushed on. "Let's say it is positive, have—"

"Nicola!" Her name came out somewhere between a groan and a command.

"Have you thought about that? Have you considered what we might do?" she demanded.

"Do?" His face was blank. "There's nothing we can do."

She brought her legs up and sat cross-legged, facing him. "But there is!"

He eyed her with suspicion, as if she had spiked her chamomile tea with gin when his back was turned and that accounted for her words. "Good God, Nicola, what could we possibly do? Other than say goodbye?"

"We could not tell anyone."

"What!"

"What if no one knew?" she asked urgently. "What if we went away somewhere, Boston maybe, where we don't know anyone, and didn't say anything?"

"Boston?" he repeated, with the air of a man picking out the only word that made sense. "You want to move to Boston?"

She shook her head, and then brushed the hair away. "No, I don't want to move to Boston! I don't want to leave San Francisco! But if we have to, if we have to go someplace where no one will know, and start fresh, then I will!"

His mouth hung open, and a red flush crept up from the neck of his sweatshirt. "You would marry your brother, and have his children, and not tell anyone?" The laugh was harsh. "Christ, Nicola, I think not telling anyone would be the least wrong part of that scenario!"

"We couldn't have children, obviously," she said quietly. "Not our own. We could adopt."

"I don't want to adopt! I don't want someone else's child, I want mine. Who knows what it would be like when it grew up?" he demanded.

His words were like a slap. "It would be like me," she said, with all the dignity she could manage.

The remorse was plain on his face, but so was the anger. "I didn't mean it to sound like that. Of course not."

She plunged on. "We couldn't marry, either. It's illegal. We could go to prison."

Greg stared at her and ran his fingers through his hair, so that it stuck up in spikes. "Illegal! Holy Christ, there goes my CPA license, on top of everything. Or if not, no one in their right mind would ever hire me after a background check." He flung his arms out. "Or wait, am I supposed to stay at home with the adopted kids while you support us all? On an editor's salary?"

"If we lived together, and didn't tell anyone, it might be all right," Nicola said, speaking quickly, getting the words out before he could protest again.

"All right? It is definitely not all right!" He fell back against the cushion, shook his head and sat up again. "But this is crazy! How did you ever come up with such an idea?"

"It was Hélène's idea," she admitted.

"Oh, that figures!" he drawled, disdain dripping from the words. "Trust a cold-blooded French atheist to think of a scheme like that!"

Nicola's breath came fast and shallow. "How dare you call her that!"

"You're right. I have no idea if she's an atheist." Arms crossed, mouth set in a grim line, Greg looked at her with eyes like chips of blue ice.

She was losing him; she could see that. "But, Greg, if no one knew—"

"I would know! You would know!"

"All I know is that I love you, and I won't give you up without a fight."

His hands closed around her upper arms like vices. "It would be wrong, Nicola! Can't you see that? It's not a matter of no one knowing, or even of it being illegal. It's a matter of right and wrong."

Her hands stroked his. "Why?" she asked. "Why is it wrong?"

"It's a sin!"

That brought her up as abruptly as if she had run headfirst into a tree in the Presidio. "A sin?" Of all the objections her mind had raised to Hélène's suggestion, this had not been one. "How can it be a sin? How can what we feel for each other be a sin? Is this a sin?" She took one of his hands and placed it on her breast.

Greg jerked his hand away as if her breast was a wasps' nest, rather than a part of her body that he had kissed and caressed more times than she could count. "Incest is a sin," he stated.

Something snapped inside her. "You damned hypocrite! Or is it that you have a flexible interpretation of sin? The thought of incest didn't stop you at any time in the past two weeks! An hour ago in the shower it sure wasn't incest, or a sin, or if it was you certainly didn't seem to care!" Nicola said, her voice shrill and cutting. "We could face prison, and you're worried about religion? I'd forgotten that your God would have a say in this!"

He rose to his feet in an abrupt movement, bumping the coffee table and knocking over the mug of her cold tea.

"Don't," he warned.

She was standing now, too, fists clenched. "Don't what? Don't mock what I don't understand? You're right, I don't understand! I don't understand how you can refuse to consider what might be our only chance."

"And I don't understand how you are able to consider such a thing! It is…heinous. A travesty of what our life should be."

Even during the argument in Death Valley, his eyes had not held this implacable coldness.

"A…travesty," she said slowly.

"What doth it profit a man if he gain the whole world, but lose his soul?" Greg said.

She backed away, away from him, and against a bookcase. Her little glass model of the Leaning Tower of Pisa crashed to the floor. "You're quoting the Bible at me? Oh, that's just great," she taunted. "Put me up on a scale with God. Of course I'm going to lose! Flesh-and-blood Nicola on one side, faith-in-things-unseen God on the other."

"I am not weighing you up against God!" he snapped. "I am trying to point out that a man must value his own honor, his sense of himself, higher than some other things!"

"Higher than me?" she whispered, stricken. "Higher than us?"

His face fell, and he took an unsteady step.

"Nicola. Please try to understand," he pleaded. He held out one hand to her.

Nicola took one step, and her fingertips touched his. "Do you remember, in Vegas, after you untied me, you said that you would do anything to keep me? Greg, what if this is what you have to do?"

His hand fell to his side. "Almost, Nicola. I said almost anything. Not this."

Greg turned on one heel and strode out of the room. She heard the door open, and close. She was alone.

* *

By the time Greg began to walk across the parking lot to the marina, the shock had faded. Every other roiling emotion, though, was as alive as if he had heard her grotesque suggestion a moment ago. Not tell anyone! That was the best part, he thought with bitterness. If no one knew, that would make everything all right.

Laughter and music spilled from the yacht club, and he glanced at the brightly lit building. He envied them. Carefree people getting happily drunk. He would like to get drunk, to wipe this crazy evening and the past two weeks from his mind, just for a while. Greg's steps faltered. No, not drunk, not with a day on the water with Sam and Peter tomorrow, but a drink or two would do no harm.

The bar was the same as any other yacht club bar he had ever seen, with too little ambiance and too many people. Greg shouldered his way through the crowd and asked for a scotch on the rocks. He didn't drink spirits often, straight spirits even less often, and he coughed as the liquid burned its way down his throat. The alcohol went straight to his head, a rush up along his spine and then a small explosion in his brain. He took another sip. Another. The edge of his emotions began to dull.

"You want a refill?" asked the bartender, gesturing with the bottle.

Greg nodded.

He swirled the ice around this one, and paused to inhale that smoky scent before drinking.

"You look lonely."

Greg couldn't believe it. Incensed, disappointed, distressed, confused – yeah, he could believe he looked any of those. What he did not look was lonely. As pick-up lines went, it needed help.

She was around 40, he guessed, with hair just too blonde and skin just too smooth. She was eyeing him up and down, and smiled when he met her gaze in what he assumed was meant to be a seductive manner.

"I'm not," he said, and looked away.

"Ah," she said, and stepped closer. "Married, then. What a shame."

He opened his mouth to say that no, he wasn't married, then shut it.

A red-painted fingernail, more like a talon, really, traced along the back of his hand. "I don't mind," she said.

Greg looked at her again. She was attractive, he realized, almost beautiful, with high cheekbones and soft brown eyes, the blonde hair falling in wisps around her face. Her red dress revealed most of her breasts and wrapped around her hips like cling film, and was short enough to show smooth thighs and long legs. If what she offered was as good as it looked, it would certainly drive Nicola from his mind.

He had not the faintest interest in finding out.

Greg knocked back the rest of his scotch. "I do mind."

Outside again, the quiet seemed unnatural after the din inside the bar. He walked towards the pontoon, and shook his head in bemusement, trying to remember when anyone had come on to him that strongly before. Then it occurred to him that she was probably a prostitute, albeit a classy one, looking for easy pickings among lonely sailors. That knocked his ego back into shape.

It was cold in *Drifter*'s cabin, with the still chill that seeps from a rocky cave in summer. He turned on the heater, and couldn't help but think of Nicola's apartment, warm with its central heating and cozy with a plump sofa and chairs. Even all those ridiculous plants made it feel warm. Or was it Nicola herself who made it feel warm?

Greg sat heavily on a bench by the table, then lay back and folded one arm over his eyes. Oh, Christ. How could he give her up?

Chapter 17

THE SOUND of pounding on the main hatch woke Greg and he struggled upright, heavy-headed and groggy. A single shaft of light from one small, uncovered hatch in the roof slanted through the dim cabin. He looked at the clock over the navigation desk: 8am! He unlocked the main hatch, squinting in the brilliant sunlight and shivering in the air that rushed in, icy cold after the stifling heat of the cabin.

Sam's face peered in, the concern turning to relief. Beside him, Peter beamed with delight. "Here we are!" he cried, oblivious to anything being wrong.

"Great," said Greg. He hauled himself up the few stairs and onto the deck, then crossed his arms and frowned down at the boy. "Are you positive you're 10 today?" he asked, striving for normality for Peter's sake. "It's men only this weekend, you know. None of those sissy nine-year-olds allowed."

Peter tucked in his chin and lowered his voice. "Damned right."

"Peter!" Sam laughed, and knocked the visor of his son's baseball cap down over his eyes. "Don't let your mother hear you say that. Not until you're at least twice as old as you are today. Now take this stuff into the cabin at the front."

"The bow, Dad. It's the bow, not the front," corrected Peter, but obediently tossed the sleeping bags down the stairs and jumped down after them.

Sam turned to Greg. "You okay? I was worried when it didn't look as if you were here."

Greg nodded. "Yeah, fine. I overslept, that's all."

"You look like shit," Sam said frankly.

That surprised Greg into a laugh.

"Nicola okay?" asked Sam. He was frowning, clearly still suspecting that something was wrong.

"She's fine. Sends her love. She wouldn't admit it, but she was glad not to have to come along," replied Greg.

Remembering his harsh words and her hurt expression, her tear-filled eyes, he figured she would probably be glad not to have to see him ever again. But…my God, what she had suggested! It was no more acceptable to him now than it had been when she said it.

Greg rubbed his hands over his face and forced himself to forget what had happened, what they had said to each other, and to focus on the weekend. He bent down to help Sam with the rest of the things.

* *

The office was empty, but Nicola did not find it peaceful. She looked around sharply every time there was a noise from beyond the cubicles in her area. She knew that was stupid, and she was mad at herself, which was not helping her to concentrate on her work.

"Damn!"

She flung down the red pen. She'd read this same opening paragraph on the page proof of next week's cover three times, and still had no idea what it said.

It wasn't the office, or the noises. She knew exactly why she couldn't concentrate.

Heinous, Greg had said. A travesty.

Nicola got up and walked over to the window, to look down on the street. Not much traffic on a Saturday afternoon, and almost no people. She rubbed her eyes, which felt gritty and puffy from lack of sleep. The red numbers on her clock had remorselessly counted down the hours that she had lain awake reliving every word they had flung at each other, every shift of expression on his face. He had never looked at her with contempt before.

How would he look at her the next time he saw her?

She wondered if Hélène had any sleeping pills. Philippe had been released from hospital this morning and Hélène had invited Nicola to join the two of them in their delayed pizza feast. Antoine's conference ended tomorrow, so, as Hélène had said, it was now or never. Nicola planned to take a bottle of red wine, and with any luck her half would send her to sleep when she got home again.

It didn't feel like her home any more, with so many of Greg's clothes in closets and drawers, or an unfamiliar book lying on the dining table. When – and why? – had he brought over that pointed metal tool he had called a marlinespike?

Nicola pressed her forehead against the cool glass, then sighed, and went back to her desk.

* *

"You going to tell me what's eating you?" Sam asked.

Greg had thought he'd got through the day as normal, but apparently not. He took a swig of his beer. "Let's go outside," he suggested. Peter was in the front berth, probably asleep but possibly not, and with the berth door open this conversation was not one he wanted the boy to hear.

They shrugged into jackets and climbed out of the main hatch. It was cold, but there wasn't much wind in the sheltered harbor where Greg had anchored. Lights twinkled on the shore, and from a handful of other boats nearby drifted talk and laughter.

In a few words, Greg outlined what Nicola had said to him last evening.

Sam breathed out sharply through his nose, and ran a hand over his head. "Boy. That's a hell of an idea." His voice held admiration.

"Yeah, well, the hell of an idea was followed by a hell of a fight," Greg said, with a short humorless laugh.

"Why?"

"You can't imagine I would ever agree to such a thing?" Greg asked. He sighed. "Sometimes, it seems like all we do now is fight. Two weeks ago in Seattle, last weekend in Death Valley, and yesterday."

There was silence for a minute, while Sam rolled his bottle between his hands. "Have you even considered it? Or did you get all high and mighty, and storm out?"

Greg blinked. "That's not exactly how I would describe it," he said stiffly.

"I would, and Debbie would, and I'm sure after these past few weeks Nicola would too, but no, I don't suppose you would.

Come on, Greg," said Sam, an impatient edge to his voice, "you can be a holier-than-thou son a bitch sometimes, and you know it."

"I know nothing of the sort, but thank you for pointing it out."

"Did you bring down the wrath of God on her head? Quote scripture at the poor girl?"

"No."

Sam sounded surprised. "Good."

"It was more of a paraphrase. I couldn't remember the precise wording," said Greg, deadpan, and they both laughed, breaking the tension. "Hand me another beer, will you?"

They drank in silence.

"You really think I get high and mighty, and storm out?"

Sam cocked his head. "How did that fight in Seattle end?"

"I walked out of the bedroom. But Mom and I were on our way to church!" he added in self-defense.

"Hmm. The one in Death Valley?"

"I, uh, slammed the car door and took off across Badwater Basin."

Sam nodded. "Friday?"

Greg fidgeted. "I left her apartment."

Sam held his hands up, and shrugged. "They all sound like storming out, to me. I suppose it's one way of ensuring you never lose an argument."

"I hate arguing with Nicola!" Greg said. "We never argued at all, until this happened."

A chuckle from Sam. "That's only because you've been together for just six months. Even without this, you would have started arguing, no matter how perfect everything seems. It doesn't take anything as terrifying as the chance of having the same mother, believe me! You should have heard me and Debbie about whether we really needed those new drapes in the living room. Completely pointless, but anyone would have thought divorce was next."

Greg smiled. "They're nice. I like the stripes." A blast of music came from a nearby boat and he turned with a frown, but it ended mid-note. "Do you think it would be a sin?"

He had no need to explain what "it" was.

"Don't ask me about sin!" protested Sam. "I can't even name the seven deadly ones, let alone the ordinary everyday ones. You know that the last time I went to church was Peter's baptism. But I do think you should get professional advice before you start flinging the word 'sin' at a lady like Nicola."

"Even if it isn't a sin, it is definitely against the law. Would you do it, Sam? Would you say yes?" Greg leaned forward, to see Sam's face in the light that shone up from the hatch above the bathroom.

What he saw was Sam's lips purse, and his high, wide forehead wrinkle in thought. "If it was me and Debbie, and she loved me so much that she would sacrifice everything else to be with me? Because that's what Nicola is prepared to do, Greg, don't you forget that. Lie. Flout convention. Break the law. That takes tremendous courage. But to answer you – I'd think long and I'd think hard before I said either way. I certainly wouldn't dismiss it out of hand. As she said, if no one knew…if there was no danger of prison, no chance of children with birth defects…." Sam's voice dwindled away.

Greg tilted up the beer bottle and drank. He regarded his old friend, then said, "You don't sound shocked or outraged by the idea, Sam."

"I guess I'm not. Hell, Greg, it's you. And Nicola. I've seen you two together. Debbie and I couldn't have been happier for you. If you really are brother and sister, then that's the sickest damned joke in the world," said Sam, shaking his head in condemnation. "When you told us Mona's story, we were both devastated for you. And for Mona, too."

"You don't think us being together would be wrong?" Greg asked intently. "Inherently wrong?"

Sam shrugged. "I'm no philosopher. I'm an accountant. Ask me numbers, not how many angels can dance on the head of a pin. But that's numbers, isn't it?" he asked with a smile. "Wrong? It's deceitful, I'd say, but more of an omission than a lie."

Greg picked at the label on the bottle. "Do you think I could lose my license?"

"I'm not following you."

"Marrying your half-sister is illegal." Greg found it nearly impossible to believe that he was saying this – but if he had to say it, he was glad it was to Sam. "You signed the same code of ethics I did. If Nicola actually is my half-sister, and we marry, we break the law. Certainly in California, so probably also in other states. We could each go to prison."

"No!" Sam's voice was harsh was shock. "You said it was against the law, but I never thought…Greg, no!"

"Yes."

Sam leaned over and put his arm around Greg's shoulder. "Shit. That's one stupid law."

Half of Greg's mouth twitched up. "Right now, I agree. I have no idea if it applies just to marriage, or also to living together. If we did, and the state found out, and we were prosecuted, I would have a criminal record." Greg shook his head in sheer disbelief at having to consider such things. "So I want to know, could I lose my license over that?"

Sam breathed out slowly. "Whoa. I have no idea. I always thought the ethics, the code of conduct, related only to our work. Our professional lives, if you like, not our personal ones. Do you think it relates to both?"

Greg shrugged. "I sure as hell hope not, the way my personal life seems to be going!"

"When I said you need advice, I was thinking religion," said Sam. "Now, I think you might need a lawyer, too."

"Great. Thanks."

They were silent for a while, listening to the gentle slap of water against *Drifter*'s hull. When Sam spoke again, it was clear where his thoughts had been. "Even if you did have a criminal record," he pointed out, "it wouldn't be for something relating to your work. It's not like you would have embezzled money or fiddled the books."

"No, I would just be that sick pervert who got off with his own sister," Greg said bitterly.

"Don't say that!"

"Other people will."

"What I don't understand is why you assume the authorities would ever know. This is all hypothetical. You and Nicola aren't going to volunteer the information, so unless someone deliberately told on you, how would the state find out? You know," said Sam thoughtfully, "it would help if you didn't look so much alike. You could dye your hair blond."

He held up both hands, thumbs and forefingers framing a rectangle, and squinted through it at Greg, who began to laugh. "Yup, you'd make a good blond. Brown contact lenses would help, too."

Greg punched him lightly on the arm. "Right."

* *

"Feast" was misleading, Nicola discovered. Philippe's doctor had reluctantly agreed that the boy could have one slice – one extremely small slice – of pizza so soon after the removal of his appendix. But no more. So, Nicola, Hélène and Philippe shared one small pizza and one extra-large salad. Philippe complained, but not as much as he would have done before the operation. Pale and tired, he went to bed at 8pm.

The women moved into the living room and finished Nicola's red wine, and then Hélène brought out the cognac.

"Oh no!" Nicola protested, the memory of that day after the wine, grappa and Southern Comfort spree far too fresh in her mind.

"Nonsense," Hélène retorted. "This is the finest cognac imaginable. I will not even tell you how much it costs. One small drink will not hurt. And it is the only sleeping pill I use, so you have no choice." She splashed a small amount into a flat-bottomed crystal glass with a short stem.

It was late now, later than Nicola had intended to stay, but they were comfortable together in the way of good friends and she was soothed by the flow of Hélène's voice. The room had worked its magic tonight, pools of light from lamps bringing the rugs to muted life, the soft colors and expensive fabrics combining to lull Nicola into a state of deep relaxation. She was curled into an armchair, draped with a cashmere throw to ward off the chill.

"Have you mentioned it yet?"

There was no need for Hélène to specify what "it" was, nor to whom "it" had been mentioned.

Nicola nodded. "Last night."

Hélène tilted her head. "It went badly," she stated.

A short, humorless laugh. "Yes, 'badly' almost begins to come close to starting to describe how extremely terribly it went. How did you know?"

"You have hardly smiled since Philippe went to bed, and I think you were pretending for his sake before that, no? You do not have the look of a happy woman," said Hélène.

"I'm not a happy woman," said Nicola. "I thought I had been unhappy before, like that day I came home to find Andrew had left, but it was nothing compared to this. I'm terrified, Hélène, terrified that Greg now has such a low opinion of me that he'll never want to see me again, let alone marry me. Two weeks ago, I was so happy! Happy was a completely new word to me. I had a shining, joyful future, a man who made me feel loved and safe and cherished and wanted; now…now, I don't know what I have." She stared into the drops of cognac in her glass.

Hélène made a not-so-polite scoffing noise. "Oh come, you exaggerate! You are…" she groped for the word in English, "melodramatic!"

She had found the word, but not the pronunciation. It came out melo-dra-ma-TEEK, and Nicola could not hold back the laugh. That feeling of hopeless doom faded. "Melodramatic," she corrected. "And I'm not. If you'd seen his face, and heard him, and watched him walk away in outrage, you wouldn't think I was being melodramatic."

"Perhaps he was?"

Nicola sat up. "Was what?"

"Melodramatic. Why walk away? Why outraged? Why did Greg not stay and discuss it?" asked Hélène.

Why not? "You know," said Nicola slowly, frowning, "that's not the first time he's done that. We never argued at all until that Sunday in Seattle, but every one since then he's just walked out."

"In high dungeon," suggested Hélène.

Nicola spluttered the last of her cognac in a fine spray over the cashmere. "I'm so sorry!" she exclaimed, wiping her hand over the drops, and laughing uncontrollably. "Dudgeon, not dungeon!"

"Ah," nodded Hélène. "I have never understood the concept of 'high dungeon,' because of course dungeons are generally underground rather than high, nor how it related to walking out in anger. It makes no more sense now that I know it is dudgeon, mind you." She rose, and walked over to the drinks cabinet.

Nicola heard the soft repetition as she passed: melodramatic, dudgeon, melodramatic, dudgeon.

"I wish I spoke another language," she said on impulse.

Hélène turned. "Why?"

"You seem to enjoy learning the obscure words in English so much. Like worrywart!" Nicola laughed.

"To hear Antoine say that word, ah, that was worth a year of my life!" She walked back towards Nicola, holding the cognac bottle.

Nicola shook her head and covered the glass with her hand. "No, Hélène! I have to walk home, and I know it's only two blocks but just imagine me weaving all over the sidewalk. I'd get arrested for walking under the influence!"

"Stay here," said Hélène with a casual shrug. "The guest room is always ready. We can talk as long as we wish, and drink cognac. I will light the fire."

Nicola hesitated, and could think of no single reason why she should go home. Greg was somewhere on the ocean and would not miraculously appear at her door tonight; if he phoned, she would receive the call as easily here as at home – not that he had shown any sign of wanting to get in touch. And it was so lonely there without him.

She held her glass up. "Thank you. I'd love to stay."

Hélène poured another splash into her glass, then walked over to the fireplace. She picked up the box of matches from the mantelpiece. "Nicola?"

"Yes?"

"Do you know how to light the fire?"

Nicola laughed, and put her glass on the table. She peeled off the cashmere, which was so soft it was like a cloud. "It looks like it's laid," she said, walking over. "Kindling, twigs, small logs, and big logs here on the side. Just light the match and hold it against the kindling."

"Kindling," repeated Hélène carefully. "*Mon Dieu*, this is my night for obscure English words, no doubt! What is the kindling?"

"There." Nicola pointed.

The match flared bright, and the flame jumped to the newspaper.

"Oh!" exclaimed Hélène, looking pleased.

"Haven't you lit the fire before?"

Hélène shook her head. "No, Antoine is in charge of the fireplace. He sweeps it, and cleans it, and he laid it just as you see now. He always lights it."

"Well then, a strike for equality," suggested Nicola.

Hélène looked aghast. "Never tell him! If he knows I can light the fire, he may expect me to cook, also!"

"I won't say a word," Nicola promised. She tried to remember ever seeing Hélène do more in the kitchen than boil water for tea, and failed.

They wandered away from the fire, Nicola to her armchair and Hélène to the chaise longue. The fire's immediate flare of light faded, but the twigs caught and the flame took hold. They were silent for a time, watching the fire and listening to the muted sound of traffic below.

"Families are funny, when you think about it," mused Hélène.

"Why? Apart from the well known fact that you can't choose them."

"That is what I mean. I was thinking of you," explained Hélène. "You were chosen. Gwen and Arthur and Bill and Alison are your family, but not due to luck or circumstance."

Nicola nodded, drowsy but puzzled. "So?"

"Would you ever have sex with Bill?"

Nicola bolted upright, wide awake. "No! Ewww, no! How can you ask such a thing?"

"This is my point. There is no shred of shared DNA between you, but he is your brother and you react with quite proper revulsion to the idea of sex with him. Yet if it happens that you and Greg do share DNA, it is expected that you should have that same reaction, despite the fact that you met only six months ago and you in no way regard him as your brother." Hélène swirled the cognac, warming it in her hand. "Why is Bill your family, but Greg not? That is what I was getting at when I said families are funny."

"Nurture over nature," proclaimed Nicola suddenly.

Hélène said, "I do not understand. The words, yes, but not the meaning."

"It's one of the few things I remember from my first-year psychology class. The debate about which is more important in determining how a person turns out – his genes, or his upbringing. In this case, I think of Bill, totally unrelated to me, as my brother because that's how I was brought up to think of him."

Hélène nodded. "I see. And by the same reasoning, you do not see Greg that way. Your genes did not recognize each other."

Nicola laughed. "I guess that's one way to put it! But you know, I remember a theory I read in a magazine. It says that we unconsciously seek out partners who are like us. Who look like we do, who are similar. So maybe our genes did recognize each other."

"Consider me and Antoine!" protested the Frenchwoman. "He is two inches shorter than me, has brown eyes and brown hair. We look nothing alike." She pointed to her own gray eyes and smoothed her blonde hair.

"So much for that theory!"

* *

The next afternoon, she thought again of Hélène's words, but this time with Bill in front of her. The two of them were in the kitchen, putting out small cakes and sandwiches cut into triangles. Their mother was a firm believer in the English custom of afternoon tea.

Nicola regarded Bill objectively, and had to admit that even if they were strangers she wouldn't have sex with him. His red hair was thinning, his watery blue eyes looked out myopically through heavy glasses, his waist was in danger of disappearing altogether. On impulse, she walked over and hugged him.

"Hey," said Bill, looking surprised but returning the hug. "What was that for?"

"Just because I love you."

His arms tightened around her. "Poor Nick." It was an old nickname from when they were children, and Bill had insisted on calling her that because he, four years old when Nicola had been adopted, had wanted a brother instead of another sister. "This thing with Greg and his mother has got you down, hasn't it?"

She nodded. He had no idea what "this thing" had led to. She still hadn't decided whether to tell her family what she had suggested to Greg. What was the point, if he was so against it? Yet having their support would give her the courage to keep suggesting it. Assuming he ever spoke to her again.

Arthur flung back the swinging door. "What are you two doing in here?" he demanded. "Picking the tea leaves by hand?"

Nicola felt like a teenager again, lazy and idling, and being chastised for not doing her chores. It was so wonderfully normal. "Sorry, Dad," she said, and began to fill the kettle.

They returned to the living room bearing trays of tea and food. The children, Bill's three and Alison's two, appeared from nowhere, piled their plates and disappeared again. The seven adults were more restrained, but afternoon tea on a Sunday was a long tradition in this house and they all examined the offerings, looking for old favorites and regarding anything new with thinly veiled suspicion.

Nicola pushed her fruit tart around the plate. She looked out the windows at the back yard and was reminded of the engagement party. It was hard to recall that unthinking happiness of three weeks ago, a time when her future was glowing and certain.

"I have to ask you something," she said abruptly.

They looked at her with expressions of interest or politeness or puzzlement.

"If the test is positive, and Greg is my bro–" she stumbled over the word, "my half-brother, what would you think if we stayed together anyway?"

Faces now held confusion or disbelief.

Alison's husband laughed, breaking the silence. "Hah, good one, Nicola!"

"No, I mean it. I'm serious. We could never have our own children, I know that, but we could still be together. We could adopt. And we couldn't marry, because it's illegal. But what real harm would it do?" she asked, searching their faces, one after the other.

Gwen's nostrils flared as she said sharply, "What harm? What harm! Nicola, how can you ask such a thing? It would be unforgivably, inexcusably wrong."

Bill put his tea to one side and rubbed his hand over his balding head. "Harm, Mom. The question is 'what harm,'" he repeated. "Not is it wrong."

"It's wrong and it's harmful!" claimed Wendy, beside him on the sofa.

The smile Bill gave Nicola, full of support and love, faded as he turned to his wife. "How? Why? What could possibly be wrong with two people who love each other like they do staying together?"

Gwen was on her feet now, glaring from Bill to Nicola. "I can't believe you could ever consider such a thing, Nicola, nor that Bill could agree with it. Why must you ask if it's wrong? Of course it's wrong!"

Arthur tugged on her hand until she sat again. "Perhaps," he said mildly, "less emotion and more reason might be useful."

Alison picked at a scone and looked around the room, eyes darting from one player to another. "I think it's wonderful and exciting! Good for you, Nicola! I never thought my little sister would be the one to make the big sacrifice for love."

"Fly in the face of convention, break the rules, live the lie. Who else but Nicola?" asked Bob with a sardonic twist of his lips. He saluted her with the cream puff in his hand.

Nicola had never especially liked Alison's husband, and right now she wanted to cram that cream puff into his oh-so-subtly mocking face.

"Put a sock in it, Bob," advised Bill. Mild-mannered dentist he might be, and long past what physical prime he'd ever had, but the look he directed at Bob convinced the other man to back off.

Prickly, uncomfortable silence filled every corner of the room.

"I can't believe Greg would go along with such an outrageous scheme," said Gwen. Her eyes were hard and her mouth set.

Nicola stared down at her hands, her fingers twisted together. The diamonds on her left hand glittered, the large central one and the swirl of chips around it, drawing her eyes as they always did. Greg had brushed aside her tentative idea of something small, so the ring she wore was bigger than she had envisioned. But it was so pretty, and she loved it. Loved the memory of the afternoon they had chosen it together. Grief pierced Nicola when she realized that if they followed her suggestion, and they were forced to live together rather than marry, she would have to stop wearing her engagement ring. Would have to pretend that marriage was not something that mattered to her, or to Greg. "He didn't go along with it. He was very much against it."

Gwen sniffed. "I knew it. He, at least, knows what's right. So there's no point in discussing this."

Arthur rose and came to sit on the arm of Nicola's chair. "What happened, sweetie?"

"He...we...a big fight." Her chin began to wobble and she rubbed the back of her hand over her mouth. "He said it would be a sin. I called him a hypocrite. We shouted at each other. It was awful. Oh, Dad," she whispered. "I haven't heard from him since he walked out. He may not want to marry me at all any more."

He gathered her to him and stroked her hair, making little sounds of comfort.

"If that bastard runs out on you," Arthur promised, "I'll cut his balls off."

"I'll hold him down while you do," offered Bill.

Into Nicola's startled mind popped the vision of a naked Greg running as fast he could, away from Kylie and Max, and her father and brother, all with knives in their hands and revenge on their minds. "Oh, Dad!" She flung her arms around him, and laughed, and scrubbed away the stupid tears. "You'd have to stand in line. But thanks for the offer. You too, Bill."

"If the worst happens, and you two do run off to Boston, or Bangalore, or wherever, you can always count on me," said her brother. His elbow dug into his wife's side.

"Oh. Yeah," said Wendy.

"Dad?"

"I'll support you 100 per cent in whatever you decide, sweetie. If you two adopt kids, I'll dandle them on my knee like any proud grandpa. I've got experience, as you know," he grinned. "Just ask those hooligans wrecking my rec room."

Nicola turned tentatively to Gwen. "Mom?"

Gwen's mouth was a thin line of disapproval. She hesitated before speaking, looking around at her family. One sharp shake of her head, then, "Nicola, no. I cannot countenance something so monstrous. Greg is right. Not only is what you're suggesting against the law of man, it is a sin against the law of God. I could never agree to or condone such a thing."

The coldness in her mother's voice turned Nicola's blood to ice. "Mom, you wouldn't…you'd still see me?"

Arthur's hand on Nicola's shoulder was firm. "Of course she would."

But he wouldn't meet her eyes.

Chapter 18

PETER TURNED around for one last wave, and Greg raised his arm in salute. He watched them get into the car, then turned back to the security gate. And stopped. He couldn't sit in the boat for hours, alone, this thing in his mind like a poison pill. He couldn't go to Nicola, either, not feeling the way he did.

Was his phone still on the boat? No, it was here, in a pocket. But what to say? He settled for texting "Back safe" and began to put the phone away, then paused, and turned it off. It was cowardly, but he couldn't face her. That reminded him of what Sam had said last night, that Nicola showed tremendous courage in being willing to give up the life she knew, to risk everything, in order to be with him.

Did he have that much courage?

Again, Greg tried to imagine them in Boston (and why Boston, of all places?), with a couple of other people's children, lying about their life to the kids and to everyone they met. He tried, and it was a blank.

He pulled up the collar of his jacket and stuffed his hands into his pockets, and walked.

It had been a relief to talk to Sam, to get the words out and hear the opinion of someone he trusted, but it had solved nothing for Greg. Still angry, still confused.

"You should get professional advice," Sam had said.

He'd like that. He'd like someone to say to him, "Oh yes, marrying your sister is an abomination and a sin." Or to say, "Oh no, people think it is but it isn't, not really." Either answer would be better than going over and over the same arguments in his head.

He wasn't far from his own church. The pastor was pleasant enough, and Greg liked him, but he balked at the idea of discussing his predicament with the man who had agreed to perform the wedding ceremony. If this all ended happily – and that was hard to believe, now – Greg couldn't see himself standing up with Nicola in front of the pastor, and wondering what thoughts were running through his head.

He walked on, down unknown streets. Pleasant suburban

streets with houses and yards, trees and gardens. The sort of place where a recently married young couple might settle, hoping to raise a family. Twilight was ending and night was drawing in, and windows glowed in soft gold.

There was a Catholic church ahead, all stone and wood, light shining through stained-glass windows. His feet slowed. Greg wasn't a Catholic; he had never been inside a Catholic church, not even for a wedding. However, he had heard of confession, and he knew it was confidential. Could he pretend to be a Catholic, and talk to a priest? He smiled grimly, imagining how the poor man would respond if Greg said, "Father, I'm afraid that I've been having sex with my sister. I think it's a sin. But I don't want to stop."

He stepped into the enclosed porch and pushed open the heavy door. The lingering scent of incense hit him first, a faint smell on the air, so unexpected in a church, or at least in churches he knew. Then he saw the enormous crucifix behind the altar, and he stumbled to a halt and stared. There was singing, and Greg feared he had barged in on a service, but the church was almost empty. Choir practice, he decided. He walked along the aisle, running shoes soundless on the black-and-white squares of marble, and then slipped onto a pew, trying to identify in which dim alcove the confessions were held. Maybe it was only at certain times, on certain days?

This was a bad idea, he decided. But the singing was comforting, and the old church was quite beautiful with its carved pews and stone pillars. He'd sit here a while, then go back to the marina.

"Hello."

The man's shoes made no more noise than Greg's runners had, and he appeared without warning. He was dressed casually, in jeans, a black shirt and a sports jacket. His balding head caught the soft light, and his eyes were full of curiosity as he peered at Greg over the tops of wireless spectacles. He looked like a professor, and Greg would never have known he was a priest if not for the white collar.

"I'm Father Michael. I don't think I've seen you here before."

"Greg." Did one shake hands with a priest? He had no hope of fooling this man. "I'm not a Catholic."

The priest laughed, and gestured at the pew. "May I?" He lowered himself onto the wooden seat, and grimaced as he rubbed his knee with a gnarled hand. "I didn't think you were a Catholic, looking around as if it was your first time in a church. But all are welcome."

"I go to church fairly often," Greg said, with a faint smile, "but it's not one like this."

Father Michael returned the smile. "Did something in particular bring you into mine?" When Greg hesitated, he continued, "It's all right. You needn't tell me. Although if you would like to talk about anything, rest assured I've probably heard it all before."

Greg bit back the line about having sex with his sister. "I was...trying to decide something."

An encouraging smile was the only reply.

"Is incest a sin?"

The priest's bushy gray eyebrows rose in surprise. "It appears I was wrong, I haven't heard it all before." He pinched his fingers around his upper lip, considering. "Leviticus 18:6-18 tells us 'You must never have sexual relations with a close relative, for I am the Lord' and goes on to list all the people you must never have sexual relations with – mother, father's wife, sister, half-sister, niece, aunt, daughter-in-law, on and on it goes. Curiously, there seems to be no rule against sexual relations with a male relative," he added.

Half-sister. Greg didn't realize he had said the words aloud until the priest began to talk again.

"Oh yes. 'Do not have sexual relations with your sister or half-sister, whether she is your father's daughter or your mother's daughter, whether she was born into your household or someone else's.' Not much room for doubt, there. And in Deuteronomy 27:22-23, we get 'Cursed is anyone who has sexual intercourse with his sister, whether she is the daughter of his father or his mother.'"

Greg leaned forward and buried his face in his hands. It was a sin; there could be no doubt. Wait a minute…. "What about Adam and Eve's children? They must have had sex with each other! And after the Great Flood, when only Noah's family survived. If we are all descended from Adam and Eve, and then from Noah, then we're all the product of incest! Why was it fine then, but a sin now?"

"Ah, it wasn't a sin until God said it was a sin," responded Father Michael with a smile.

"How convenient," observed Greg, and was surprised to hear the older man laugh.

The priest continued, sounding like a man debating academic details rather than tearing Greg's life to shreds. "We must keep in mind that sexual relations between close relatives was deemed a sin in order to prevent giving birth to damaged children, in a time when they had no knowledge of genetics and it wasn't possible to choose not to have children. Farther back, at the time of Adam and Eve, and Noah, presumably our genes were in better shape. But how relevant is that today, when a couple can choose? I am, of course, for the sake of argument, glossing over the fact that the Roman Catholic Church forbids the use of artificial contraception."

Greg nodded, bemused by this discourse on sex and gene pool viability from an elderly Catholic priest.

"So," mused the priest, "should that proscription still be valid? Perhaps it depends on how strictly one interprets the Bible. There are many things in the Bible that are directed for or against, and which no one today would consider following. According to Deuteronomy 23.13, we should carry a stick with us, so that when we defecate we can dig a hole and cover it up. I think you will find that most people use a toilet. Why do we adhere to one ancient law, but not another?"

Greg shifted on the uncomfortable seat, and faced the priest. "Are you saying incest might not be considered a sin if there was no chance of children being born?"

When Father Michael looked up from his folded hands, his eyes were full of a compassion that made Greg uneasy. Had he guessed?

"I'm saying that in our day and age, nothing is clear cut. It probably wasn't back then, either; we merely see it that way through the lens of time. They were no different to us. They loved, they yearned, they wanted, and I'm sure they could reason as well as we can. To know a thing to be wrong, but to want it nonetheless, to ache for it…." His words, so soft, faded to nothing.

In their silence, the singing of the choir faded, leaving one pure, high treble note floating in the air.

"So it is wrong? Even if it wasn't a sin, it would be wrong?" Greg leaned back and looked ahead, towards the altar, at the face of the crucified Jesus with his surreal expression of peace.

"I regret that I cannot trot out quotations for you on that front," the priest said. "I will answer for myself, though, rather than for God, if that's all right. I would say that if coercion or force is involved, or one party hasn't the wherewithal to refuse, then yes, absolutely, it would be wrong. But if we are talking about consenting adults, two people who choose such a thing in full awareness of what they do – two people who, above all, love each other? Then, is that wrong? How do we define wrong in such a case? Thirty years ago, homosexuality was considered wrong. Now? No one bats an eyelid."

Greg smiled. "Not in San Francisco, at least. So you think right and wrong are flexible? They change, like fashion? It's that simple?"

The priest sighed. "I think right and wrong are things with which good people will always wrestle. Like the age-old conundrum that if God exists, and He loves us, how then can there be suffering and evil in the world? Nothing is simple."

"No." Greg stared at his runners. "No, it's not."

"Have I helped you at all?" asked Father Michael. "I fear you are still troubled by this question."

Greg gave him a sideways smile. "Let's say I'm still wrestling." He got to his feet. "Thank you."

He sidled along the pew. When he reached the aisle, the priest's voice stopped him.

"I know you aren't a Catholic, Greg, but we're all children of the same Father." He raised his hand and sketched the sign of the cross. "Go with God, my son."

Greg nodded. "Thank you, Father."

A whisper floated after him. *"Ego te absolvo a peccatis tuis."*

* *

Nicola lay in bed. Alone, for the fourth night in a row. How long had it been since she had gone so long without Greg beside her? She couldn't remember. Since the first time they had made love, on *Drifter* at China Camp, it seemed they had been together every night.

She told herself she wouldn't look, but the clock drew her eyes like a magnet: 1:14am.

"I'll be back here Sunday night," he had said. "Promise."

Promises, as everyone knows, are made to be broken.

With an exclamation of impatience, Nicola threw back the covers. She rose, plumped the pillows, shook out the blankets vigorously and floated them back onto the mattress – and then walked out of the bedroom. It was empty without Greg, full only of memories and longing.

She felt her way down the dark hallway and into the living room. It was lighter here, the streetlights and city lights seeping through the plants at the window and falling in jungle patterns on the floor. She pulled a woven throw off the chair and wrapped it around her, and curled into a corner of the sofa, staring at the shadows and listening to the tick of the clock.

* *

Nicola was in her bedroom, dressing for work, when a knock sounded on the door. She flinched, and dropped the blouse she had just taken from a hanger. Heavy dread fought with the tingle of anticipation. She snatched up the blouse and hurried from the bedroom, doing up buttons as she went, and flung open the door without bothering to look through the peephole.

He stood at a slight angle, dressed in suit and tie. Two days of sailing had darkened his face, so that his jaw line, closely shaved this morning, looked pale. His expression was difficult to read against the dazzling fall of light from a window behind him. He didn't say anything. Then his left hand, behind his back, came forward and she saw the single red rose.

"Yes."

Nicola's breath was a sob, and her hands flew up to cover her mouth.

His arms were around her and he was walking her backwards, into the apartment. He kicked the door shut.

"Yes," Greg said again. He stepped back, and she could see his face now. Tired and drawn, but there was an underlying peace, too.

"Yes, I will leave San Francisco, and never father your children, and be estranged from any of my family and friends who won't accept us. I will risk prison and the loss of my chosen livelihood. I will do anything it takes to be with you. If our love is a sin, then I am damned already." In one violent movement, he pulled her to him and buried his face against her shoulder. "I'll do it, but, oh, Nicola, that's not what I want!"

"Neither do I! But if it's the only way?" A weekend of emotions battered and stretched hair-thin was taking its toll, and her voice cracked.

His lips were against hers as he said, "I've been without you for two days. I couldn't bear a lifetime. Oh darling, don't cry. It's all right! I'm here, I'll never leave."

"I thought you would say no!" she gasped, hating the weakness of the tears but unable to stop them. "I thought you despised me for even thinking of such a thing. I was afraid you would break it off even if the results are negative, because of that."

"I could never do that," he murmured. "Think you're crazy, and a lunatic, and utterly outrageous, yes, but never that. I don't know how we'll pull this off if it comes to that, but I'm sure you'll figure it out."

Somehow, during the course of this exchange, they had ended up on the bed. Nicola snuggled against him, her fingers playing with his tie. "You'll have to help, you know. If."

"I hope we find out today!" Greg said with sudden vehemence. "Either way. I can't bear much more of this." A pause. "You said you might go to your parents' house yesterday. Did you?"

Nicola pulled her head back to look at him, and then couldn't resist hugging him in sheer joy because he was in her bed again. On her bed, really, both of them fully clothed and Greg still wearing his shoes, but that wasn't the point. "Yes."

"Did you tell them your suggestion?"

"Yes."

"And?" The single syllable was long and drawn out.

"And what do you think?" she asked sharply, rising on an elbow. "They were shocked. Once they got over that, it ranged from one extreme to the other. Mom...." Her voice faltered. "Mom refuses to consider it. She was...adamant, Greg." Again, Nicola saw the pursed mouth and the frown, the crossed arms, the cold disappointment in her mother's eyes, which she had never seen before.

His hand reached up to smooth back her hair. "She'll come around."

"If she doesn't?"

Greg's eyes were steady. "If we do this, darling, it won't come without a price. Your relationship with Gwen may be part of that price." He hesitated, then said, "Even if the results are negative, what happened yesterday might have changed it already. I'm sorry, Nicola. Sorry to come between you and Gwen."

Loss welled up inside her like a black tide. Her mother, gone? Or if not gone, then changed? No more that easy, unthinking telling of anything? And, on the other side, the loss of Greg.

Nicola flopped back down and pressed herself against him, hugging him so hard that Greg grunted in protest. "If that's the price, I'll pay it!" she vowed. Her lips sought his once more. They were firm and warm, slightly chapped from two days of sailing, and she had longed since Friday to feel them again.

Reassured, she said, "You know who surprised me most, yesterday?"

"No, but I wasn't there, so you'll have to tell me," he said, sounding as if he was humoring Peter.

She dug an elbow into his ribs, and he grunted again. "Bill. He was completely behind us."

"Bill?" The surprise in his voice was clear.

"I know. I would have thought the same thing. Boring Bill, old before his time," chuckled Nicola. "You should have seen him, checking Mom and dragging Wendy into line. Bob was being his typical obnoxious self, but Bill told him to put a sock in it." She debated telling him about her father's and Bill's plan for dealing with Greg if he left her, but thought he might not appreciate the humor of it.

She felt his laugh. "Did he? Bill's a good man. I've always liked him," said Greg.

"Especially since he fixed that molar for you," Nicola observed.

"Yes, I admit, I have liked him even more since then."

Nicola wrapped her legs around his, and rested her head against his chest. "Greg? Did you tell your family?"

His chest beneath her cheek rose and fell. "No. Dad says Mom is becoming more convinced every day that she is your mother. I can't throw this at her unless it's absolutely necessary. Dad is very worried about her," he said.

"What do you mean?"

"I'm not sure myself. That's what he said last night. I called, when I got back from talking to the priest. But Dad wouldn't elaborate," Greg said. His fingers stroked through her hair.

The flash of jealousy and anger that knifed her when she learned that he had called Edward last night, not her, was nothing compared to her curiosity about a priest. "Greg, you don't have a priest. You have a pastor."

His soft laugh whispered against her cheek. "Last evening I did. Father Michael, a fully fledged Roman Catholic priest. That man knows his Bible, I'll tell you."

She twisted around so she could see his face. "Why did you talk to a Catholic priest?"

"Oh, Nicola," he sighed. His arms tightened around her. "I envy you. You believe in God, yes, but you don't care very much about him, or about religion. You don't judge yourself, or your life, against it."

"Do you?" She'd had no idea. "Does it really matter that much to you?"

"I spent an hour last night sitting on a stiff wooden bench in a cold stone church, discussing the nature of sin and right versus wrong with a Catholic priest, because I couldn't bring myself to say such things to my own pastor – the man I still hope will marry us," Greg said. His lips brushed her hair. "Yes, Nicola, it matters that much to me. Sometimes, I wish it mattered that much to you."

She pulled away, her back stiffening, but before she could say anything, his fingers were against her mouth.

"But most of the time," he said with a smile, "I couldn't care less about your views of God and sin and what the Bible tells us. If I want religious debate, I'll go see Father Michael. If I want a beautiful, smart, sexy woman to share my life with," his mouth was against hers now, and he'd rolled her onto her back, "I'll stick with you."

"We're going to be very late for work," Nicola murmured a while later.

"Too bad." Greg gathered her closer, and rested his chin on her head. When he spoke again, there was a note of diffidence in his voice, which was not something she was used to hearing. "I want to ask you something."

"Shoot."

"Do you think I'm a holier-than-thou son of a bitch at times?"

She resisted the smile, given how serious he sounded. "I think we've established that we have very different views on religion, both its interpretation and its importance, but as long as you don't think you're going to drag me off to church every Sunday, I can handle that. I don't believe you think you're better than I am just because you have a greater faith. And I can't recall you ever acting holier than me. Not that I'd recognize it if you did!"

"What about high and mighty?" he asked.

Now Nicola did laugh. "What's got into you?"

"Sam. He said you were a lady and had tremendous courage. The way he described me was less flattering," said Greg, lips twisted in a wry smile. "He didn't pull any punches."

"Good friends don't," replied Nicola.

"So am I?"

She straightened his tie, and sat up. "We're late for work already."

His fingers closed on her shoulders as she tried to slide off the bed. "Do I have to tie you up again to get an answer?"

"Then we'd be incredibly late," she smiled. "Okay. You can be, I don't know, like you've already made your mind up about things. You know best, and be damned to other opinions. But," Nicola stressed as she turned to him, "I love you despite this extraordinary character flaw. And over the next 50 or so years, I can work on you."

His hand stopped her kiss, and although his face was serious, his eyes twinkled. "And no doubt I can spend the time correcting your own extraordinary character flaws."

She caught his hand in hers, and leaned closer. "This should be an interesting 50 years."

* *

"It's about time you turned up, Nicky!" exclaimed Kylie when Nicola hurried past her desk not too many minutes before 10am. "You won't believe what happened to me on the weekend!"

"Sorry, Kylie. I was kind of tied up this morning," Nicola said, and pressed her lips together to stop the laugh when she realized what she'd said. "You'll have to tell me later."

Max's expression was wary as she slid onto her chair. "How are things? If I'm allowed to make an observation, you look happier than you did last week."

"I am happier. Much! And I'm sorry if I was short or snappish at all. You're a good friend, Max." Nicola smiled at him and touched his arm.

Max looked startled, but pleased, and then smiled self-consciously and shook his head. "Nah."

Nicola woke up her computer, launched a few programs, signed into her email and went to the kitchen to make a coffee. It was really just a corner with kettle, microwave, sink and fridge, and the coffee came out of a can, but it would do.

"Nicky!"

She turned, to see Max waving his arm. "It's that space tourism article guy. I'm transferring him to you."

Nicola told the freelance writer one more time that, no, the paper would not pay for him to take a trip into near-Earth orbit on a souped-up airplane, and swore that she was convinced he would write a fantastic article even without experiencing weight-lessness. She hung up. Blowing on her coffee, she moved one hand to the mouse and clicked onto her email.

The scalding coffee splashed onto her pants when adrenaline shot through her at the sight of her inbox. She fumbled the cup onto her desk and seized a handful of tissues, dabbing them against her thigh as she groped in her purse for her phone.

"It's here."

A pause. "What is?"

"The email!"

"And…?"

"I haven't read it!" she exclaimed, but in a low tone. "I'm not doing that on my own."

Greg's sharp intake of breath was loud in her ear. "Not in the office! Christ, Nicola, not with all those people. Meet me downstairs."

Nicola was closer to the ground floor than Greg was, and had managed to pull up her email on the phone by the time he arrived. He had the breathless air of a man who had taken the stairs two at a time. One hand on her arm, he pulled her outside.

It was cold, and drizzling, and the wind whistling up the canyons of office buildings cut through her blouse and his shirt. Greg pulled her to him fiercely, warmth flaring where their bodies touched. His dark blue eyes bored into hers. "Regardless of what it says, I will stay with you, Nicola. Remember that. I'm yours for as long as you will have me."

Calm washed through her, and an invincible peace. "Forever," she said.

Nicola opened the email.

They both scanned the text, which told them nothing other than that what they really wanted to read was in the attachment.

She tapped the attachment. A lifetime passed as they stood in the inadequate shelter of that corner of the building, just a man and woman pressed together with a cell phone between them, waiting for the report to open.

An image materialized first, a company logo. Then words, from the top down: the date, the address, the salutation, more meaningless words. Then details of the samples, the testing dates, the results–

Chapter 19

"NEGATIVE." Nicola's breath caught. Was that really what it said? Or was that what she saw because that was what she so badly wanted to see? "Greg? Is that what it says?"

The answer was in his face, alight with joy and relief. "Yes. Oh yes, my darling, my completely unrelated darling, yes!"

He whooped, and swung her into the air. "Negative!"

Nicola laughed, and clutched his shoulders for balance. "Put me down, you fool!"

Greg put her down, and then he dropped to one knee on the busy sidewalk. People who were bustling by stopped, and gawked, and smiled.

"Get up!" she hissed, plucking at his sleeve. Her face was fiery with embarrassment, but that didn't stop her from smiling.

Greg took her hand, and kissed it. "Nicola, will you marry me?"

"If she says no, I will!" called a woman's voice.

"If she says no, then I will!" retorted a man.

Greg was gazing up at her, his eyes full of love and amusement. The lips that she would never tire of kissing were curved into a teasing smile. Even that ridiculous dimple was back. Nicola's hands cupped his face, and her thumbs stroked his cheekbones. "I said yes the first time, didn't I?" she said softly. "I'm not likely to change my mind now, after everything."

"What did she say?"

"I don't know, I couldn't hear."

"Speak up, lady!"

Nicola leaned down and kissed Greg, feeling his hands slide up her arms and into her hair, pulling her closer.

"Woo hoo!"

"That's a yes, man, for sure!"

She straightened up and pulled him to his feet, then turned to the crowd that had gathered. Her face split into a grin, and she cried, "Yes!"

* *

"Negative!" shouted Nicola, the moment her mother answered the phone. A quiet shout, because she was in the newspaper's lobby, but full of delight and triumph. "Negative, negative, negative! You're back on venue-booking duties!"

Silence.

"Mom?"

"You're sure?" Gwen sounded doubtful.

"Of course I'm sure! You're the best venue booker in San Francisco," laughed Nicola.

"I mean, are you sure it's negative?"

"Oh yes! In big, bold, beautiful letters. The most wonderful thing I've ever read," she replied.

There was note of challenge in Gwen's voice as she said, "Would you forward it to me?"

"Why?"

"I would like to read it for myself."

The joy rushed out of Nicola like air from a punctured tire. "You sound as if you don't believe me."

"Well, Nicola, after your outrageous words yesterday, and your shocking lack of any sense of what's right, can you blame me?" asked her mother stiffly. "If you can seriously contemplate living with your half-brother, you can certainly lie about the results."

"He is not my half-brother! He's not any sort of brother at all!" Nicola hissed. She sagged against the wall. "Mom, how can you say these things to me?" She heard the outrage and anger in her voice, and forced herself to calm down. "It's me. You know me."

"I thought I did." The response was crisp.

"I thought I knew you, too," said Nicola slowly. She wiped a hand over her cheek. "I've never heard you talk like this."

Gwen said, "I've never had any need. Until yesterday, you always behaved decently."

Nicola stared through the glass doors to the street, the people and vehicles blurred by tears. She swallowed. "I'll find a venue myself, Mom. I have to get back to work now."

* *

"Well?" demanded Edward.

Greg laughed. "Isn't 'hello' the customary way to answer the phone?"

"It's 11.25, we're both at work and I don't think you're calling for a social chat. You've heard, haven't you?" asked Edward.

"Negative, Dad! Negative!"

Edward's sigh gusted down the phone. "Oh, thank heavens. How wonderful. I'm speechless. I never believed that Nicola really could be Mona's daughter, of course. But still, it's wonderful."

"You'll be pleased to know that your operation was unexpectedly brought forward a week. You are on the road to recovery and looking forward to dancing at our wedding. That's what we're telling everyone," explained Greg. "I tried Mom, but there's no answer, not at home or on her cell. I've forwarded the message from the lab to her email. I thought she would want to read it."

"She's probably at church." His father's voice was grim.

Greg frowned. "Now?"

"Every day. I don't know if she's begging forgiveness from God, or praying, or what. And if she is praying, I very much fear it's for the wrong thing," said Edward, sounding tired and, for the first time that Greg could recall, old. "She's obsessed. Or possessed. I'm not sure which. If she's possessed, then at least she's in the right place, I guess." He tried for a laugh, and failed.

"Oh, God," said Greg, unable to think of anything else.

"Precisely my point."

Greg managed a chuckle. "Dad! This is no time for bad puns. Or good ones," he added with a smile. "How do you think she'll take the news?"

Silence. "I honestly don't know. I hope it will make her see sense, and she'll go back to how she was."

"I'm not sure any of us can go back to how we were," said Greg slowly. "We've all had to face things in the past two weeks that we had never dreamed of facing. Gwen…Gwen got all righteous and condemnatory yesterday, and she as much as told Nicola this morning that she didn't believe her when Nicola called to say the results were negative. Nicola is very upset." Too late, Greg remembered that he hadn't told his father.

Sure enough, Edward asked in puzzlement, "Righteous and condemnatory about what?"

He told him, as briefly as possible.

A long breath. "What a girl!" Edward exclaimed. "You hold on to her, son."

"I intend to, Dad."

"Poor Nicola," said Edward. "I got the impression she's very close to Gwen."

"Yeah. I'll call Gwen this afternoon myself, and Arthur. He's a good man. I hope that between the two of us, we can bring Gwen around," explained Greg. He'd go to Sausalito and shake some sense into Gwen in person, if that's what it took to get Nicola's mother to their wedding.

"Greg…what did you say, when Nicola made her suggestion?"

His laugh was wry. "I got all high and mighty, and holier than thou – that's how Sam described it, by the way – and then stormed out, and avoided Nicola until this morning. And then I said yes," he finished.

"Good," approved Edward. "A hell of a decision to have to make, but I would have thought less of you if you had said no."

"Thanks, Dad. That means a lot to me. I didn't tell you because I didn't know how Mom would react," he explained.

"Neither do I." His father paused, then asked, "Do you think I should suggest she talk to someone?"

"I know a good Catholic priest," Greg said lightly.

Edward sounded startled when he asked, "You've converted to Catholicism? Don't tell your mother that, either!"

"No, I haven't. He…explained some things to me. He helped," said Greg, remembering that calm, quiet voice in the still of the church, and the sound of the choir rising and falling in the back-ground. "But as for Mom, I think a therapist would be better than a priest. Someone she doesn't know, a professional who can help her deal with all this. She's tried for 36 years to bury her past, and now it's smacked her in the face. So to speak. Yeah, I think talking to someone would be a great idea."

"That's what I think, too. I simply can't imagine how to sug-gest it," confessed Edward.

"Straight up, Dad. Tell her we're worried about her."

"You want to do it?"

"No way. And besides," said Greg with a grin, "I've got a fian-cée again, and she needs some attention tonight."

* *

Nicola opened her bedroom door far enough to call, "Can I come out yet?"

There was silence, and a dim light that flickered and wavered. She pushed open the door and looked down the hallway at the tealight candles spaced along the floor. "Oh!" Directly in front of the door lay one perfect pink peony. She stooped to pick it up, cradling the fragrant blossom in her hands. How had he found a peony in November?

When they had, finally, got home from a day at the office that had seemed as if it would never end, Greg had banished her to the bedroom. "Make yourself beautiful," he had said. "Even more beautiful than you already are, I mean. Don't come out, no matter what you hear!"

The things she had heard had only increased her curiosity. The door buzzer had sounded three times, and there had been voices and muffled thumps. And something in the kitchen smelled divine.

"Greg?" she called now.

His head poked around the living room door. "Did I say you could come out yet?"

She smiled. "No."

"Do I have to tie you to the bed to make you stay there?"

One hand trailed up her leg, lifting the hem of the midnight-blue dress she knew he liked and revealing quite a length of thigh. "Maybe."

Even in the light of just the candles, and from the other end of the hallway, she could see how his eyes followed the rising hem. "Oh, all right," he said. "Since you're here anyway." He opened the door all the way and she could see the flicker of more tea-lights in holders, and then heard the sound of a violin.

Nicola stepped into the living room, holding her peony, and

stopped in amazement. The violin was not a recording: a stranger in a tuxedo stood in the corner of her living room, playing something that was joyous and sad at the same time, the notes sweeping and spinning. Greg, too, was wearing a tuxedo, something she had never seen. It suited him, and at the sight of its dark formality, she was glad she had taken time with her own appearance.

The dining table had been brought in and placed in the center of the room, draped in a white cloth she didn't recognize and laid with silver and china she did not own. Nor did she own the crystal glasses that caught the candlelight. And there were more peonies, dozens of them, pink and white and red, in vases on the shelves and end tables.

"Oh!" she said again.

Nicola whirled around at the loud pop of a champagne cork behind her, and there was a waiter, white cloth over his arm and bottle in his hand.

"How did you manage all this?" she marveled.

Greg grinned, and hooked an arm behind her to pull her against him. "You'd be amazed what a credit card and a few phone calls can pull off. We could have gone out, but I wanted us to be at home. Is that all right?" Unbelievably, he looked anxious, as if thinking she might conceivably say that it was not.

"All right?" she repeated. "Greg, it's wonderful. Miraculous. Extraordinary."

The waiter extended a silver tray holding the full champagne glasses, and then slipped out the door.

"There's a chef, too," explained Greg. "Don't worry, they take all this stuff away with them when we're done. No dishes to wash!"

She glanced at the violinist, who gave her a small smile and a flourish of notes.

"And he's only here for the first course," Greg whispered, under the pretext of kissing her ear. "I thought any longer would be too much."

"I wonder what the neighbors think of him?" she whispered back, her arms around his neck.

Greg was nibbling on her neck, but answered, "They probably wish you'd turn your stereo down."

The waiter was back. He placed his tray on a side table – the only one not covered in peonies – and pulled out a chair, indicating with a sweeping gesture that Nicola should sit. She sat. He flicked the napkin and floated it onto her lap, then turned to Greg, who with a look of mild alarm forestalled the man by snatching it up himself. Nicola smiled into her glass.

"Coquilles St Jacques," murmured the waiter as he placed a shell-shaped plate before her. Or maybe it was a real shell. Delicately browned, piped mashed potato ringed something lumpy in a white sauce.

"Do you know what this is?" asked Greg, when the waiter had gone.

She shook her head. "No idea. It sounds French. I can phone Hélène and ask! Don't you know?"

"No, I didn't have time to choose menus. I said no tomatoes, and then left it up to them. It smells incredible." He picked up his fork.

"It tastes incredible, too," said Nicola a moment later. "It's scallops."

He tapped his fork against the shell. "This should have been a clue."

When the waiter returned for the shells, scraped bare of every last delicious morsel, the violinist produced a soaring arpeggio of notes and swept his bow into the air.

"Wonderful!" enthused Nicola, clapping.

He bowed, and with a smile said, "May I offer you both my warmest congratulations on your engagement?"

Greg rose to shake the man's hand, and Nicola saw the folded money discreetly change hands. She had always envied men the ease with which they did that – that, and the fact that all their clothes had pockets, so handy for carrying small amounts of money for tips.

"I was surprised when your fiancée came in," the violinist confided with a laugh. "You look so alike, I thought she was your sister!"

"Did you really?" asked Greg, looking surprised. The merest hint of a wink was directed at Nicola. "No one has ever said that before."

Nicola buried her face in the arrangement of peonies, stifling the laugh.

"No doubt it was the lighting in here," replied the other man. "You know how deceptive candles can be. Goodnight!"

Eyes wide and lips pressed together to hold in the laughter, they listened to his footsteps down the hall, the opening of the door, that slow squeak that no amount of oil ever seemed to fix, then the soft snick as he pulled it closed behind him.

"Oh dear God!" Greg collapsed against his chair, shaking with laughter. "We'll never escape this!"

"But now we can laugh about it. That was perfect," Nicola said, and reached for his hand. "This whole evening is perfect. You're perfect." She lifted his hand and kissed it.

He turned his palm to her face and stroked her cheek. "If I get him to come back, will you repeat that in front of a witness? According to Sam, we are bound to argue about drapes, if nothing else, and I would like to remind you of my perfection at that time."

"Fat chance."

The scallops were followed by chicken in a light sauce with vegetables, followed by a tangy, fruity dessert, followed by coffee and petits fours. They decamped to the sofa for the coffee and cakes, in part because the waiter and the chef had to whisk the table back into the kitchen. A few more bangs and murmurs from the kitchen, and then they left, waving and wishing Greg and Nicola a pleasant evening.

"Pleasant?" said Nicola, when Greg returned from seeing them out. "Only a pleasant evening? It's already been incredible." And it was only going to get better, judging from the way he was looking at her as he crossed the room. She kicked off her shoes, and opened her arms.

His own arms went around her shoulders and Nicola leaned towards him eagerly. Then he stopped, and frowned, and sat back. He gathered both her hands in his. "The last time we sat here, I said some cruel things to you. I apologize for that."

She gazed into his eyes, so blue and so clear, so full of love. "Oh Greg, don't. I was no better. Let's not bring it up again. I'm just so glad it's over." She rested her forehead against his shoulder.

"Like waking up from a nightmare," he said. His fingers played with the tab of the zipper that ran down the back of her dress.

Nicola pulled on one end of his bow tie, and nothing happened. "Isn't this supposed to come undone when I do that?"

"If I had actually tied it in the first place, yes. But I'd still be standing in front of a mirror trying to figure it out. This is a ready-made one. It comes with the outfit," he said.

She laughed, and tweaked it again. "You can tie all those knots on your boat, and tie my hands in Vegas so that the silk came undone with one pull, but you couldn't manage this?"

He shrugged. "Different kind of knot."

"You look wonderful, by the way," she remarked. "Even if you did cheat on the tie. When I walked in and saw you…well, if the violin player and the waiter hadn't been here, I would have taken all these clothes off you hours ago. Ripped them off."

"You liked them so much you wanted to rip them off?" he asked in amusement.

She was busy with the tie's fastening, but spared a moment to correct him. "I liked *you* so much."

His tie came off, along with the jacket and cummerbund. She started on the shirt, and felt air against the skin of her back as the zipper came down.

"I phoned that venue this afternoon. The one we booked before," she clarified. "They've had a cancellation so can take us two weeks from this coming Saturday. Then there's nothing until late January. I thought if you talk to the pastor tomorrow and he can do the wedding itself sometime near the Saturday, I'll book it."

"January might be better," said Greg slowly, a thoughtful note in his voice.

Her fingers stilled. "Why?"

"It would give everyone a chance to get over the past two

weeks. You and I aren't the only ones whose lives were turned upside down," he pointed out.

"You mean Mona," said Nicola, with some reluctance.

"Not just Mom. Mostly, yes," he admitted. "I'd prefer my mother to be at our wedding, happy for us, rather than clinging to an irrational belief that you are her daughter, or that her real daughter will suddenly turn up and everything will be all right. If Dad can persuade her to get some therapy, I think she'll be better."

Shame and remorse trickled through Nicola as she acknowledged that she had been so focused on herself, and what Mona's revelations had meant for her and Greg, that she had pushed Mona to a corner of her mind. Had branded her "the enemy," and managed to overlook that on the first evening in Seattle, and during their day together, she had liked Mona very much, and that Mona was suffering, too.

"I can wait two months," she said.

"I'm not going anywhere," Greg assured her.

"You better not!" She tapped one finger against his chest in warning. "Oh, how will we explain this new delay to everyone at work?"

Greg grinned. "Dad had a relapse?"

"Poor Edward!" She laughed, and returned her attention to those finicky studs. "Greg, what are you doing back there?"

Something large and soft was playing up and down her back. He smiled, and moved the peony blossom he had been brushing over her skin so that it tickled her under her nose. Nicola stopped his hand, and inhaled the scent.

"I've never seen so many peonies," she said.

"This morning, I realized the only flower I've given you is that marigold I stole. Roses were all they had at the gas station," he explained with a grin. "So I thought I'd make up for it tonight."

She kissed him, stated, "You have nothing to make up for," and went back to the tiny studs that marched down the front of his shirt.

"What about your dress?" he asked.

She glanced down at herself. The dress was hanging off her

shoulders in front and gaping open at the back. "One pull on the sleeves, and it's pretty much off."

Greg laughed, and pulled on the sleeves. The dress puddled around her waist. "Yup. But I meant wedding dress."

"Oh! I'll get something from a store. You know I'm not too fussy. Hélène will help, I'm sure," she said, perhaps too brightly.

"Just Hélène?"

Nicola bit her lip. "Maybe Mom, too. She called me while I was getting ready, when you wouldn't let me come out of the bedroom. I think Dad must have read her the riot act, because she apologized. I'm not sure how sincere she was, though." She could still hear the stiffness in her mother's voice.

"It hasn't been easy for her, either," said Greg.

"It looked pretty easy yesterday, making me feel so small and dirty! And like a liar today!"

He caught both her hands in his, and looked at her with a frown. "Have you not considered how she must have felt? You're her daughter in every way but genetically. You're closer to her than Alison is, I've seen that. And suddenly you might have found your real mother? Gwen must have been nervous, uneasy, worried; scared of losing you. Perhaps all that manifested itself in her disapproval. Or perhaps that was her way of trying to keep you, by parting us, so that you didn't move to Boston."

Nicola leaned back, to see his face better. "You don't believe she truly thinks I'm contemptible?"

"I believe that if the results had been positive, she truly would have disapproved very strongly of us staying together. That's how Gwen is. But contemptible?" He kissed the tip of her nose. "No one could possibly think you are contemptible, and certainly not the woman who has loved you since you were nine months old!"

She sniffed. "How'd you get to be so smart?"

"Lucky, I guess. Maybe it will rub off on you, over the next 50 years or so," he teased.

"Ha ha," she retorted. "Okay, January it is. Maybe by then the mother of the bride will be speaking to the bride, and the mother of the groom will be…better." Then Nicola laughed. "Or we could go back to Vegas and get it over with. Like that woman at the show suggested. She really liked you. 'Oh, he is so handsome' and 'Oh my, he's just to die for' was all I heard when she followed me to the ladies' room."

"Were you jealous?" Greg teased.

"Nah! She confirmed my own good taste, that's all. It's lucky she never saw you in this outfit, or I would have had to fight for you!"

Greg looked down at the shirt, which she had managed to undo almost as far as the waistband of his pants. "As much as I enjoy having you undress me, my darling, I haven't made love to you since the shower on Friday and I don't think I can wait until you finish this." He tugged the ends free and swiftly dealt with the remaining studs. "And that thing you do with your tongue every time you remove a stud is not helping."

She ran her hands up the warm skin of his bare back as he pulled her to him, and reveled in the taste of his mouth, the feel of his hands. Willingly, she lay back against the sofa as his body pressed her down. His fingers trailed down to her waist and she felt them hook into her clothes.

"Lift up," he murmured, and when she obediently raised her hips, he stripped off nylons, panties and dress in one movement. "Take your bra off."

Nicola raised her eyebrows, stretched, and slowly crossed her arms behind her head. "By myself?"

He deposited a swift kiss on her belly button, then stood up. "I'm sure you'll manage."

She unhooked the bra and pulled it off, but she was puzzled. Greg had been known to spend 15 minutes just removing her bra, 15 glorious minutes that left her weak and reeling, and now he had better things to do? He walked to a bookcase and pulled a paper bag out from behind books. Back beside the sofa, holding it in one hand, he smiled down at her. "Close your eyes."

Instead, she narrowed them, and asked with suspicion, "What's in that bag? Something left over from Las Vegas?"

"Nicola, Nicola. So untrusting," he tut-tutted. "Now close your eyes."

A rustle of paper, then something feather-light landed on a

breast, one on an arm, her face, a flurry as soft as snowflakes on her tummy and legs. Nicola plucked one whatever-it-was from her thigh, and rubbed it between her finger and thumb. It felt like velvet, but more slick, and was so delicate that it tore.

"Petals!" she exclaimed, and opened her eyes to see that Greg had sprinkled hundreds of peony petals over her.

"There's another bag in the hall closet, too," he said. "I wasn't sure where we'd end up."

"You thought we'd end up in the closet?" she asked, trying to imagine them doing anything in that tiny space. "That would be a first."

More petals drifted down as he emptied the bag. "No. But I could hardly stash it in the bedroom with you in there." His face softened and his pupils widened. "You look so amazing with all those petals. As if you're lying on freshly fallen snow. Pink snow." He braced one hand against the back of the sofa and leaned down to kiss her, slow and tantalizing. The other hand, just as slow, burrowed through the soft heap of petals caught between her legs.

Nicola moaned, and her legs parted as if by their own volition. If she didn't stop him now, she knew, she would be lost. It was three days since he had touched her there, three long days during which she had sometimes doubted that he would ever touch her again, and desire for him burned hot and fierce. But there was something she wanted to do first. She pushed at his shoulders and for a moment he resisted, then he relented and straightened up.

"What's wrong?" Greg asked, running both hands through his hair and frowning.

She struggled to her feet, petals whispering to the floor. "Nothing is wrong, my love. It's just that the sofa is too small for what I have in mind." She scooped a double handful of the petals off the sofa and rubbed them over his chest, and then with a laugh she placed one on top of his head. "And I want to see how you look wearing nothing but peony petals." He still had on the formal black pants, and she twitched them.

His smile was slow and wide. "And what exactly might you have in mind?"

"Bring some of those candles, and follow me." They walked to the bedroom, the candles in their hands throwing monstrous shadows on the walls. "Get those pants off, buster," she commanded.

"Bossy all of a sudden, aren't you?" he remarked, but his hands were busy with the zipper.

She pointed, and he scrambled onto the bed.

"You don't know the half of it," she replied. She reached into a drawer, sat on the edge of the bed and extended one leg, then slipped the fishnet stocking over her pointed toes and with provocative deliberation she drew it up to her thigh.

"Oh," Greg said. He started to sit up, but she pointed at him again.

The second stocking went on, and then the scarlet shoes with four-inch stiletto heels. Tuesday evening, after Pilates, she had teetered around the apartment in them, so was fairly certain she wouldn't fall off or twist an ankle now.

"Uh," said Greg. He licked his lips, and stared at her as if mesmerized.

Nicola stood up and walked over to the closet in what she hoped was a domineering yet still seductive manner. She tried not to laugh. "The bustier is red, I couldn't find a black one. I hope that's okay."

"Uh," he said again. "You don't need the bust thing too."

She turned back to face him, and folded her arms under her breasts. She tapped one foot. "You sure?"

He cleared his throat. "I'm sure."

Hands on hips now, she glared at him, still trying not to laugh. "I am going to get the other bag. Don't move."

His eyes ran over her, down to the shoes and back up the stockings. "Don't be long, in that case."

She stalked out of the room, and clapped her hand over her mouth to stifle the giggle. She felt ridiculous walking around in nothing but stockings, heels and jewelry. Ridiculous, yes, but... powerful, too. A man couldn't fake a reaction like that. Nicola found it hard to believe that Greg could be so turned on by such an outfit, but, then, wasn't that the whole point of a fantasy?

It wasn't something you could control. Well, let's do it right, she thought. Nicola bent over and fluffed her fingers through her hair, then flipped up and tossed it back. She bit her lips and pinched her cheeks; old-fashioned, but it worked.

Bag in hand, she started to close the door. Then stopped, and with a soft laugh she reached to the back of the shelf.

Deep breath, shoulders back and breasts out, and she sauntered into the bedroom. Nicola leaned against the doorjamb and idly swiveled one foot from side to side on the point of the absurd heel.

Greg's eyes followed the shoe like a cat with a dangling piece of string.

She tossed the bag in her hand, and its contents gave a silken rustle.

"What are you hiding behind your back?" he asked, eyes darting from her shoe to her arm.

Her eyes opened wide. "Me? Nothing." One step, one exaggerated sway of her hips; another step, another sway, his eyes following every step, until she was beside the bed.

Nicola shook the bag again, and peony petals wafted down.

He twitched, and smiled, and brushed at the petals. "That tickles."

"I don't care," she said.

Nicola bent from the waist, and now his eyes moved from her legs to her breasts. "I am not going to tie you up," she said. "As you will have noticed by now, there is no headboard, so there's nothing to tie you to. But I want you to stretch out your arms, and leave them there."

Greg grinned.

"Farther. I'm sure you can reach the edge of the mattress if you try."

His fingers curled around the edges.

"Now, promise me you'll stay like that." She leaned even closer. "Promise. No matter what."

He licked his lips. "I promise."

More petals fell from the bag, and Greg twitched again, and laughed, but he didn't move.

"Nicola?"

She stepped back far enough that he could see her feet, and did the shoe swiveling thing again. "Yes?"

"I ask again, what are you hiding behind your back?"

Inch by inch, Nicola drew her hand forward. She pursed her lips and blew softly, and Janine's red ostrich feather quivered.

"Time to beg for mercy."

THE END

Acknowledgements

Once again, I would like to thank two people who generously gave their time to help improve this book.

To Jennifer Hashimoto – your editorial input is invaluable. You caught some embarassing bloopers, and your "inquiries" regarding character and plot resulted in a tighter, more focused novel. "Too Close" is a better book because of you.

A huge thanks to my mother, Flo, chief beta reader and proof-reader. Your help in finding typos and missing words undoubtedly improved the final result. Any such errors that remain are entirely my own fault!

Also, thanks are due to my four beta readers. Their suggestions and comments on an early draft helped to shape the final version.

About Elizabeth Krall

Elizabeth Krall grew up in Canada and lived in London, England, for many years. She has now settled in Sydney, Australia.

Most of her career was spent as an editor, but now she works as a print and digital graphic designer. An unexpected side-effect of leaving editing was the resurgence of an interest in writing. Her first novel, Ship to Shore, was published in February 2012; her second, Too Close, in February 2013. She is somewhat apprehensive about the expectation this pattern may give rise to regarding February 2014!

She is also the author of an occasional series of short stories themed around holidays, called Holiday Romances.

Elizabeth's interests include travel, tall ship sailing and cocktails.

You can connect with Elizabeth Krall at
http://elizabethkrallwriter.wordpress.com/

Novels by Elizabeth Krall

SHIP TO SHORE

Storms at sea. Heartbreak on land.

Sally meets Dermid on a tall ship sailing across the Atlantic and is drawn to him, despite what she considers to be his unfortunate passion for bagpipes. Their tentative romance ends badly: she feels guilty and he feels betrayed, and they part in hurt, angry silence.

In spite of what happened on the ship, Sally can't forget Dermid, although when she takes a job on a Scottish island she claims that the fact he lives on a nearby island has nothing to do with it. Not a thing.

On the Isle of Lewis, city girl Sally runs head-on into small-town Scotland, complete with inquisitive neighbors and more things tartan than she had ever imagined existed.

When her job ends, Sally must choose between building a life with Dermid or returning to her carefree, wandering ways. Someone from Dermid's past sparks a crisis that sends Sally fleeing back to London – and may tear them apart forever.

And could she ever learn to love the bagpipes?

Set against the tempestuous North Atlantic and the windswept beauty of the Hebrides, 'Ship to Shore' is a story of two people who must learn to trust their feelings, and to trust each other.

About the Holiday Romances series

Holiday Romances is an occasional series of short stories with a holiday theme.

1. Valentine's Day – 'Toast To Go'
2. Easter – 'The Perfect Chocolate Martini'
   (available Easter 2013)

Don't forget to check for additional stories in the series!

Please go to http://elizabethkrallwriter.wordpress.com/about-holiday-romances for the latest information.

CPSIA information can be obtained at www.ICGtesting.com
Printed in the USA
LVOW01s1618120315

430303LV00006B/145/P